WAVES OF TERROR
Weird Stories About the Sea

WAVES OF TERROR

Weird Stories About the Sea

edited by

MICHEL PARRY

LONDON
VICTOR GOLLANCZ LTD
1976

© Selection and original material Michel Parry 1976

ISBN 0 575 02184 5

MADE AND PRINTED IN GREAT BRITAIN BY
THE GARDEN CITY PRESS LIMITED
LETCHWORTH, HERTFORDSHIRE SG6 1JS

CONTENTS

ACKNOWLEDGEMENTS

THE EDITOR WISHES to thank the following authors, or their executors or agents, and publishers for permission to include copyright material in this book:

Curtis Brown Ltd. for "Log the Man Dead" by Eugene Burdick, © 1953 by Popular Publications Inc. for *Argosy* magazine, May 1953.

Penguin Books Ltd. for "At Sea" by Guy de Maupassant, translated by H. N. P. Sloman. Translation © H. N. P. Sloman, 1946. Reprinted from *Boule de Suif and Other Stories* (Penguin Classics 1946).

Glenn Lord for "Sea Curse" by Robert E. Howard, © 1928 by the Popular Fiction Publishing Company for *Weird Tales*, May 1928; Copyright renewed 1956 by Mrs P. M. Kuykendall.

Buhler, King & Buhler for "Fishhead" by Irvin S. Cobb, © 1914 by Irvin S. Cobb. Reprinted from *The Escape of Mr Trimm*.

Hill, Quale & Hartmann and Arkham House, publishers, for "Dagon" by H. P. Lovecraft, © 1923 by the Popular Fiction Publishing Company for *Weird Tales*, October 1923.

The Atlantic Monthly Company for "Fire In the Galley Stove" by Captain William Outerson, © 1937 by the Atlantic Monthly Company, Boston, Mass. Reprinted by permission of Mr William Outerson.

Mrs Lili Russell for "The Slaver" by John Russell, © 1923 by John Russell. Reprinted from *In Dark Places*.

The Society of Authors and the Estate of John Masefield for "The Devil and the Old Man", © 1905 by John Masefield. Reprinted from *A Mainsail Haul*.

"From the Dark Waters" by David Drake, © 1976 by David A. Drake.

Selection and original material © 1976 by Michel Parry.

Every effort has been made to trace the copyright holders of these stories. The editor offers his apologies in the event of any necessary acknowledgement being accidentally omitted.

While, in the sea, far down between Storm's knees
I saw a bloated Horror watching there—
A waiting shape, a shark, and deeper still,
A hideous, loathsome, writhing mass that claimed
The Ocean's silent bed—a foul affront
To Nature's strange and wondrous handiwork,
Smirching the very deep with darker hue.
                    William Hope Hodgson, *The Place of Storms*

INTRODUCTION

To MY MIND there is no better way of illustrating the mysterious and inviolate nature of the Sea than by reference to Loch Ness. This Scottish lake, the alleged residence of a famous monster, is twenty-three miles long and has a depth of less than a thousand feet at its deepest point, a mere drop in the ocean when measured against the vast tracts of water which cover two-thirds of our planet's surface. For the past two decades or so, Loch Ness has been under almost constant observation by various teams of investigators hoping to prove conclusively that the monster really does exist. Huge amounts of money have been spent on this endeavour. Teams of divers have plunged repeatedly into the icy water in an effort to locate the camera-shy creature. The latest techniques in sonar and underwater photography from the United States and Japan have been used to try to penetrate the loch's murky water. Bathyscaphes have gone up and down like yo-yos and even an experimental submarine has plumbed the depths in vain. But after all these years of effort and expenditure, no one has yet been able to prove—or disprove—the monster's existence. If there is a monster down there, his privacy is comfortably assured by the opaque waters of the loch.

This failure to resolve the mystery of even a comparative pond such as Loch Ness emphasises just how little we know about the underwater areas of our planet. Vast stretches of the Earth's sea-bed remain unprobed and unfathomed, as inaccessible to the human eye as the clouded surface of Venus. And, once in a while, the Sea casts up some anomaly such as the monstrous cœlacanth, a hint of what sort of thing might be lurking down in the far depths of the ocean.

Even today a sea voyage is still something of a voyage into the Unknown. Just four centuries ago, seamen lived in terror of sailing off the edge of the world. These days ships' navigators have a better idea of where they are headed but still cannot guarantee with absolute certainty that they will ever reach their destination. For too many sailors and passengers every year, the next port of call turns out to be Davy Jones's Locker. As for those unfortunate souls who vanish in the waters of the Bermuda Triangle, who can say *where* they end up! It is obvious that man still has much to learn before he can claim to have mastered the Sea. So far, his presence on the water has been scarcely tolerated. And to believe any different suggests the same kind of reckless optimism shown by the owners of the "unsinkable" *Titanic*.

For centuries now, the Sea has been regarded as a symbol, if not the actual physical embodiment, of the Great Unknown which surrounds mortal man. Hardly surprising then that it has also been the source and inspiration of innumerable myths, legends, superstitions and plain tall tales. A good many of the oldest and most durable epics that have come down to us deal with adventurers who braved the perils of unknown waters—Sinbad, Ulysses, Jason and other heroes. In the not-so-distant past when maps and sea-charts were pale with blanks, the strangest things might be expected to happen once a ship was out of sight of familiar land—and usually had by the time some old salt spun out the yarn over a noggin of rum.

If sailors provided the yarn, writers were not slow in providing the embroidery, for the Sea offered them the perfect backcloth against which to let their imaginations run wild. Sea stories, especially those fortified by encounters with sea serpents, mysterious islands and cannibal tribes, were immensely popular in the eighteenth and nineteenth centuries, periods when the claim that *Britannia Rules the Waves* was less of an idle boast than it has become. In many ways, weird sea stories served the same function then as science fiction does today. The two genres have much in common. Both give plausibility to the implausible by setting it in a situation which is conveniently remote—the Sea or outer space—but at the same time, acceptable as familiar and real. Many of the basic situations and even plots of the two genres have proved to be interchangeable. For example, Shakespeare's shipwreck fantasy, *The Tempest*, was readily adapted into the basis for a SF film called *Forbidden Planet* whilst there is hardly a world of difference between

Sinbad the Sailor and Jim Kirk, captain of *Star Trek*'s starship *Enterprise*. Significantly, science fiction never really attained its present mass market status until after the Russians made space travel a concrete reality. That should have sounded the death-knell for the weird sea story but the enormous success of Peter Benchley's *Jaws*, which is basically the traditional theme of the Monster from the Deep in modern guise, proves that there is still a demand for fiction of this kind.

In making this selection of outstanding weird stories of the Sea, I have attempted to choose stories which illustrate the wide diversity of themes within the genre. At the same time I have tried to avoid stories with which the reader is already likely to be familiar. For this reason I have excluded such old favourites as "The Upper Berth" by F. Marion Crawford and Edgar Allan Poe's "Descent into the Maelstrom" and "MS Found in a Bottle". These are all splendid stories but readily available in other collections. In their place I have substituted stories which I hope will prove less familiar but no less entertaining.

Here there be Monsters, the warning once to be found on old sea-charts, would be entirely appropriate to this collection as I have included several stories featuring monstrous sea-beasts. Monsters have always had an important part to play in sea fiction as *Jaws* recently reaffirmed. The Great White Shark of Peter Benchley's book actually has a long line of literary ante-cedents that include Leviathan, the Hydra, the Kraken and Moby Dick. My own favourite monster story in this collection is "From the Tideless Sea" by William Hope Hodgson. It is worth noting that this story, which first appeared in 1906, is set in the Sargasso Sea, a becalmed area of the Atlantic south of Bermuda. Being an experienced seaman, it is entirely possible that Hodgson knew of strange and inexplicable incidents occurring in this area long before the present much-publicised interest in the so-called Devil's Triangle.

Phantom ships are another staple ingredient of sea stories. The best known of such vessels is, of course, *The Flying Dutchman*, a sighting of which inspired Wagner's famous opera. The legend of the sea captain doomed to sail his ship through stormy seas for all eternity has many fascinating variants. One German version has the ship manned by the ghosts of suicides with a

lively skeleton as their captain. An apparition of a similar sor
is sighted in one of the stories in this book, "Sea Curse" by
Robert E. Howard, whilst that master of the sea story, Joseph
Conrad, writes about a doomed ship of another kind in "The
Brute".

Derelict vessels found adrift with no sign of their crews have
always provided a subject for wild conjecture. The best-known
example of such a mystery is the *Marie Celeste*, the crew of
which inexplicably vanished in 1873. An even more curiou
incident took place a few years later in 1881. An American
clipper, the *Ellen Austin*, sighted a derelict schooner adrif
about six hundred miles off the coast of Ireland. On being
boarded, the schooner was found to be deserted and had apparently been in that condition for some time. The *Ellen Austin's*
skipper decided to claim the abandoned vessel as salvage and
haul her back to New York. A party of volunteers was accord-
ingly put aboard to keep his prize seaworthy. Shortly afterwards
a storm blew up which made communication between the two
vessels impossible. Eventually the storm subsided and the
skipper anxiously hailed his men aboard the derelict. There was
no answer for, as further investigation soon showed, the salvage
party had vanished from the ship. With some apprehension a
second salvage team was put aboard, this time with orders to
maintain a careful watch and to sound the alarm at the first sign
of trouble. The night passed quietly. But in the morning, the
Ellen Austin's skipper discovered that the derelict—and his
salvage crew—had disappeared from sight, never to be seen
again.

In his story "Fire in the Galley Stove", Captain William
Outerson provides a chilling account of how another ship
came to be found abandoned and adrift under similar
circumstances.

A far more common occurrence, even today, is for a ship to
go down, sometimes taking all hands with her. Readers are
advised to keep their life-jackets handy as they have a number
of shipwrecks ahead of them. The most unusual of these is
probably to be found in "A Psychological Shipwreck", a story
by that neglected American master of the macabre, Ambrose
Bierce. Of course, at such times it is traditional for the captain

o go down with his ship. In an unusual variation on this theme, Robert Louis Stevenson's tale of "The Sinking Ship" tells of a kipper who preferred to go *up* with his ship.

Despite the many modern improvements in shipbuilding and communications, the job of fisherman remains one of the most hazardous of all occupations. Consider then how dangerous the job must have been a century ago, the period about which Guy de Maupassant writes in "At Sea". His cold, detached account of a serious accident aboard a trawler makes for truly horrifying reading. Even more unfortunate was the individual who found himself unexpectedly press-ganged into service in the Royal Navy. Quite apart from the usual hazards of life at sea and the likelihood of death or mutilation in battle, he also had to contend with the frequently sadistic discipline enforced aboard ship by martinets of the officer class. Eugene Burdick's "Log the Man Dead" vividly recreates the inhuman punishments once meted out to sailors found guilty of even the smallest infraction of naval regulations.

Whilst men who found themselves in such a situation might have welcomed any opportunity to escape ashore, there have always been others equally eager to spirit themselves aboard. Stowaways, as will be seen in William Clark Russell's "The Phantom Death" and John Russell's "The Slaver", come in all shapes and sizes, none of them welcome.

The right to the title of monarch of the Sea has often been fiercely disputed. Both Poseidon and his twin brother, Neptune, have had their eye on the crown for some time now, whilst Britannia has modestly claimed to rule the waves for almost as long. In his contribution, the American weird-story writer, H. P. Lovecraft proposes a new contender to the throne—the fish-god, "Dagon". Unfortunately, Dagon proves to have expansionist ambitions that bode ill for landlubbers everywhere. Even the Devil has had a crack at ruling the waves if John Masefield's story of "The Devil and the Old Man" is to be believed. Luckily, Old Nick appears to be no more competent at the job than was King Canute.

Finally, to show that terror, like charity, begins at home, I have included a story which takes place ashore. "Fishhead" by

Irvin S. Cobb concerns some strange goings-on in a lake. An
that seems to bring us back full-circle to Loch Ness and it
monster.

Here then, without any further ado, is a selection of eeri
sea stories that should shiver even the stoutest timbers...

MICHEL PARRY

FROM THE TIDELESS SEA
by William Hope Hodgson

Like Joseph Conrad, William Hope Hodgson (1875–1918) went
to sea at an early age. In the words of his friend, the publisher,
A. St John Adcock, Hodgson "left home to spend eight years
aboard ship, roughing it at the ends of the earth in all manner
of picturesque places and voyaging three times round the
world". During this time he was awarded the Royal Humane
Society's bronze medal for saving a fellow seaman from drowning in shark-infested waters. Experiences such as these were to
prove invaluable to Hodgson when he turned his hand to
writing later in life. He showed himself to be a versatile writer
with many different kinds of story to his credit: fantasy, science
fiction, detective mysteries, romances and even westerns—but it
was at writing eerie tales of the sea that he excelled. Tragically,
whilst he was at the peak of his imaginative powers, Hodgson
met his death in action during the Great War.

He was a writer of exceptional imagination whose best
work is distinguished by images of the fantastic worthy of
the surrealist masters. His novel, *The House on the Borderland*,
in particular, attains moments of cosmic resonance which have
few equals elsewhere in imaginative literature. Amongst his
other works are *The Boats of the "Glen Carrig"* (1907), *The
Night Land* (1912), *Carnacki the Ghost-Finder* (1913), *The Luck
of the Strong* (1916) and *Captain Gault* (1917). The following
story and its sequel, "More News From the *Homebird*", are
from a collection entitled *Men of Deep Water* (1914). When this
collection first appeared, a reviewer commented: "These stories
of the sea are enthralling... Mister Hodgson is a writer on
whom the mantle of Poe has fallen."

THE CAPTAIN OF the schooner leant over the rail, an
stared for a moment, intently.

"Pass us them glasses, Jock," he said, reaching a hand behin
him.

Jock left the wheel for an instant, and ran into the littl
companionway. He emerged immediately with a pair of marine
glasses, which he pushed into the waiting hand.

For a little, the captain inspected the object through th
binoculars. Then he lowered them, and polished the objec
glasses.

"Seems like er water-logged barr'l as sumone's been doin
fancy paintin' on," he remarked after a further stare. "Shove
ther 'elm down er bit, Jock, an' we'll 'ave er closer look at it."

Jock obeyed, and soon the schooner bore almost straight for
the object which held the captain's attention. Presently, it was
within some fifty feet, and the captain sung out to the boy in
the caboose to pass along the boathook.

Very slowly, the schooner drew nearer, for the wind was no
more than breathing gently. At last the cask was within reach,
and the captain grappled at it with the boathook. It bobbed in
the calm water, under his ministrations; and, for a moment,
the thing seemed likely to elude him. Then he had the hook
fast in a bit of rotten-looking rope which was attached to it. He
did not attempt to lift it by the rope; but sung out to the boy
to get a bowline round it. This was done, and the two of them
hove it up on to the deck.

The captain could see now, that the thing was a small water-
breaker, the upper part of which was ornamented with the
remains of a painted name.

"H—M—E—B——" spelt out the captain with difficulty,
and scratched his head. " 'ave er look at this 'ere, Jock. See wot
you makes of it."

Jock bent over from the wheel, expectorated, and then stared
at the breaker. For nearly a minute he looked at it in silence.

"I'm thinkin' some of the letterin's washed awa'," he said at
last, with considerable deliberation. "I have ma doots if ye'll
be able to read it."

"Hadn't ye no better knock in the end?" he suggested, after

further period of pondering. "I'm thinkin' ye'll be lang comin'
t them contents otherwise."

"It's been in ther water er thunderin' long time," remarked
ιe captain, turning the bottom side upwards. "Look at them
arnacles!"

Then, to the boy: —

"Pass erlong ther 'atchet outer ther locker."

Whilst the boy was away, the captain stood the little barrel
ιn end, and kicked away some of the barnacles from the under-
ιde. With them, came away a great shell of pitch. He bent, and
ιspected it.

"Blest if ther thing ain't been pitched!" he said. "This 'ere's
ιeen put afloat er purpose, an' they've been mighty anxious as
ιer stuff in it shouldn't be 'armed."

He kicked away another mass of the barnacle-studded pitch.
'hen, with a sudden impulse, he picked up the whole thing and
ιhook it violently. It gave out a light, dull, thudding sound, as
ιough something soft and small were within. Then the boy
ame with the hatchet.

"Stan' clear!" said the captain, and raised the implement.
'he next instant, he had driven in one end of the barrel. Eagerly,
ιe stooped forward. He dived his hand down and brought out
little bundle stitched up in oilskin.

"I don' spect as it's anythin' of valley," he remarked. "But
guess as there's sumthin' 'ere as 'll be worth tellin' 'bout w'en
ιe gets 'ome."

He slit up the oilskin as he spoke. Underneath, there was
ιnother covering of the same material, and under that a third.
'hen a longish bundle done up in tarred canvas. This was
ιemoved, and a black, cylindrical shaped case disclosed to view.
ιt proved to be a tin canister, pitched over. Inside of it, neatly
ιrapped within a last strip of oilskin, was a roll of papers,
ιhich, on opening, the captain found to be covered with writing.
'he captain shook out the various wrappings; but found noth-
ιng further. He handed the MS across to Jock.

"More 'n your line 'n mine, I guess," he remarked. "Jest you
ιead it up, an' I'll listen."

He turned to the boy.

"Fetch ther dinner erlong 'ere. Me an' ther mate 'll 'ave it

comfertable up 'ere, an' you can take ther wheel. . . . Now ther
Jock!"

And, presently, Jock began to read.

"The Losing of the *Homebird*"

"The *'Omebird!*" exclaimed the captain. "Why, she were lo
w'en I wer' quite a young feller. Let me see—seventy-three
That were it. Tail end er seventy-three w'en she left 'ome, ai
never 'eard of since; not as I knows. Go a'ead with ther yarr
Jock."

"It is Christmas eve. Two years ago today, we became lo
to the world. Two years! It seems like twenty since I had m
last Christmas in England. Now, I suppose, we are already for
gotten—and this ship is but one more among the missing! M
God! to think upon our loneliness gives me a choking feelin;
a tightness across the chest!

"I am writing this in the saloon of the sailing ship, *Homebir*
and writing with but little hope of human eye ever seeing tha
which I write; for we are in the heart of the dread Sargasso Se
—the Tideless Sea of the North Atlantic. From the stump c
our mizzen mast, one may see, spread out to the far horizor
an interminable waste of weed—a treacherous, silent vastitud
of slime and hideousness!

"On our port side, distant some seven or eight miles, there i
a great, shapeless, discoloured mass. No one, seeing it for th
first time, would suppose it to be the hull of a long lost vesse.
It bears but little resemblance to a sea-going craft, because of
strange superstructure which has been built upon it. An examin
ation of the vessel herself, through a telescope, tells one that sh
is unmistakably ancient. Probably a hundred, possibly tw
hundred, years. Think of it! Two hundred years in the mids
of this desolation! It is an eternity.

"At first we wondered at that extraordinary superstructure
Later, we were to learn its use—and profit by the teaching o
hands long withered. It is inordinately strange that we shoul
have come upon this sight for the dead! Yet, thought suggests
that there may be many such, which have lain here through th
centuries in this World of Desolation. I had not imagined tha

ιe earth contained so much loneliness, as is held within the ιrcle, seen from the stump of our shattered mast. Then comes ιe thought that I might wander a hundred miles in any direc- ιon—and still be lost.

"And that craft yonder, that one break in the monotony, ιat monument of a few men's misery, serves only to make the ιlitude the more atrocious; for she is a very effigy of terror, ιlling of tragedies in the past, and to come!

"And now to get back to the beginnings of it. I joined the *Iomebird*, as a passenger, in the early part of November. My ιealth was not quite the thing, and I hoped the voyage would ιelp to set me up. We had a lot of dirty weather for the first ιouple of weeks out, the wind dead ahead. Then we got a ιoutherly slant, that carried us down through the forties; but a ιood deal more to the westward than we desired. Here we ran ιght into a tremendous cyclonic storm. All hands were called ι shorten sail, and so urgent seemed our need, that the very ιfficers went aloft to help make up the sails, leaving only the ιaptain (who had taken the wheel) and myself upon the poop. ιn the main deck, the cook was busy letting go such ropes as ιe mates desired.

"Abruptly, some distance ahead, through the vague sea-mist, ιut rather on the port bow, I saw loom up a great black wall of ιloud.

" 'Look, Captain!' I exclaimed; but it had vanished before ι had finished speaking. A minute later it came again, and this ιme the captain saw it.

" 'O, my God!' he cried, and dropped his hands from the ιheel. He leapt into the companionway, and seized a speaking ιrumpet. Then out on deck. He put it to his lips.

" 'Come down from aloft! Come down! Come down!' he ιhouted. And suddenly I lost his voice in a terrific mutter of ιound from somewhere to port. It was the voice of the storm— ιhouting. My God! I had never heard anything like it! It ιeased as suddenly as it had begun, and, in the succeeding quiet- ιess, I heard the whining of the kicking-tackles through the ιlocks. Then came a quick clang of brass upon the deck, and ι turned quickly. The captain had thrown down the trumpet, ιnd sprung back to the wheel. I glanced aloft, and saw that

many of the men were already in the rigging, and racing down
like cats.

"I heard the captain draw his breath with a quick gasp.

" 'Hold on for your lives!' he shouted, in a hoarse, unnatural
voice.

"I looked at him. He was staring to windward with a fixed
stare of painful intentness, and my gaze followed his. I saw
not four hundred yards distant, an enormous mass of foam and
water coming down upon us. In the same instant, I caught the
hiss of it, and immediately it was a shriek, so intense and awful
that I cringed impotently with sheer terror.

"The smother of water and foam took the ship a little fore
side of the beam, and the wind was with it. Immediately, the
vessel rolled over on to her side, the sea-froth flying over her
in tremendous cataracts.

"It seemed as though nothing could save us. Over, over we
went, until I was swinging against the deck, almost as against
the side of a house; for I had grasped the weather rail at the
captain's warning. As I swung there, I saw a strange thing
Before me was the port quarter boat. Abruptly, the canvas
cover was flipped clean off it, as though by a vast, invisible
hand.

"The next instant, a flurry of oars, boats' masts and odd gear
flittered up into the air, like so many feathers, and blew to
leeward and was lost in the roaring chaos of foam. The boat
herself, lifted in her chocks, and suddenly was blown clean
down on to the main deck, where she lay all in a ruin of white
painted timbers.

"A minute of the most intense suspense passed; then, sud
denly, the ship righted, and I saw that the three masts had
carried away. Yet, so hugely loud was the crying of the storm
that no sound of their breaking had reached me.

"I looked towards the wheel; but no one was there. Then
made out something crumpled up against the lee rail. I struggled
across to it, and found that it was the captain. He was insensible
and queerly limp in his right arm and leg. I looked round
Several of the men were crawling aft along the poop. I beckoned
to them, and pointed to the wheel, and then to the captain. A
couple of them came towards me, and one went to the wheel

hen I made out through the spray the form of the second
ate. He had several more of the men with him, and they had
coil of rope, which they took forrard. I learnt afterwards that
ey were hastening to get out a sea-anchor, so as to keep the
hip's head towards the wind.

"We got the captain below, and into his bunk. There, I left
im in the hands of his daughter and the steward, and returned
n deck.

"Presently, the second mate came back, and with him the
emainder of the men. I found then that only seven had been
aved in all. The rest had gone.

"The day passed terribly—the wind getting stronger hourly;
hough, at its worst, it was nothing like so tremendous as that
rst burst.

"The night came—a night of terror, with the thunder and
iss of the giant seas in the air above us, and the wind bellow-
ag like some vast elemental beast.

"Then, just before the dawn, the wind lulled, almost in a
moment; the ship rolling and wallowing fearfully, and the water
oming aboard—hundreds of tons at a time. Immediately after-
ards it caught us again; but more on the beam, and bearing
he vessel over on to her side, and this only by the pressure of
he element upon the stark hull. As we came head to wind
gain, we righted, and rode, as we had for hours, amid a
housand fantastic hills of phosphorescent flame.

"Again the wind died—coming again after a longer pause,
nd then, all at once, leaving us. And so, for the space of a
errible half hour, the ship lived through the most awful, wind-
ess sea that can be imagined. There was no doubting but that
e had driven right into the calm centre of the cyclone—calm
nly so far as lack of wind, and yet more dangerous a thousand
mes than the most furious hurricane that ever blew.

"For now we were beset by the stupendous Pyramidal Sea;
sea once witnessed, never forgotten; a sea in which the whole
osom of the ocean is projected towards heaven in monstrous
ills of water; not leaping forward, as would be the case if there
ere wind; but hurling upwards in jets and peaks of living
rine, and falling back in a continuous thunder of foam.

"Imagine this, if you can, and then have the clouds break

away suddenly overhead, and the moon shine down upon th
hellish turmoil, and you will have such a sight as has been give
to mortals but seldom, save with death. And this is what w
saw, and to my mind there is nothing within the knowledge c
man to which I can liken it.

"Yet we lived through it, and through the wind that cam
later. But two more complete days and nights had passe
before the storm ceased to be a terror to us, and then, onl
because it had carried us into the seaweed-laden waters of th
vast Sargasso Sea.

"Here, the great billows first became foamless; and dwindle
gradually in size as we drifted further among the floating mass
of weed. Yet the wind was still furious, so that the ship dro
on steadily, sometimes between banks, and other times ov
them.

"For a day and a night we drifted thus; and then astern
made out a great bank of weed, vastly greater than any whic
hitherto we had encountered. Upon this, the wind drove us ste
foremost, so that we over-rode it. We had been forced som
distance across it, when it occurred to me that our speed wa
slackening. I guessed presently that the sea-anchor, ahead, ha
caught in the weed, and was holding. Even as I surmised thi
I heard from beyond the bows a faint, droning, twanging soun
blending with the roar of the wind. There came an indistin
report, and the ship lurched backwards through the weed. Th
hawser, connecting us with the sea-anchor, had parted.

"I saw the second mate run forrard with several men. The
hauled in upon the hawser, until the broken end was aboar
In the meantime, the ship, having nothing ahead to keep h
'bows on', began to slew broadside towards the wind. I sa
the men attach a chain to the end of the broken hawse
then they paid it out again, and the ship's head came back t
the gale.

"When the second mate came aft, I asked him why this ha
been done, and he explained that so long as the vessel was en
on, she would travel over the weed. I inquired why he wishe
her to go over the weed, and he told me that one of the me
had made out what appeared to be clear water astern, and th
—could we gain it—we might win free.

"Through the whole of that day, we moved rearwards across the great bank; yet, so far from the weed appearing to show signs of thinning, it grew steadily thicker, and, as it became denser, so did our speed slacken, until the ship was barely moving. And so the night found us.

"The following morning discovered to us that we were within a quarter of a mile of a great expanse of clear water—apparently the open sea; but unfortunately the wind had dropped to a moderate breeze, and the vessel was motionless, deep sunk in the weed; great tufts of which rose up on all sides, to within a few feet of the level of our main deck.

"A man was sent up the stump of the mizzen, to take a look round. From there, he reported that he could see something, that might be weed, across the water; but it was too far distant for him to be in any way certain. Immediately afterwards, he called out that there was something, away on our port beam; but what it was, he could not say, and it was not until a telescope was brought to bear, that we made it out to be the hull of the ancient vessel I have previously mentioned.

"And now, the second mate began to cast about for some means by which he could bring the ship to the clear water astern. The first thing which he did, was to bend a sail to a spare yard, and hoist it to the top of the mizzen stump. By this means, he was able to dispense with the cable towing over the bows, which, of course, helped to prevent the ship from moving. In addition, the sail would prove helpful to force the vessel across the weed. Then he routed out a couple of kedges. These, he bent on to the ends of a short piece of cable, and, to the bight of this, the end of a long coil of strong rope.

"After that, he had the starboard quarter boat lowered into the weed, and in it he placed the two kedge anchors. The end of another length of rope, he made fast to the boat's painter. This done, he took four of the men with him, telling them to bring chain-hooks, in addition to the oars—his intention being to force the boat through the weed, until he reached the clear water. There, in the marge of the weed, he would plant the two anchors in the thickest clumps of the growth; after which we were to haul the boat back to the ship, by means of the rope attached to the painter.

" 'Then,' as he put it, 'we'll take the kedge-rope to the capstan, and heave her out of this blessed cabbage heap!'

"The weed proved a greater obstacle to the progress of the boat, than, I think, he had anticipated. After half an hour's work, they had gone scarcely more than some two hundred feet from the vessel; yet, so thick was the stuff, that no sign could we see of them, save the movement they made among the weed, as they forced the boat along.

"Another quarter of an hour passed away, during which the three men left upon the poop, paid out the ropes as the boat forged slowly ahead. All at once, I heard my name called. Turning, I saw the captain's daughter in the companionway, beckoning to me. I walked across to her.

" 'My father has sent me up to know, Mr Philips, how they are getting on?'

" 'Very slowly, Miss Knowles,' I replied. 'Very slowly indeed. The weed is so extraordinarily thick.'

"She nodded intelligently, and turned to descend; but I detained her a moment.

" 'Your father, how is he?' I asked.

"She drew her breath swiftly.

" 'Quite himself,' she said; 'but so dreadfully weak. He——'

"An outcry from one of the men, broke across her speech: —

" 'Lord 'elp us, mates! wot were that!'

"I turned sharply. The three of them were staring over the taffrail. I ran towards them, and Miss Knowles followed.

" 'Hush!' she said, abruptly. 'Listen!'

"I stared astern to where I knew the boat to be. The weed all about it was quaking queerly—the movement extending far beyond the radius of their hooks and oars. Suddenly, I heard the second mate's voice: —

" 'Look out, lads! My God, look out!'

"And close upon this, blending almost with it, came the hoarse scream of a man in sudden agony.

"I saw an oar come up into view, and descend violently, as though someone struck at something with it. Then the second mate's voice, shouting: —

" 'Aboard there! Aboard there! Haul in on the rope! Haul in on the rope——!' It broke off into a sharp cry.

"As we seized hold of the rope, I saw the weed hurled in all directions, and a great crying and choking swept to us over the brown hideousness around.

" 'Pull!' I yelled, and we pulled. The rope tautened; but the boat never moved.

" 'Tek it ter ther capstin!' gasped one of the men.

"Even as he spoke, the rope slackened.

" 'It's coming!' cried Miss Knowles. 'Pull! Oh! Pull!'

"She had hold of the rope along with us, and together we hauled, the boat yielding to our strength with surprising ease.

" 'There it is!' I shouted, and then I let go of the rope. There was no one in the boat.

"For the half of a minute, we stared, dumfounded. Then my gaze wandered astern to the place from which we had plucked it. There was a heaving movement among the great weed masses. I saw something waver up aimlessly against the sky; it was sinuous, and it flickered once or twice from side to side; then sank back among the growth, before I could concentrate my attention upon it.

"I was recalled to myself by a sound of dry sobbing. Miss Knowles was kneeling upon the deck, her hands clasped round one of the iron uprights of the rail. She seemed momentarily all to pieces.

" 'Come! Miss Knowles,' I said, gently. 'You must be brave. We cannot let your father know of this in his present state.'

"She allowed me to help her to her feet. I could feel that she was trembling badly. Then, even as I sought for words with which to reassure her, there came a dull thud from the direction of the companionway. We looked round. On the deck, face downward, lying half in and half out of the scuttle, was the captain. Evidently, he had witnessed everything. Miss Knowles gave out a wild cry, and ran to her father. I beckoned to one of the men to help me, and, together, we carried him back to his bunk. An hour later, he recovered from his swoon. He was quite calm, though very weak, and evidently in considerable pain.

"Through his daughter, he made known to me that he wished me to take the reins of authority in his place. This, after a slight demur, I decided to do; for, as I reassured myself, there were no duties required of me, needing any special knowledge of ship-craft. The vessel was fast; so far as I could see, irrevocably fast. It would be time to talk of freeing her, when the captain was well enough to take charge once more.

"I returned on deck, and made known to the men the captain's wishes. Then I chose one to act as a sort of bo'sun over the other two, and to him I gave orders that everything should be put to rights before the night came. I had sufficient sense to leave him to manage matters in his own way; for, whereas my knowledge of what was needful, was fragmentary, his was complete.

"By this time, it was near to sunsetting, and it was with melancholy feelings that I watched the great hull of the sun plunge lower. For a while, I paced the poop, stopping ever and anon to stare over the dreary waste by which we were surrounded. The more I looked about, the more a sense of lonesomeness and depression and fear assailed me. I had wondered much upon the dread happening of the day, and all my ponderings led to a vital questioning:—What was there among all that quiet weed, which had come upon the crew of the boat, and destroyed them? And I could not make answer, and the weed was silent—dreadly silent!

"The sun had drawn very near to the dim horizon, and I watched it, moodily, as it splashed great clots of red fire across the water that lay stretched into the distance across our stern. Abruptly, as I gazed, its perfect lower edge was marred by an irregular shape. For a moment, I stared, puzzled. Then I fetched a pair of glasses from the holdfast in the companion. A glance through these, and I knew the extent of our fate. That line, blotching the round of the sun, was the conformation of another enormous weed bank.

"I remembered that the man had reported something as showing across the water, when he was sent up to the top of the mizzen stump in the morning; but, what it was, he had been unable to say. The thought flashed into my mind that it had been only *just* visible from aloft in the morning, and now it was in sight from the deck. It occurred to me that the wind might be compacting the weed, and driving the bank which surrounded the ship, down upon a larger portion. Possibly, the clear stretch of water had been but a temporary rift within the heart of the Sargasso Sea. It seemed only too probable.

"Thus it was that I meditated, and so, presently, the night found me. For some hours further, I paced the deck in the darkness, striving to understand the incomprehensible; yet with no better result than to weary myself to death. Then, somewhere about midnight, I went below to sleep.

"The following morning, on going on deck, I found that the stretch of clear water had disappeared entirely, during the night, and now, so far as the eye could reach, there was nothing but a stupendous desolation of weed.

"The wind had dropped completely, and no sound came from all that weed-ridden immensity. We had, in truth, reached the Cemetery of the Ocean!

"The day passed uneventfully enough. It was only when I served out some food to the men, and one of them asked whether they could have a few raisins, that I remembered, with a pang of sudden misery, that it was Christmas day. I gave them the fruit, as they desired, and they spent the morning in the galley, cooking their dinner. Their stolid indifference to the late terrible happenings, appalled me somewhat, until I remembered what their lives were, and had been. Poor fellows! One of them ventured aft at dinner time, and offered me a slice of what he called 'plum duff'. He brought it on a plate which he had found in the galley and scoured thoroughly with sand and water. He tendered it shyly enough, and I took it, so graciously as I could, for I would not hurt his feelings; though the very smell of the stuff was an abomination.

"During the afternoon, I brought out the captain's telescope, and made a thorough examination of the ancient hulk on our port beam. Particularly did I study the extraordinary superstructure around her sides; but could not, as I have said before, conceive of its use.

"The evening, I spent upon the poop, my eyes searching wearily across that vile quietness, and so, in a little, the night came—Christmas night, sacred to a thousand happy memories. I found myself dreaming of the night a year previous, and, for a little while, I forgot what was before me. I was recalled suddenly—terribly. A voice rose out of the dark which hid the main deck. For the fraction of an instant, it expressed surprise; then pain and terror leapt into it. Abruptly, it seemed to come from above, and then from somewhere *beyond* the ship, and so in a moment there was silence, save for a rush of feet and the bang of a door forrard.

"I leapt down the poop ladder, and ran along the main deck, towards the fo'c'sle. As I ran, something knocked off my cap. I scarcely noticed it *then*. I reached the fo'c'sle, and caught at the latch of the port door. I lifted it and pushed; but the door was fastened.

" 'Inside there!' I cried, and banged upon the panels with my clenched fist.

"A man's voice came, incoherently.

" 'Open the door!' I shouted. 'Open the door!'

" 'Yes, sir—I'm com-ming, sir," said one of them, jerkily.

"I heard footsteps stumble across the planking. Then a hand fumbled at the fastening, and the door flew open under my weight.

"The man who had opened to me, started back. He held a flaring slush-lamp above his head, and, as I entered, he thrust it forward. His hand was trembling visibly, and, behind him, I made out the face of one of his mates, the brow and dirty, clean-shaven upper lip drenched with sweat. The man who held the lamp, opened his mouth, and gabbered at me; but, for a moment, no sound came.

" 'Wot—wot were it? Wot we-ere it?' he brought out at last, with a gasp.

"The man behind, came to his side, and gesticulated.

" 'What was what?' I asked sharply, and looking from one to the other. 'Where's the other man? What was that screaming?'

"The second man drew the palm of his hand across his brow; then flirted his fingers deckwards.

" 'We don't know, sir! We don't know! It were Jessop! Somethin's took 'im just as we was comin' forrid! We—we— He—he—HARK!'

"His head came forward with a jerk as he spoke, and then, for a space, no one stirred. A minute passed, and I was about to speak, when, suddenly, from somewhere out upon the deserted main deck, there came a queer, subdued noise, as though something moved stealthily hither and thither. The man with the lamp caught me by the sleeve, and then, with an abrupt movement, slammed the door and fastened it.

" 'That's IT, sir!' he exclaimed, with a note of terror and conviction in his voice.

"I bade him be silent, while I listened; but no sound came to us through the door, and so I turned to the men and told them to let me have all they knew.

"It was little enough. They had been sitting in the galley, yarning, until, feeling tired, they had decided to go forrard and turn-in. They extinguished the light, and came out upon the deck, closing the door behind them. Then, just as they turned to go forrard, Jessop gave out a yell. The next instant they heard him screaming in the air above their heads, and, realising that some terrible thing was upon them, they took forthwith to their heels, and ran for the security of the fo'c'sle.

"Then I had come.

"As the men made an end of telling me, I thought I heard something outside, and held up my hand for silence. I caught the sound again. Someone was calling my name. It was Miss Knowles. Likely enough she was calling me to supper—and she had no knowledge of the dread thing which had happened. I sprang to the door. She might be coming along the main deck in search of me. And there was something out there, of which I had no conception—something unseen, but deadly tangible!

" 'Stop, sir!' shouted the men, together; but I had the door open.

" 'Mr Philips!' came the girl's voice at no great distance. 'Mr Philips!'

" 'Coming, Miss Knowles!' I shouted, and snatched the lamp from the man's hand.

"The next instant, I was running aft, holding the lamp high, and glancing fearfully from side to side. I reached the place where the main mast had been, and spied the girl coming towards me.

" 'Go back!' I shouted. 'Go back!'

"She turned at my shout, and ran for the poop ladder. I came up with her, and followed close at her heels. On the poop, she turned and faced me.

" 'What is it, Mr Philips?'

"I hesitated. Then:—

" 'I don't know!' I said.

" 'My father heard something,' she began. 'He sent me. He——'

"I put up my hand. It seemed to me that I had caught again the sound of something stirring on the main deck.

" 'Quick!' I said sharply. 'Down into the cabin!' And she, being a sensible girl, turned and ran down without waste of time. I followed, closing and fastening the companion-doors behind me.

"In the saloon, we had a whispered talk, and I told her everything. She bore up bravely, and said nothing; though her eyes were very wide, and her face pale. Then the captain's voice came to us from the adjoining cabin.

" 'Is Mr Philips there, Mary?'

" 'Yes, father.'

" 'Bring him in.'

"I went in.

" 'What was it, Mr Philips?' he asked, collectedly.

"I hesitated; for I was willing to spare him the ill news; but he looked at me with calm eyes for a moment, and I knew that it was useless attempting to deceive him.

" 'Something has happened, Mr Philips,' he said, quietly. 'You need not be afraid to tell me.'

"At that, I told him so much as I knew, he listening, and nodding his comprehension of the story.

" 'It must be something big,' he remarked, when I had made an end. 'And yet you saw nothing when you came aft?'

" 'No,' I replied.

" 'It is something in the weed,' he went on. 'You will have to keep off the deck at night.'

"After a little further talk, in which he displayed a calmness that amazed me, I left him, and went presently to my berth.

"The following day, I took the two men, and, together, we made a thorough search through the ship; but found nothing. It was evident to me that the captain was right. There was some dread Thing hidden within the weed. I went to the side and looked down. The two men followed me. Suddenly, one of them pointed.

" 'Look, sir!' he exclaimed. 'Right below you, sir! Two eyes like blessed great saucers! Look!'

"I stared; but could see nothing. The man left my side, and ran into the galley. In a moment, he was back with a great lump of coal.

" 'Just there, sir,' he said, and hove it down into the weed immediately beneath where we stood.

"Too late, I saw the thing at which he aimed—two immense eyes, some little distance below the surface of the weed. I knew instantly to what they belonged; for I had seen large specimens of the octopus some years previously, during a cruise in Australasian waters.

" 'Look out, man!' I shouted, and caught him by the arm. 'It's an octopus! Jump back!' I sprang down on to the deck. In the same instant, huge masses of weed were hurled in all directions, and half a dozen immense tentacles whirled up into the air. One lapped itself about his neck. I caught his leg; but he was torn from my grasp, and I tumbled backwards on to the deck. I heard a scream from the other man as I scrambled to my feet. I looked to where he had been; but of him there was no sign. Regardless of the danger, in my great agitation, I leapt upon the rail, and gazed down with frightened eyes. Yet, neither of him nor his mate, nor the monster, could I perceive a vestige.

"How long I stood there staring down bewilderedly, I cannot say; certainly some minutes. I was so bemazed that I seemed incapable of movement. Then, all at once, I became aware that a light quiver ran across the weed, and the next instant, something stole up out of the depths with a deadly celerity. Well it was for me that I had seen it in time, else should I have shared the fate of those two—and the others. As it was, I saved myself only by leaping backwards on to the deck. For a moment, I saw the feeler wave above the rail with a certain apparent aimlessness; then it sank out of sight, and I was alone.

"An hour passed before I could summon a sufficiency of courage to break the news of this last tragedy to the captain and his daughter, and when I had made an end, I returned to the solitude of the poop; there to brood upon the hopelessness of our position.

"As I paced up and down, I caught myself glancing continuously at the nearer weed tufts. The happenings of the past two days had shattered my nerves, and I feared every moment to see some slender death-grapple searching over the rail for me. Yet, the poop, being very much higher out of the weed than the main deck, was comparatively safe; though only comparatively.

"Presently, as I meandered up and down, my gaze fell upon the hulk of the ancient ship, and, in a flash, the reason for that great superstructure was borne upon me. It was intended as a protection against the dread creatures which inhabited the weed. The thought came to me that I would attempt some similar means of protection; for the feeling that, at any moment, I might be caught and lifted out into that slimy wilderness, was not to be borne. In addition, the work would serve to occupy my mind, and help me to bear up against the intolerable sense of loneliness which assailed me.

"I resolved that I would lose no time, and so, after some thought as to the manner in which I should proceed, I routed out some coils of rope and several sails. Then I went down on to the main deck and brought up an armful of capstan bars. These I lashed vertically to the rail all round the poop. Then I knotted the rope to each, stretching it tightly between them, and over this framework stretched the sails, sewing the stout canvas to the rope, by means of twine and some great needles which I found in the mate's room.

"It is not to be supposed that this piece of work was accomplished immediately. Indeed, it was only after three days of hard labour that I got the poop completed. Then I commenced work upon the main deck. This was a tremendous undertaking, and a whole fortnight passed before I had the entire length of it enclosed; for I had to be continually on the watch against the hidden enemy. Once, I was very nearly surprised, and saved myself only by a quick leap. Thereafter, for the rest of that day, I did no more work; being too greatly shaken in spirit. Yet, on the following morning, I recommenced, and from thence, until the end, I was not molested.

"Once the work was roughly completed, I felt at ease to begin and perfect it. This I did, by tarring the whole of the sails with Stockholm tar; thereby making them stiff, and capable of resisting the weather. After that, I added many fresh uprights, and much strengthening ropework, and finally doubled the sail-cloth with additional sails, liberally smeared with the tar.

"In this manner, the whole of January passed away, and a part of February. Then, it would be on the last day of the month, the captain sent for me, and told me, without any preliminary talk, that he was dying. I looked at him; but said nothing; for I had known long that it was so. In return, he stared back with a strange intentness, as though he would read my inmost thoughts, and this for the space of perhaps two minutes.

" 'Mr Philips,' he said at last, 'I may be dead by this time tomorrow. Has it ever occurred to you that my daughter will be alone with you?'

" 'Yes, Captain Knowles,' I replied, quietly, and waited.

"For a few seconds, he remained silent; though, from the changing expressions of his face, I knew that he was pondering how best to bring forward the thing which it was in his mind to say.

" 'You are a gentleman——' he began, at last.

" 'I will marry her,' I said, ending the sentence for him.

"A slight flush of surprise crept into his face.

" 'You—you have thought seriously about it?'

" 'I have thought very seriously,' I explained.

" 'Ah!' he said, as one who comprehends. And then, for a little, he lay there quietly. It was plain to me that memories of past days were with him. Presently, he came out of his dreams, and spoke, evidently referring to my marriage with his daughter.

" 'It is the only thing,' he said, in a level voice.

"I bowed, and after that, he was silent again for a space. In a little, however, he turned once more to me:—

" 'Do you—do you love her?'

"His tone was keenly wistful, and a sense of trouble lurked in his eyes.

" 'She will be my wife,' I said, simply; and he nodded.

" 'God has dealt strangely with us,' he murmured, presently, as though to himself.

"Abruptly, he bade me tell her to come in.

"And then he married us.

"Three days later, he was dead, and we were alone.

"For a while, my wife was a sad woman; but gradually time eased her of the bitterness of her grief.

"Then, some eight months after our marriage, a new interest stole into her life. She whispered it to me, and we, who had borne our loneliness uncomplainingly, had now this new thing to which to look forward. It became a bond between us, and bore promise of some companionship as we grew old. Old! At the idea of age, a sudden flash of thought darted like lightning across the sky of my mind:—*FOOD!* Hitherto, I had thought of myself, almost as of one already dead, and had cared naught for anything beyond the immediate troubles which each day forced upon me. The loneliness of the vast Weed World had become an assurance of doom to me, which had clouded and dulled my faculties, so that I had grown apathetic. Yet, immediately, as it seemed, at the shy whispering of my wife, was all this changed.

"That very hour, I began a systematic search through the ship. Among the cargo, which was of a 'general' nature, I discovered large quantities of preserved and tinned provisions, all of which I put carefully on one side. I continued my examination until I had ransacked the whole vessel. The business took me near upon six months to complete, and when it was finished, I seized paper, and made calculations, which led me to the conclusion that we had sufficient food in the ship to preserve life in three people for some fifteen to seventeen years. I could not come nearer to it than this; for I had no means of computing the quantity the child would need year by year. Yet it is sufficient to show me that seventeen years *must* be the limit. Seventeen years! And then——

"Concerning water, I am not troubled; for I have rigged a great sailcloth tun-dish, with a canvas pipe into the tanks; and from every rain, I draw a supply, which has never run short.

"The child was born nearly five months ago. She is a fine little girl, and her mother seems perfectly happy. I believe I could be quietly happy with them, were it not that I have ever in mind the end of those seventeen years. True! we may be dead long before then; but, if not, our little girl will be in her teens—and it is a hungry age.

"If one of us died—but no! Much may happen in seventeen years. I will wait.

"My method of sending this clear of the weed is likely to succeed. I have constructed a small fire-balloon, and this missive, safely enclosed in a little barrel, will be attached. The wind will carry it swiftly hence.

"Should this ever reach civilised beings, will they see that it is forwarded to:—"

(Here followed an address, which, for some reason, had been roughly obliterated. Then came the signature of the writer)

"Arthur Samuel Philips."

The captain of the schooner looked over at Jock, as the man made an end of his reading.

"Seventeen years pervisions," he muttered thoughtfully. "An' this 'ere were written sumthin' like twenty-nine years ago!" He nodded his head several times. "Poor creetures!" he exclaimed. "It'd be er long while, Jock—a long while!"

LOG THE MAN DEAD
by Eugene Burdick

Conditions in the navy have improved somewhat since the days when discipline was enforced by keelhauling and the cat-o'-nine-tails and the only reliable method of recruitment was the press-gang. "Log the Man Dead" is about this dark side of naval history and suggests that Captain Bligh was by no means a unique individual. Its author, Eugene Burdick (1918–1965), first came to prominence as the co-writer, with William Lederer, of *The Ugly American* (1958), a prophetic indictment of American foreign policy in south-east Asia. Marlon Brando was the star of the film version. Eugene Burdick's other best-known novel is *Fail Safe* (written in collaboration with Harvey Wheeler), a chilling story of the world brought to the brink of nuclear annihilation by a mechanical fault that sends American bombers winging towards Moscow. His other works include *The Ninth Wave* (1956), *The Blue of Capricorn* (1961), *The 480* (1964) and *Nina's* Book (1965).

IN THE HARBOUR of Plymouth, in England, the ship-building firm of Hawkins and Company was working day and night on the ship. During the day men, naked to the waist, chipped at huge raw logs, converting them into ribs and spars. At night, torches and cressets were lit and, in the fitful light, hot creosote and tallow were poured over the caulking which had been pounded into the seams. In the sail shops, yards of bright-red cloth were converted into sails. The great, gaunt ribs of the ship grew higher than the shops and were finally planked over and sanded into a slick surface. The masts were inserted into their locks and the long task of fitting the sails begun.

Crimping crews began to drive impressed crewmen aboard the ship. Among these was a tall, slim boy named Simon Jonson, from Devonshire. This was the first time he had ever seen salt water. As he filed aboard he looked up at the masts, their tips vanishing into the mist. The ship seemed enormous.

Finally a carpenter chiselled the letters T—I—G—E—R into the overhanging stern of the vessel. The next day the ship slid down the ways, heaved gently in the quiet waters and then rested, ready for the sea.

Four months later the ship was six hundred miles off Africa and becalmed in a great, dead circle of water. Occasionally a ground swell would bulge the grey, hot surface and the ship would creak. Under the steady blast of unrelieved brightness, the sea began to smell like iodine, quenched iron and dead fish.

But the *Tiger* was taut with excitement. For a man was on trial for his life and the man was Simon Jonson. He stood on the quarter deck in front of a table over which the officers of a court-martial eyed him. Behind him the entire crew was drawn up in three straight lines.

The men stood stiffly and sweat streaked their clothes black, poured down their faces, ran in trickles into their shoes. Simon Jonson, facing the sun, was almost blinded, so that the figures of the officers behind the table seemed to be tiny black figures, all identical and all very far away. Occasionally a salty drop of sweat ran into his eye, but he patiently blinked it away. He was thinking of an event that had occurred three weeks before. In exact and precise outlines, the memory came back to him. As the voice of the prosecutor droned on, endlessly and far away, Simon thought back to that rotten, irresistible memory.

It had started with a simple argument between Watson, the boatswain's mate, and Blake, the sailmaker. They had stood arguing by the hatch leading into the fo'c'sle and Simon had been listening. Suddenly, in one of those blinding seconds of action, the argument had grown heated and Blake had swung his sail needle at Martin. Quite by accident, the curved, ugly needle caught in Watson's shoulder muscle and jutted out, turning the shirt red as the blood seeped out. In a moment, Mr Galbraith, the second mate, was on the scene, and had arrested Blake for attacking another man.

"He didn't mean anything, Mr Galbraith," Watson said through his clenched teeth. As if to minimise his injury he reached up and jerked the needle out of his shoulder. The blood ran in a gush down his arm. "We was just fooling around."

"We'll let the captain decide that," Mr Galbraith said coldly. "There are regulations to govern such matters."

Two days later the captain had called the crew together and read the verdict against Blake. The captain was a tall, thin, aristocratic man who wore immaculate white linen at his throat. He looked somehow like a preacher as his Adam's apple worked in his long neck. When he finished two men seized Blake and dragged him to a block situated in the middle of the quarter deck. Blake screamed a long, quivering shriek and then stared with bulging eyes up at the sky.

One of the men forced the sail needle into Blake's open hand and then forced the hand down on to the block. At the same time another man stepped forward with a sharp hatchet. Simon had been standing numbly, hardly knowing what was happening. But as he saw the hatchet he guessed what was to come. With a quick, sliding jerk, he was out of the right ranks of the crew, had stepped across the deck and, tearing the hatchet from the man's hand, threw it over the side. Then, wheeling about, he swung accurately and powerfully at one of the men holding Blake's hand. The man fell and the other man let go. Blake stood frozen, staring up at the sky, paralysed with fear, unable to move.

In a moment Simon was subdued by a brace of seamen and was standing in front of the captain. He had not been excited when he left the ranks and he was not excited now, only impatient to explain to the captain the true story of the needle-stabbing episode.

"It was not a fight, sir," Simon started to say in a deliberate voice. "They were really only joking. It was not——"

The captain's already thin face had drawn sharp with anger. Two spots of colour burned in his cheeks.

"It states in the Rules for the Regulation of the Navy that any man who draws the blood of another shall have the hand that inflicted the damage chopped off," the captain said in a crisp, rigidly controlled voice.

"But any rule that doesn't recognise that this was just a joke between friends is a bad rule," Simon said. He could not conceive that the captain would not see the justice of this.

"The Regulations also state that anyone that interferes with the administrations of justice aboard a naval ship shall be confined to the bowsprit," the captain said. His narrow red tongue came out, flicked at the corners of his mouth, left his lips moist. "You shall stand court-martial for that offence."

And then, as the crew held Simon back, although he was calm and cool, the two men again held Blake's hand on the block. With a swish a new hatchet cut the air. A dark spray of blood shot over the deck, the severed hand opened with a jerk, and the gleaming, bright needle rolled out on the deck. Blake shrieked once, then groaned and fainted. Simon watched the proceedings coldly, his eyes moving from the hand to the captain's face.

"And Seaman Jonson was, to your best knowledge, not suffering from sunstroke, brain fever or other disease when he interfered with the administration of justice on last June fifteenth?" Lieutenant Galbraith, the prosecuting officer, was asking the ship's surgeon.

The surgeon, a squat fat man, with a red face, shook his head. "He was of sound mind and body." He turned his bloodshot drunkard's eyes towards Simon and then glanced quickly away.

Simon still could not believe that he would not be able to explain his actions. To his methodical, Devonshire mind it seemed a simple case of righting a wrong. He waited patiently for the moment when he would be asked to explain what had happened.

In a few more moments Lieutenant Galbraith finished his interrogation. He turned to the captain saying, "Sir, I have finished the presentation of the case for His Majesty's Navy."

"In your opinion, Mr Galbraith, does this offence fall under those crimes which call for automatic confinement to the bowsprit until dead?" the captain asked casually, although he was watching Simon while he spoke.

"Well, sir, it might be interpreted in another manner if

extenuating circumstances were found." Lieutenant Galbraith hedged, unwilling to face the reality of such a sentence.

"What would such extenuating circumstances be?" the captain asked in an icy voice. Without waiting for an answer he stood up and announced, "Gentlemen, the court-martial shall retire to my cabin to reach a verdict."

So suddenly that he could scarcely comprehend what had happened, the officers had left the quarter deck and Simon realised that he would never have a chance to plead his case; that the decision would be reached on the basis of the evidence that the court-martial had now taken. For the first time he thought seriously of "bowspritting". It was one of the most dreaded words in the navy and Simon had heard endless stories of former "bowspritting" sentences in the crew's quarters.

This was the most hideous of punishments. A sailor sentenced to be "spitted" was led to the bow of the ship where the power-ful jutting beak of the ship, reaching far out over the cut-water, constituted the bowsprit. At the foot of the bowsprit he was given a ration of beer, a half-loaf of bread and a sharp sail knife. Then two boatswain mates tied his body to the bowsprit, leaving his arms free. There, after finishing the bread and beer, he had three alternatives.

First, he could kill himself with the knife and have a speedy death. Or he could cut himself loose and fall into the ocean, where he would either drown or fall victim to the shark or the sharp slashing teeth of the barracuda. Or, finally, he could starve to death on the bowsprit. The thing he could not do was to come back off the bowsprit on to the ship. Five yards behind the victim the ship was going about its normal life, but he could only eye that life as his own existence was slowly squeezed out.

If the man stayed on the bowsprit and died, his body was not removed, and for months there would be the thick, rotten odour of death about the bowsprit as the elements and the sharp, pecking beaks of sea-birds reduced the body. Finally there would be nothing left but a jiggling, clean-picked skeleton, held to the spar by the few remaining lines. And no man would, or could, touch the lines on the skeleton. They must wait until the line rotted off and the skeleton slipped loose and fell into the sea.

"They won't spit you, Simon," one of the crew members murmured to him. "You did nothing wrong."

"Quiet there," the sergeant snarled.

The crew fell silent and then, after a pause, began to whisper among themselves. From the sound of their whispers Simon knew they thought he would get the bowsprit. He began to feel as if he were involved in a hot, steaming nightmare which had gripped him in some strange way, but which would release him before it was too late. The sun suddenly seemed to increase in size and warmth. His head felt empty and burned out. He knew he was afraid.

In ten minutes the officers filed back out of the cabin. The surgeon licked a smear of Demerara rum off his lips, the captain touched his hands to the linen at his neck, Lieutenant Galbraith looked deliberately past Simon. They assembled quickly around the table and Lieutenant Galbraith stood up. He cleared his throat and spoke.

"We find Apprentice Seaman Jonson guilty of obstructing the administration of justice and under the Regulations of the Navy we order him confined to the bowsprit, never to return. God rest his soul. Ship's Clerk, strike his name from the record. Boatswain, carry out the sentence. All hands splice the main brace."

Simon heard the crew stiffen in anger behind him, even before he realised what the sentence was. Then Simon felt his cheeks burn hot; behind his eyes he felt blackness loom up; the table and officers angled before his eyes and then vanished. He had fainted.

The captain turned and walked into his cabin. The officers walked slowly towards the limp, unconscious body of the boy. They picked him up and carried him to the bowsprit and bound him to the long spar. It was a hot, sultry day and Simon did not regain consciousness for some time. An officer was stationed at the foot of the bowsprit to make sure that Jonson did not return to the ship. As far as the British Navy was concerned, Simon Jonson was already dead. The ship's clerk drew a line through his name on the roster and put these words after it: "Died at sea."

Simon had been on the bowsprit only a half hour when the whole aspect of the sea suddenly altered. The bottle-green colour changed, a flat, black bank of clouds came bustling down out of the middle distance, and, with a sudden jerk, the sails filled, the frigate heeled over and began to scud across the ocean. The Canaries dropped away and the ship lurched swiftly towards the equatorial seas. The shock of the cool wind brought young Simon back to consciousness and as soon as he looked around he could see what had happened. He glanced at the sea, down the bowsprit to where the officer stood. Then he glanced at the worsening sea. He tucked the bread, the bottle of beer and the knife into his shirt, tightened the ropes around his chest and waist and locked his arms around the bowsprit.

Simon was tough, intelligent and determined to live. When he looked over his shoulder at the men, who gathered at the foot of the bowsprit to shout encouragement to him, his eyes bulged slightly with fear, but his jaw was strong and tight. As the seas got higher the bowsprit would occasionally dip deep into the green water, lurch back, and Simon would come to the surface dripping water, his fingers biting into the smooth, tough wood of the bowsprit.

The storm lasted six days. During that time Simon drank and ate nothing. His only refreshment was the shock of the seas passing over his body as the bowsprit lunged into the tropical waters. When it rained, he turned his head towards the sky, stuck his tongue out and caught a pitiful few drops of water. With his hands, he scooped the thin, slick layer of rainwater off of the surface of the spar and obtained a few more drops. Meanwhile the *Tiger* pitched and wallowed down the length of Africa, passed Dakar, and finally began to head south-east to swing in under the great belly of Africa and to run along the Gold Coast.

On the seventh day the winds died and the sun came up hot and clear. The sails began to flap again, the ship rolled listlessly. They were within a hundred miles of the equator. The bowl of the sea and sky became brassy with heat, the ocean steamed. The sun burned the salt water off of Simon's skin, leaving streaks of pure-white salt behind. In the storm his cap and shoes had washed away, and now the exposed skin on his feet, hands and face turned pink, then red, and as blisters formed, a painful white.

By the tenth day the boy's tongue began to protrude from his mouth and he chewed on a small piece of the bread, trying to work up some saliva. On the eleventh day Martin advised him to take some of the beer, and for the first time the boy uncorked the bottle and took a mouthful of the rich bitter stuff. Martin was the boatswain of the *Tiger* and although he had spent twenty years at sea he was bitterly opposed to the navy method of discipline. A tough, wizened, sun-blackened man, he had much admired Simon's calm performance before the court-martial. The beer revived Simon at once and he waved a hand at the crew members who stood at the foot of the bowsprit. The crew roared support back to him.

"Just a mouthful, Simon. That's all you can have today," Martin called to him. "Cork up the bottle and put it back in your shirt."

The boy obeyed reluctantly, his bleary, bloodshot eyes fastened on the bottle of beer. Martin now spent his nights sleeping at the foot of the bowsprit, awakening throughout the night to give the boy encouragement and, occasionally, to pray with him.

On the thirteenth day two things happened. The lines holding Simon had become loose because of the weight he had lost. It took him six hours to untie the knots and tighten up the lines around his shrunken body. The second thing that happened was that he began to moan—an occasional desolate, low scream of pain that hung over the ship like a curse before the tropical winds swept it away.

By now the ship had swung under the great overhanging belly of Africa and was heading towards the tiny island of Sao Thomé, which was almost exactly on the equator. Each day the sun came up hot and clear and beat down on the boy on the unprotected bowsprit. During the hottest part of the day the helmsman tried to steer so that the sails made a shadow over Simon, but the captain insisted relentlessly that they hold to the true compass course.

By now the boy's tongue was black and swollen. The exposed skin of his feet and neck had formed into hard brown scabs of burnt flesh. He lay like a sack of rags, only his hands, clinging like claws to the bowsprit, seemed alive. He gave a cry of despair two or three times a day. Once a day he took a single mouthful of beer from the bottle. He could no longer chew the bread. Several times when the members of the crew were swabbing down decks they would throw a bucket of cool sea-water over his dry body. This would revive him and he would wave a thin hand in thanks. The crew members cheered wildly whenever this happened. The officer on watch would beat the offending crew member, but it went on despite this.

On the seventeenth day, Sao Thomé was sighted and the ship steadied on a direct course for the island. The boy had not stirred for a day now and the crew feared he was dead. As the ship threaded its way through the channel the crew stood watching him. The ship was finally warped alongside the dock.

"Boy, you've made it, you're safe," Martin said in a low voice. "Come on, boy, wake up. Cut yourself loose. We've made a port."

Nothing happened, and a groan went up from the crew. Martin's voice went higher, a note of despair in it, as he repeated the words.

Then the bundle of rags stirred, the boy's head, now balancing on an incredibly thin neck, came up. Through the puffed and lacerated eyelids there was a gleam of light. Thick, swollen fingers laced with blood reached into his shirt, took out the knife. With weak, grotesque motions he sawed at the ropes, cutting through a thread at a time. He finished one rope and then collapsed, unconscious. In a half hour he revived and doggedly cut through the last rope. Then he turned and looked dully at the crew without speaking.

"You can't come back down the bowsprit," Martin shouted. "It's against the King's Regulations. Drop into the water."

The words slowly worked through to Simon's mind. He let go of the knife, half-turned on the bowsprit and fell into the still water alongside the dock with a loud splash.

The boatswain, Martin, and two other sailors dived over the side. They collared Simon and swam over to the pier with him. Two other sailors had sprinted off down the dock. They came back with oranges, sugar lumps and a beaker of water. They squeezed the juice of several oranges into his mouth, past the swollen, blackened tongue; then gradually and slowly they gave him water. By that afternoon the tough fibre of the boy's body was already knitting and he was asking for meat. He was going to live. But the seventeen days on the bowsprit had changed Simon Jonson. He was no longer a boy. He had become a hard and bitter man. Although he recovered quickly from the ravages of exposure, lines remained about his mouth and eyes. Whenever the *Tiger* was mentioned his face became a flat, implacable mask in which his eyes glittered with a cold hatred.

Martin explained that it had never been contemplated that a man would return alive from the trip to the bowsprit. In the eyes of the captain, Simon was now dead. In the eyes of the Navy and of England, Simon was also dead, and his family would be notified that he had died at sea. He was without passport, nationality, money, family or profession. Simon nodded grimly as Martin talked, his eyes occasionally wandering down the dock to the black, empty outline of the bowsprit on which he had lived for so many days.

"I'll live somehow," Simon said flatly. "Can you teach me how to build a boat before the *Tiger* sails? If you can, I'll have a trade that I can work at. Then I won't starve to death on this miserable island."

"I'll try, my boy," Martin said. "But it is a difficult craft. It takes time."

Eighteen hours a day, for the time the *Tiger* remained in port, Martin taught Simon the craft. Simon's gaunt hands were weak at first, but they were sure and deft. He learned quickly. In all that time, however, Simon did not once talk of England and he would not permit Martin to mention the Royal Navy or the humiliation of his bowspritting. Martin was disturbed by the steel-hard bitterness he found in Simon. Once he began to talk of Christian forgiveness, but Simon only stared at him with glazed and cynical eyes. Martin's voice trailed off inconclusively, disconcerted by the hardness in Simon's face which appeared to intensify.

Finally the *Tiger* sailed. Everyone on the island was on the docks to watch it leave—except Simon Jonson. He was on the far side of the island cutting a rosewood tree into spars for a sloop he had already started to build. He had his trade, and was hard at work.

During the next year Simon built furniture, homes, canoes—anything to keep alive. In his spare time he worked on his sloop. It took two years to finish it.

The day it was finished he took on a crew of four Gold Coast Negroes and began to roam the under part of Africa. He bought hardwoods, spices, gold, pearls, and an occasional diamond. These goods he then resold to European merchants. He gained a reputation for being a fair and honest dealer and he worked at a grinding pace. He confided in no one, made no friends, was never known to smile. Within five years he was one of the richest men to be found along the Gold Coast.

Four times a year he wrote long letters to Martin. In these letters his furious, raging hatred of the British Navy was put into words. Martin, now retired to his cottage in Oxford, wrote Simon to soften his attitude, to let bygones be bygones. Each reply was the same: a restatement of Simon's quiet, deadly hatred for the men who had tortured him and whom he would never forget.

Finally, seven years after the bowspritting of Simon, Martin wrote a letter in which he offered to send his youngest daughter, Nancy, to Sao Thomé in the hopes that she and Simon would be married. The girl was eighteen, tall, clean-limbed and cheerful. Martin wrote that she was the only thing that could save Simon from the cancerous hate that was eating inside him.

For six months there was no response to his letter.

Then, suddenly and unexpectedly, Simon Jonson was given his revenge. He was in a dirty, hot anchorage north of Cape Lopez, negotiating for the purchase of six huge pearls that had been passed from one native hand to another halfway around the globe. He had almost completed the sale when a canoe with three natives in it came flying across the anchorage. They reported that they had seen an English man-of-war drifting hopelessly with the current, far out at sea. And, they reported, there was a man tied to the bowsprit.

Simon completed his sale, gathered his crew and set sail in the direction the natives indicated. After two days of sailing he located the ship. As soon as he saw it, he knew what had appened. It was the victim of what was called a line hurricane.

Line hurricanes are short-lived storms of a terrible intensity. The horizon is suddenly obscured by a black, solid line of clouds that is laced with lightning flashes around the surface of he sea, the sea in front of the storm becomes flat, the whole universe seems to stop and to wait dully for a few seconds. The hurricane strikes like a coiled snake. In a matter of seconds the wind rises to enormous velocities and pulls the tops of the waves after it, so that there is a flat, flying sheet of water a few feet off the surface. Beneath this, great combers of green-and-white water crash insanely against one another. For several minutes he whole ocean turns dark, and the hissing of water and wind is so great that normal voices are utterly lost. Then it is suddenly over. The sea falls flat, the sun reappears, a few wounded fish lie gasping and dying on the surface. But if a sailing vessel is caught in such a storm with sail on, either its sails will be ripped to shreds or its mast snapped. A poorly handled ship will simply vanish and a well-handled one will be badly damaged at the very best.

As Simon approached the ship, he saw it was a large man-of-war. It carried thirty-three guns and the name *India* was on its stern. All the masts had been broken, the decks were a tangle of broken spars and lines, there were gaping holes in the gun decks where the guns had come adrift and smashed their way overboard, the rails were splintered and torn, bits of sail, mattresses, shattered casks, wet powder were scattered over everything.

And the natives had been right . . . from the bowsprit dangled he body of a man.

As Simon bore down on the *India*, the desultory activity of he men aboard the ship stopped. Men staggered to the rails, looked with bleary eyes at Simon's sloop. A hatch opened and the captain walked out on deck. Simon hove-to a hundred feet from the damaged ship.

"What happened to you?" he shouted to the captain.

"Hit by a line hurricane," the captain said in a rasping voice. 'No time to batten down or secure. Our guns came adrift and smashed half the crew before they went overboard. Compass ruined. All our water kegs smashed into pieces."

WOT * *

The captain ran a dry tongue over even drier lips. Simon realised that all of the men along the rail were half dead with thirst.

"You are a hundred and fifteen miles south-west of Calbar. I advise you to make for it at once," Simon said. He motioned for his black crew to set sail and he began to veer away from the *India*.

"Wait, man," the captain cried. "Do you have water? My God, we are dying of thirst. We can never make land in this condition. If you have water, in the name of mercy give it to us."

"Yes, I have five large kegs of fresh water," Simon said.

"Look, you talk English; you must be an Englishman," the captain croaked. "I order you to come alongside and give us water and supplies. I further order you——"

"I am no English subject," Simon said coldly. "I am a citizen of the seas. I am under no obligation to obey your orders."

He ran back alongside the ship, but carefully stayed out of gunshot. The captain, reeling slightly under the impact of the tropical sun, stared down at him unbelievingly.

"Then I request you to aid us in the name of common humanity," the captain said.

"Ah, common humanity, that is another thing," Simon said, but his voice was colder and more deadly than before. "Then, in the name of common humanity, I order you to take that man down from the bowsprit."

"That is impossible," the captain said. "That man was sentenced to the bowsprit several days ago under the authority of His Majesty's Regulations for the Government of the Royal Navy. It is impossible for me or anyone else to order him cut loose."

The men on the rail, the captain and Simon all looked down the ship towards the bowsprit. The poor wretch tied there raised his head, his eyes glittering with hope. The captain turned and looked down at Simon.

There was a long silence while all the vast and massive authority of the British Navy matched wills with a single individual in a small sloop.

"It is impossible for me to aid you as long as that man is tied to the bowsprit," Simon said deliberately and slowly. He

stured to his crew and the sails of his sloop went up. As the
nvas ballooned slowly, the sloop picked up way and began
move away from the *India*.

"No man was ever allowed to come down off the bowsprit
the ship," the captain screamed.

Simon did not reply. He merely glanced once at the captain,
en at the man on the bowsprit. Then he turned his back to
e ship.

The captain's tongue came out, his hot, dry breath whistled
t through the dry passages of his nose. Then he threw back
s head and shouted after Simon, suddenly afraid that he could
t be heard.

"Cut the man loose from the bowsprit. I pardon him
conditionally."

The crew began a ragged cheer. Men stumbled down the
ck towards the bowsprit, clambered over the debris to set
eir shipmate free. The man on the bowsprit waved his hands
ebly, unable to realise fully what had happened.

Simon heard the command and put his tiller hard over. The
oop bore down on the shattered hulk of the *India*. As lines
me from the ship and were tied to huge water casks in the
oop, Simon did something he had not done in seven years. He
t his head back and smiled up at the crew. As the men stove
the end of the first cask and stuck their dry heads into the
esh water he continued to smile at them.

Two weeks later when he returned to Sao Thomé, after aiding
e *India* to make port, he sat down to answer the last letter of
s friend Martin.

"My dear and only friend Martin," he began. "Since you
rote, something has happened which has much changed my
rmer attitude. You will now find that I am more kindly dis-
osed towards His Majesty's Navy in particular and the English
ople in general. I would now be most grateful if you would
nd your youngest daughter Nancy to Sao Thomé as you pro-
osed in your last letter. She will not have an easy life here, but
e can be assured that I shall give her all the love and care and
votion of which I am capable . . ."

THE PHANTOM DEATH
by William Clark Russell

Born in New York of English parents (his mother believe
herself related to Wordsworth), William Clark Russell (1844
1911) went to sea as a ship's apprentice at an early age an
served eight arduous years aboard a merchantman, voyagin
to India and Australia and other distant ports of call. He gav
up the seaman's life in 1866 to become a journalist but foun
greater success writing novels and short stories inspired by h
shipboard experiences. His first major work was *The Wreck (*
the Grosvenor (1877), now regarded as a classic of maritim
literature. Amongst his other notable works are *The Froze*
Pirate (1877), *Round the Galley Fire* (1883), *On the Fo'c's*
Head (1884), *The Death Ship* (1888) and *An Ocean Traged*
(1891). Russell was the author of fifty-seven books altogethe
including several biographies of naval personalities such a
Nelson, Collingwood and Dampier and some collections of se
shanties. Although William Clark Russell is now largely fo
gotten, his fiction was much in demand in the late Victoria
period. His success may even have led William Hope Hodgso
to pursue a literary career along similar lines.

One by-product of Russell's writing was that his work ex
posed the cruelties and hardships suffered by merchant seame
and helped bring about some sorely-needed reforms in th
Merchant Navy.

On the 24th of April, 1840, having finished the busines
that had carried me into the Brazils, I arrived at Rio de Janeir
where I found a vessel lying nearly loaded, and sailing for th
port of Bristol in four or five days. In those times, passenge

affic between Great Britain and the eastern coast of South
merica was almost entirely carried on in small ships, averag-
g from two hundred to five hundred tons. The funnel of the
:ean mail steamer, with her gilded saloons and side wheels,
hich, to the great admiration of all beholders, slapped twelve
1ots an hour out of the composite fabric, had not yet hove into
ght above the horizon of commerce, and folks were very well
.tisfied if they were no longer than three months in reaching
e Brazilian coast out of the River Thames.

The little ship in which I took passage was a barque called
e Lord of the Isles; her burthen was something under four
1ndred tons. She was a round-bowed waggon of a vanished
pe, with a square, sawed-off stern, painted ports, heavy over-
1nging channels, and as loftily rigged, I was going to say, as
line-of-battle ship, owing to her immense beam, which gave
:r the stability of a church. I applied to the agent and hired
cabin, and found myself, to my secret satisfaction, the only
1ssenger in the ship. Yes, I was rejoiced to be the sole
1ssenger; my passage out had been rendered memorably miser-
•le by the society of as ill-conditioned, bad-tempered, sulky
lot of wretches as ever turned in of a night into bunks, and
1rsed the captain in their gizzards in a calm for not being able
whistle a wind up over the sea-line.

The name of the skipper of the Lord of the Isles was Joyce.
e was unlike the average run of the men in that trade. Instead
being beef-faced and bow-legged, humid of eye and gay with
og-blossoms, he was tall, pale, spare; he spoke low and in a
elancholy key; he never swore; he drank wine and water, and
ere was little or nothing in his language to suggest the sailor.
is berth was right aft on the starboard side; mine was right
t also, next his. Three cabins on either hand ran forward from
ese two after-berths. Two of them were occupied by the first
d second mates. Between was a roomy "state-cabin", as the
rm then was; a plain interior furnished with an oblong table
d fixed chairs, lighted by day by a large skylight, by night
• a couple of brass lamps.

We sailed away on a Monday morning, as well I recollect,
1t of the spacious and splendid scene of the harbour of Rio,
1d under full breasts of canvas, swelling to the height of a

main-skysail big enough to serve as a mizzen topgallant-sail fc
a thousand-ton ship of today, and with taut bowlines and yearn
ing jibs, and a heel of hull that washed a two-foot-wide strea
of greenish copper through the wool-white swirl of froth tha
broke from the bows, the *Lord of the Isles* headed on a straigl
course for the deep solitudes of the Atlantic.

All went well with us for several days. Our ship's compan
consisted of twelve men, including a boatswain and carpente
The forecastle hands appeared very hearty, likely fellow
despite their pier-head raiment of Scotch cap and broken sma
clothes, and open flannel shirt, and greasy sheath-knife belte
to the hip. They worked with a will, they sang out cheerily a
the ropes, they went in and out of the galley at meal-time witl
out faces of loathing, and but one complaint came aft befor
our wonderful, mysterious troubles began: the ship's brea
crawled, they said, and, being found truly very bad, good whit
flour was served out in lieu.

We had been eight days at sea, and in that time had mac
fairly good way; it drew down a quiet, soft, black night with th
young moon gone soon after sunset, a trembling flash of sta
over the mastheads, a murky dimness of heat and of stagnatic
all round about the sea-line, and a frequent glance of sea-fir
over the side when a dip of the barque's round bends drove th
water from her in a swelling cloud of ebony. I walked th
quarter deck with the captain, and our talk was of England an
of the Brazils, and of his experiences as a mariner of thirt
years' standing.

"What of the weather?" said I, as we came to a pause at th
binnacle, whose bright disc of illuminated card touched int
phantom outlines the hairy features of the Jack who graspe
the wheel.

"There's a spell of quiet before us, I fear," he answered, in h
melancholy, monotonous voice. "No doubt a day will come, N
West, when the unhappy sea-captain upon whose forehead th
shipowner would be glad to brand the words 'Prompt Despatc
will be rendered by steam independent of that most capriciot
of all things—wind. The wind bloweth as it listeth—which
very well whilst it keeps all on blowing; for with our machiner
of trusses, and parrels, and braces, we can snatch a sort

propulsion out of anything short of hurricane antagonism within six points of what we want to look up for. But of a dead night and of a dead day, with the wind up and down, and your ship showing her stern to the thirty-two points in a single watch, what's to be done with an owner's request of *look sharp*? Will you come below and have some grog?"

The second mate, a man named Bonner, was in charge of the deck. I followed the captain into the cabin, where he smoked a cigar; he drank a little wine and water, I drained a tumbler of cold brandy grog, then stepped above for an hour of fresh air, and afterwards to bed, six bells, eleven o'clock, striking as I turned in.

I slept soundly, awoke at seven o'clock, and shortly afterwards went on deck. The watch were at work washing down. The crystal brine flashed over the white plank to the swing of the bucket in the boatswain's powerful grasp, and the air was filled with the busy noise of scrubbing-brushes, and of the murmurs of some live-stock under the long-boat. The morning was a wide radiant scene of tropic sky and sea—afar, right astern on the light blue verge, trembled the mother-o'-pearl canvas of a ship; a small breeze was blowing off the beam; from under the round bows of the slightly-leaning barque came a pleasant, brook-like sound of running waters—a soft shaling as of foam over stones, sweet to the ear in that heat as the music of a fountain. Mr Bonner, the second mate, was again in charge of the deck. When I passed through the companion hatch I saw him standing abreast of the skylight at the rail: the expression of his face was grave and full of concern, and he seemed to watch the movements of the men with an inattentive eye.

I bade him good morning; he made no reply for a little, but looked at me fixedly, and then said, "I'm afraid Captain Joyce is a dead man."

"What is wrong with him?" I exclaimed eagerly, and much startled.

"I don't know, sir. I wish there was a medical man on board. Perhaps you'd be able to tell what he's suffering from if you saw him."

I at once went below, and found the lad who waited upon us in the cabin preparing the table for breakfast. I asked him if

the captain was alone. He answered that Mr Stroud, the chief
mate, was with him. On this I went to the door of Captain
Joyce's cabin and lightly knocked. The mate looked out, and
seeing who I was, told me in a soft voice to enter.

Captain Joyce lay in his bunk dressed in a flannel shirt and
a pair of white drill trousers. All his throat and a considerable
portion of his chest were exposed, and his feet were naked.
looked at him scarcely crediting my sight: I did not know him
as the man I had parted with but a few hours before. He was
swelled from head to foot as though drowned: the swelling
contorted his countenance out of all resemblance to his familiar
face; the flesh of him that was visible was a pale blue, as
rubbed with a powder of the stuff called "blue" which the
laundresses use in getting up their linen. His eyes were open
but the pupils were rolled out of sight, and the "whites", as they
are called, were covered with red blotches.

I had no knowledge of medicine, and could not imagine what
had come to the poor man. He was unconscious, and evidently
fast sinking. I said to Mr Stroud, "What is this?"

The mate answered, "I'm afraid he's poisoned himself acci
dentally. It looks to me like poison. Don't it seem so to you, sir
See how his fingers and toes are curled."

I ran my eye over the cabin and exclaimed, "Have you
searched for any bottles containing poison?"

"I did so when he sent for me at four o'clock, and complained
of feeling sick and ill. He was then changing colour, and his
face was losing its proper looks. I asked him if he thought he
had taken anything by mistake. He answered no, unless he had
done so in his sleep. He awoke feeling very bad, and that was
all he could tell me."

I touched the poor fellow's hand, and found it cold. His
breathing was swift and thin. At moments a convulsion, like
wrenching shudder, passed through him.

"Is it," I asked, "some form of country sickness, do you
think—some kind of illness that was lying latent in him when
we sailed?"

"I never heard of any sort of sickness," he answered, "that
made a man look like that—not cholera even. And what but

poison would do its work so quickly? Depend upon it he's either been poisoned, or poisoned himself unawares."

"Poisoned!" I exclaimed. "Who's the man in this ship that's going to do such a thing?"

"It's no natural illness," he answered, looking at the livid, bloated face of the dying man; and he repeated with gloomy emphasis, "he's either been poisoned, or he's poisoned himself unawares."

I stood beside Mr Stroud for about a quarter of an hour, watching the captain and speculating upon the cause of his mortal sickness; we talked in low voices, often pausing and starting, for the convulsions of the sufferer made us think that he had his mind and wished to sit up and speak; but the ghastly, horrid, vacant look of his face continued fixed by the stubborn burial of the pupils of his eyes; his lips moved only when his frame was convulsed. I put my finger upon his pulse and found the beat thread-like, terribly rapid, intermittent, and faint. Then, feeling sick and scared, I went on deck for some air.

The second mate asked me how the captain was and what I thought. I answered that he might be dead even now as I spoke; that I could not conceive the nature of the malady that was killing him, that had apparently fastened upon him in his sleep, and was threatening to kill him within the compass of four or five hours, but that Mr Stroud believed he had been poisoned, or had poisoned himself accidently.

"Poisoned!" echoed the second mate, and he sent a look in the direction of the ship's galley. "What's he eaten that we haven't partaken of? A regular case of poisoning, does the chief officer think it? Oh no—oh no—who's to do it? The captain's too well liked to allow of such a guess as that. If the food's been fouled by the cook in error, how's it that the others of us who ate at the cabin table aren't likewise seized?"

There was no more to be said about it then, but in less than half an hour's time the mate came up and told us the captain was gone.

"He never recovered his senses, never spoke except to talk in delirium," he said.

"You think he was poisoned, sir?" said the second mate.

"Not wilfully," answered Mr Stroud, looking at me. "I never

said that; nor is it a thing one wants to think of," he added
sending his gaze round the wide scene of flashing ocean.

He then abruptly quitted us and walked to the galley, wher
for some while he remained out of sight. When he returned h
told the second mate with whom I had stood talking that h
had spoken to the cook, and thoroughly overhauled the dressin
utensils, and was satisfied that the galley had nothing to do wit
the murderous mischief which had befallen the skipper.

"But why be so cock-certain, Mr Stroud," said I, "that th
captain's dead of poisoning?"

"I *am* cock-certain," he answered shortly, and with som
little passion. "Name me the illness that's going to kill a ma
in three or four hours, and make such a corpse of him as lie
in the captain's cabin."

He called to the second mate, and they paced the deck to
gether deep in talk. The men had come up from breakfast, an
the boatswain had set them to the various jobs of the mornin
but the news of the captain's death had gone forward; it wa
shocking by reason of its suddenness. Then, again, the deat
of the master of a ship lies cold and heavy upon the spirits of
company at sea; 'tis the head gone, the thinking part. The mat
may make as good a captain, but he's not the man the cre
signed articles under. The seamen of the *Lord of the Isles* wor
grave faces as they went about their work; they spoke softl
and the boatswain delivered his orders in subdued notes. Afte
a bit the second mate walked forward and addressed the boats
wain and some of the men, but what he said I did not catch.

I breakfasted and returned on deck: it was then ten o'cloc
I found the main topsail to the mast and a number of seame
standing in the gangway, whilst the two mates hung together o
the quarter deck, talking, as though waiting. In a few minute
four seamen brought the body of the captain up through th
companion hatch, and carried it to the gangway. The corpse wa
stitched up in a hammock and rested upon a plank, over whic
the English ensign was thrown. I thought this funeral ver
hurried, and dreaded to think that the poor man might b
breathing and alive at the instant of his launch, for after all w
had but the mate's assurance that the captain was dead; an
what did Mr Stroud know of death—that is, as it would be ir

dicated by the body of a man who had died from some swift, subtle, nameless distemper, as Captain Joyce seemingly had?

When the funeral was over, the topsail swung, and the men returned to their work, I put the matter to the mate, who answered that the corpse had turned black, and that there could be no more question of his being dead than of his now being overboard.

The breeze freshened that morning. At noon it was blowing strong, with a dark, hard sky of compacted cloud, under which curls and shreds of yellow scud fled like a scattering of smoke, and the mates were unable to get an observation. Mr Stroud seemed engrossed by the sudden responsibilities which had come upon him, and talked little. That afternoon he shifted into the captain's berth, being now, indeed, in command of the barque. It was convenient to him to live in that cabin, for the necessary nautical appliances for navigating the ship were there along with facilities for their use. Mr Bonner told me that he and the mate had thoroughly examined the cabin, overhauled the captain's boxes, lockers, shelves and the like for anything of a poisonous nature, but had met with nothing whatever. It was indeed an amazing mystery, he said, and he was no longer of opinion with Mr Stroud that poison, accidentally or otherwise taken, had destroyed the captain. Indeed, he now leaned to my view, that Captain Joyce had fallen a victim to some disease which had lain latent in him since leaving Rio, something deadly quick and horribly transforming, well known, maybe, to physicians of the Brazils, if, indeed, it were peculiar to that country.

Well, three days passed, and nothing of any moment happened. The wind drew ahead and braced our yards fore and aft for us, and the tub of a barque went to leeward like an empty cask, shouldering the head seas into snowstorms off her heavy round bow, and furrowing a short scope of oil-smooth wake almost at right angles with her sternpost. Though Mr Stroud had charge of the ship, he continued from this time to keep watch and watch with Mr Bonner as in the captain's life, not choosing, I dare say, to entrust the charge of the deck to the boatswain. On the evening of this third day that I have come to, I was sitting in the cabin under the lamp writing down some memories of the past week in a diary, when the door of the captain's berth was opened, and my name was faintly called. I saw Mr Stroud, and instantly went to him. His hands were clasped upon his brow, and he swayed violently as though in pain, with greater vehemence than the heave of the deck warranted; his eyes were starting, and, by the clear light of the brace of cabin lamps, I easily saw that his complexion was unusually dusky, and darkening even, so it seemed to me, as I looked.

I cried out, "What is the matter, Mr Stroud?"

"Oh, my God!" he exclaimed, "I am in terrible pain—I am horribly ill—I am dying."

I grasped him by the arm and conducted him to his bunk, into which he got, groaning and holding his head, with an occasional strange short plunge of his feet such as a swimmer makes when resting in the water on his back. I asked him if he was only just now seized. He answered that he was in a deep sleep, from which he was awakened by a burning sensation throughout his body. He lay quiet awhile, supposing it was a sudden heat of the blood; but the fire increased, and with it came torturing pains in the head, and attacks of convulsions; and even whilst he told me this the convulsive fits grew upon him, and he broke off to groan deeply as though in exquisite pain and distress of mind; then he'd set his teeth, and then presently scream out, "Oh, my God! I have been poisoned—I am dying!"

I was thunderstruck and terrified to the last degree. What was this dreadful thing—this phantom death that had come into the ship? Was it a contagious plague? But what distemper is there that, catching men in their sleep, swells and discolours them even as the gaze rests upon them, and dismisses their souls to God in the space of three or four hours?

I ran on deck, but waited until Mr Bonner had finished bawling out some orders to the men before addressing him. The moon was young, but bright, and she sheared scythe-like through the pouring shadows, and the light of her made a marvellous brilliant whiteness of the foam as it burst in masses from the plunge of the barque's bows. When I gave the news to Mr Bonner, he stared at me for some moments wildly and in silence, and then rushed below. I followed him as quick as he went, for I had often used the sea, and the giddiest dance of a deck-plank was all one with the solid earth to my accustomed feet. We entered the mate's berth, and Mr Bonner lighted the bracket lamp and stood looking at his shipmate, and by the aid of the flame he had kindled, and the bright light flowing in through the open door, I beheld a tragic and wonderful change in Mr Stroud, though scarce ten minutes had passed since I was with him. His face was bloated, the features distorted, his eyes rolled continuously, and frequent heavy twitching shudders convulsed his body. But the most frightful part was the dusky hue of his skin, that was of a darker blue than I had observed in the captain.

He still had his senses, and repeated to the second mate what he had related to me. But he presently grew incoherent, then fell delirious, in about an hour's time was speechless and lay racked with convulsions; of a horrid blue, the features shockingly convulsed, and the whites of the eyes alone showing as in the captain's case.

He had called me at about nine o'clock, and he was a dead man at two in the morning, or four bells in the middle watch. Both the second mate and I were constantly in and out with the poor fellow; but we could do no good, only marvel, and murmur our astonishment and speculations. We put the captain's steward, a young fellow, to watch him—this was an hour before his death—and at four bells the lad came out with a white face, and said to me, who sat at the table, depressed and awed and overwhelmed by this second ghastly and indeterminable visitation, that the chief mate was dead, had ceased to breathe, and was quickly turning black.

Mr Bonner came into the cabin with the boatswain, and they went into the dead man's berth and stayed there about a quarter of an hour. When they came out the boatswain looked at me hard. I recollect that that man's name was Matthews. I asked some questions, but they had nothing to tell, except that the body had turned black.

"What manner of disease can it be that kills in this fashion?" said I. "If it's the plague, we may be all dead men in a week."

"It's no plague," said the boatswain, in a voice that trembled with its own volume of sound.

"What is it?" I cried.

"Poison!" he shouted, and he dropped his clenched fist with the weight of a cannon-ball upon the table.

I looked at the second mate, who exclaimed, "The boatswain swears to the signs. He's seen the like of that corpse in three English seamen who were poisoned up at Chusan."

"Do you want to make out that both men have committed suicide?" I exclaimed.

"I want to make out that both men have been poisoned!" shouted the boatswain, in his voice of thunder.

There was a significance in the insolence of the fellow that confounded and alarmed me, and the meaning was deepened by the second mate allowing his companion to address me in this roaring, affronting way without reproof. I hoped that the man had been drinking, and that the second mate was too stupid with horror to heed his behaviour to me, and without giving either of them another word I walked to my cabin and lay down.

I have no space here to describe the wild and terrifying fancies which ran in my head. For some while I heard the boatswain and the second mate conversing, but the cabin bulkhead was stout, the straining and washing noises all about the helm heavy and continuous, and I caught not a syllable of what they said. At what hour I fell asleep I cannot tell; when I awoke my cabin was full of the sunshine that streamed in through the stern window. I dressed, and took hold of the handle of the door, and found myself a prisoner. Not doubting I was locked up in error, I shook the door, and beat upon it, and called out loudly to be released. After a few minutes the door was opened, and the second mate stood in the threshold. He exclaimed—"Mr West, it's the wish of the men that you should be locked up. I'm no party to the job—but they're resolved. I'll tell you plainly what they think: they believe you've had a hand in the death of the captain and the chief mate—the bo'sun's put that into their heads; I'm the only navigator left, and they're afraid you'll try your hand on me if you have your liberty. You'll be regularly fed and properly seen to; but it's the crew's will that you stop here."

With that, and without giving me time to utter a word, he closed and secured the door. I leaned against the bulkhead and sought to rally my wits, but I own that for a long while I was as one whose mind comes slowly to him after he has been knocked down insensible. I never for an instant supposed that the crew really believed me guilty of poisoning the captain and chief mate: I concluded that the men had mutinied, and arranged with Mr Bonner to run away with the ship, and that I should remain locked up in my cabin until they had decided what to do with me.

By-and-by the door was opened, and the young steward put a tray containing some breakfast upon the cabin deck. He was but a mule of a boy, and I guessed that nothing but what might still further imperil me could come of my questioning him, so in silence I watched him put down the tray and depart. The meal thus sent to me was plentiful, and I drew some small heart out of the attention. Whilst I ate and drank, I heard sounds in the adjoining berth, and presently gathered that they were preparing the body of the chief mate for its last toss over the side. After a bit they went on deck with the corpse, and then all was still in the cabin. I knew by the light of the sun that the vessel was still heading on her course for England. It was a bright morning, with a wild windy sparkle in as much of the weather as I could see through the cabin window. The plunge of the ship's stern brought the water in a roar of milky froth all about the counter close under me, and the frequent jar of rudder and jump of wheel assured me that the barque was travelling fast through the seas.

What, in God's name, did the men mean by keeping me a prisoner? Did they think me a madman? Or that I, whose life together with theirs depended upon the safe navigation of the barque, would destroy those who alone could promise me security? And what had slain the two men? If poison, who had administered it? One man might have died by his own hand, but not both. And since both had perished from the same cause, self-murder was not to be thought of. What was it, then, that had killed them, visiting them in their sleep, and discolouring, bloating, convulsing, and destroying them in a few hours? Was it some deadly malady subtly lurking in the atmosphere of the after part of the vessel? If so, then I might be the next to be taken. Or was there some devilish murderer lying secretly hidden? Or was one of the crew the doer of these things? I seemed to smell disease and death, and yearned for the freedom of the deck, and for the sweetness of the wide, strong rush of wind.

The day passed. The second mate never visited me. The lad arrived with my meals, and when he came with my supper I asked him some questions, but obtained no more news than that the second mate had taken up his quarters in the adjoining berth as acting captain, and that the boatswain was keeping watch and watch with him.

I got but little rest that night. It blew hard, and the pitching of the vessel was unusually heavy. Then, again, I was profoundly agitated and in deep distress of mind; for, supposing the men in earnest, it was not only horrible to be thought capable of murder, there was the prospect of my being charged and of having to clear my character. Or, supposing the men's suspicion or accusation a villainous pretext, how would they serve me? Would they send me adrift, or set me ashore to perish on some barren coast, or destroy me out of hand? You will remember that I am writing of an age when seafaring was not as it now is. The pirate and the slaver were still afloat doing a brisk business. There often went a desperate spirit in ships' forecastles, and the maritime records of the time abound with tragic narratives of revolt, seizure, cruelty of a ferocious sort.

Another day and another night went by, and I was still locked up in my cabin, and, saving the punctual arrival of the lad with my meals, no man visited me.

Some time about eight o'clock on the morning of the third day of my confinement, I was looking through the cabin window at the space of grey and foaming sea and sallow flying sky which came and went in the square of the aperture with the lift and fall of the barque's stern, when my cabin door was struck upon, and in a minute afterwards opened, and the boatswain appeared.

"Mr West," said he, after looking at me for a moment in silence with a face whose expression was made up of concern and fear and embarrassment, "I've come on my own part, and on the part of the men, sir, to ask your pardon for our treatment of you. We was mistook. And our fears made us too willing to believe that you had a hand in it. We dunno what it is now, but as Jesus is my God, Mr West, the second mate he lies dead of the same thing in the next cabin!"

I went past him too stupefied to speak, and in a blind way sat down at the cabin table and leaned my head against my hand. Presently I looked up, and on lifting my eyes I caught sight of two or three sailors staring down with white faces through the skylight.

"You tell me that the second mate's dead?" said I.

"Yes, sir, dead of poison, too, so help me God!" cried the boatswain.

"Who remains to navigate the ship?" I said.

"That's it, sir!" he exclaimed, "unless you can do it?"

"Not I. There's no man amongst you more ignorant. May I look at the body?"

He opened the door of the cabin in which the others had died, and there, in the bunk from which the bodies of Captain Joyce and Mr Stroud had been removed, lay now the blackened corpse of the second mate. It was an awful sight and a passage of time horrible with the mystery which charged it. I felt no rage at the manner in which I had been used by that dead man there and the hurricane-lunged seaman alongside of me and the fellows forward; I could think of nothing but the mystery of the three men's deaths, the lamentable plight we were all in through our wanting a navigator, with the chance, moreover, that it *was* the plague, and not poison mysteriously given, that had killed the captain and mates, so that all the rest of us, as I have said, might be dead men in another week.

I returned to the cabin, and the boatswain joined me, and we stood beside the table conversing, anxiously watched by several men who had stationed themselves at the skylight.

"What we've got to do," said I, "is to keep a bright look-out for ships, and borrow some one to steer us home from the first vessel that will lend us a navigator. We're bound to fall in with something soon. Meanwhile, you're a smart seaman yourself, Matthews, as well qualified as any one of them who have died to sail the ship, and there's surely some intelligent sailor amongst the crew who would relieve you in taking charge of the deck. I'll do all I can."

"The question is, where's the vessel now?" said the boatswain.

"Fetch me the log-book," said I, "and see if you can find the chart they've been using to prick the courses off on. We should be able to find out where the ship was at noon yesterday. I can't enter that cabin. The sight of the poor fellow makes me sick."

He went to the berth and passed through the door, and might have left me about five minutes, evidently hunting for the chart, when he suddenly rushed out, roaring in his thunderous voice, "I've discovered it! I've discovered it!" and fled like a madman up the companion steps. I was startled almost to the very stopping of my heart by this sudden furious wild behaviour in him: then wondering what he meant by shouting "he had discovered it!" I walked to the cabin door, and the very first thing my eye lighted upon was a small snake, leisurely coiling its way from the head to the feet of the corpse. Its middle was about the thickness of a rifle-barrel, and it then tapered to something like whipcord to its tail. It was about two feet long, snow white, and speckled with black and red spots.

This, then, was the phantom death! Yonder venomous reptile it was, then, that, creeping out of some secret hiding-place, and visiting the unhappy men one after another, had stung them in their sleep, in the darkness of the cabin, and vanished before they had struck a light and realised indeed that something desperate had come to them!

Whilst I stood looking at the snake, whose horror seemed to gain fresh accentuation from the very beauty of its snow-white speckled skin and diamond-bright eyes, the boatswain, armed with a long handspike, and followed by a number of the crew, came headlong to the cabin. He thrust the end of the handspike under the belly of the creature, and hove it into the middle of the berth.

"Stand clear!" he roared, and with a blow or two smashed the reptile's head into a pulp. "Open that cabin window," said he. One of the men did so, and the boatswain with his boot scraped the mess of mashed snake on to the handspike and shook it overboard.

"I told you they was poisoned," he cried, breathing deep;

"and, oh my God, Mr West—and I humbly ask your pardon again for having suspected ye—do you know, sir, whilst I was a-talking to you just now I was actually thinking of taking up my quarters in this here cabin this very night."

Thus much: and now to end this singular experience in a sentence or two. Three days after the discovery of the snake we sighted and signalled a large English merchantman bound to London from the Rio de la Plata. Her chief officer came aboard, and we related our story. He asked to see the snake. We told him we had thrown it overboard. On my describing it, he informed me that he guessed it was the little poisonous reptile known in certain districts of South America as the Ibiboboko. He returned to his ship, and shortly afterwards the commander sent us his third officer, with instructions to keep in company as long as possible.

AT SEA

by Guy de Maupassant

"Cruel" is an adjective often applied to the Sea, but in this story it is human cruelty that Guy de Maupassant is primarily concerned with. Although still young at the time of his death, de Maupassant (1850–1893) was sufficiently talented and prolific a writer to fill thirty thick volumes with his work and to establish a lasting reputation as one of France's greatest story-tellers. In his later years, however, he developed an obsessive fear of impending madness; an obsession which inevitably made itself felt in his work and which prompted him to write many stories of an unrelenting grimness. Writing about these *contes cruels*, H. P. Lovecraft commented that they were the "morbid outpourings of a realist mind in a pathological state [rather] than the healthy imaginative products of a vision naturally disposed towards fantasy and sensitive to the normal illusions of the unseen".

De Maupassant's fears were not unfounded for he died incurably insane.

THE FOLLOWING PARAGRAPH recently appeared in the press:

Boulogne-sur-Mer, January 22nd: from our correspondent:
There is consternation among the sea-faring community here, which has been so hard hit during the last two years, at a frightful tragedy a few days ago. The fishing-boat commanded by Captain Javel was driven too far to the west, as it was coming into port, and foundered on the rocks of the breakwater protecting the pier. In spite of the efforts of the lifeboat

and the use of the rocket apparatus, four men and the cabin-boy lost their lives. The bad weather continues. Further disasters are feared.

I wonder who this Captain Javel is. Is he the brother of the one-armed Javel?

If the poor fellow who was washed overboard and now lies dead, perhaps under the wreck of his shattered vessel, is the man I am thinking of, he was involved, eighteen years ago, in another tragedy, terrifying, yet simple, like all the tragedies of the deep.

At that time the elder Javel was skipper of a trawler.

The trawler is the best type of fishing-boat. Strongly built to face any weather, and broad in the beam, she is always tossing about on the waves, like a cork; at sea all the time, continually lashed by the heavy, salt-laden Channel gales, she combs the sea tirelessly, with all sail set, dragging over the side a great net, which scours the ocean-bed, sweeping off and bringing up all the creatures that lurk in the rocks—flat fish clinging to the sand, heavy crabs with crooked claws and lobsters with pointed whiskers.

When the breeze is fresh and the water choppy, fishing starts. The net is attached along the whole length of a pole cased in iron, which is lowered by means of two cables working on two windlasses fore and aft. And the boat, drifting to leeward with wind and tide, drags along with her this device for stripping and ransacking the sea-bed.

Javel had his younger brother on board, with a crew of four and a cabin-boy. He had sailed from Boulogne in fine, clear weather to go trawling.

Soon the wind got up and, increasing to gale force, compelled the trawler to run before it. She reached the English coast, but mountainous seas were lashing the cliffs and pounding the beaches, so that it was impossible to come alongside the piers, the approaches to the harbours being dangerous with flying foam and roaring waves.

The trawler put about once more, rising to the rollers, tossed, battered, drenched with spray, buffeted with deluges of water, but undismayed in spite of everything, for she was accustomed to this sort of heavy weather, which sometimes kept her at sea for five or six days between the two neighbouring countries, unable to make harbour in either.

At last the gale dropped, while she was still some distance out, and, though it was still rough, the skipper ordered the trawl-net to be put down.

So the great net was heaved over the side, and two men forward and two in the stern began to let the cables holding it run out over the windlasses. Suddenly it touched bottom, but, as a huge wave made the boat heel over, the younger Javel, who happened to be forward superintending the paying out of the rope, staggered, and his arm got caught between the cable, momentarily slackened by the heeling of the boat, and the wood of the gunwale over which it passed. He made a desperate effort, trying to raise the rope with his other hand, but the net was already drawing and the tightened cable would not give.

The man cried out in pain. Everyone ran to his help. His brother left the tiller. They tugged at the rope in an attempt to free the limb, which was being crushed. It was useless.

"We must cut it," said one of the sailors, taking from his pocket a large knife, two slashes of which could have saved the younger Javel's arm.

But cutting the cable meant losing the net, and the net was worth money, a great deal of money—fifteen hundred francs; and it was the property of the elder Javel, with whom having was keeping.

In an agony of anxiety he shouted: "No! don't cut it; wait a moment; I'll bring her head up into the wind." And he ran to the tiller and put it hard over.

The boat hardly answered the helm, hampered as she was by the net, which checked her way, and there was also the drag of drift and wind.

The younger Javel had fallen to his knees, with clenched teeth and haggard eyes. He did not say a word.

His brother came back, still afraid that one of the sailors would use his knife. "Wait, wait, don't cut, we'll cast anchor."

The anchor was let go, and the whole length of the chain paid out. Then they began to heave at the capstan to slacken the cables of the net. At last the rope relaxed, and the arm, now useless inside the sleeve of the bloodstained jersey, was freed.

The younger Javel seemed dazed. They took off his jersey, revealing a ghastly sight—a mass of pulped flesh, from which blood was spurting as if under the action of a pump. The man looked at his arm and murmured: "Buggered!"

As the haemorrhage was making a pool on the deck, one of the crew cried: "He'll bleed to death; the artery must be tied."

So they took a piece of coarse, brown, tarred string and, putting it round the limb above the wound, they pulled it tight with all their force. The flow of blood gradually lessened and finally stopped altogether.

The younger Javel got up, with the arm hanging limp at his side. He took hold of it with the other hand, raised it, turned it round and shook it. Everything was broken, all the bones shattered; it was only joined to the shoulder by the muscles. He examined it sadly and thoughtfully. Then he sat down on a furled sail, and his comrades advised him to bathe the place to prevent gangrene.

They put a bucket near him, and every few minutes he filled a glass with water and bathed the ghastly wound, letting a trickle of fresh water run over it.

"You'd be more comfortable below," said his brother.

He went below, but came up again an hour later, not liking to be alone. Besides, he preferred the fresh air. He sat down on the sail again and went on bathing his arm.

They were having a good catch. The broad, white-bellied fish were lying about near him, wriggling in their death-throes. He kept his eyes on them, bathing his crushed limb all the time.

As they were just getting back to Boulogne, the wind got up again suddenly; and the little vessel began her mad career once more, pitching and tossing, jarring the poor fellow's injured arm.

Night came on. The weather remained dirty till dawn. When the sun rose, England was in sight, but, as the sea was going down, they set course back for France, beating up against the wind.

Towards evening the younger Javel called his comrades and showed them ugly-looking black marks, where mortification of the mangled portions of the limb was setting in.

The sailors examined it, giving their advice.

"It looks precious like gangrene," opined one.

"You'd better put salt water on it," declared another.

So they brought salt water and poured it over the wound. The injured man turned green, ground his teeth and flinched a little; but he did not cry out.

When the smarting ceased, he said to his brother: "Give me your knife." His brother handed him the knife. "Now hold my arm out straight and keep it stretched."

They did as he asked.

Then he began carving his own flesh. He worked quietly, reflectively, severing the last tendons with the razor-edged blade; and soon there was only the stump left. He uttered a deep sigh and declared: "It was the only thing to do; I was buggered."

He seemed relieved, and was breathing heavily, as he resumed his bathing of the stump.

The night was rough again and they could not make land.

When daylight appeared, the younger Javel picked up his severed arm and scrutinised it carefully. Putrefaction was setting in. His comrades also came to examine it; they passed it round from hand to hand, felt it, turned it over and sniffed it.

His brother said: "You'd better throw it overboard now."

But the younger Javel fired up at that: "No, I won't! It's mine, I'd have you know; it's my arm, after all."

He picked it up again and put it between his legs.

"That won't prevent it putrefying," said the elder brother.

The injured man had an inspiration. When they were long at sea, they used to pack the fish in barrels of salt to preserve them.

He asked: "I suppose I couldn't put it into brine?"

"That's an idea," declared the others.

So they emptied one of the barrels which had been filled with the last few days' catch; and they put the arm at the bottom. They heaped salt on the top of it and replaced the fish one by one.

One of the sailors made a joke about it: "We must take care not to sell it at the auction."

And everyone laughed except the two Javels.

The wind was still high. They tacked about in sight of

Boulogne till ten o'clock the next morning. The injured man went on bathing his arm.

At intervals he got up and walked from one end of the boat to the other. His brother at the tiller watched him, shaking his head.

At last they made the harbour.

The doctor examined the wound and pronounced it quite healthy. He dressed it carefully and ordered rest. But Javel refused to go to bed till he had recovered his arm, and went back as quickly as he could to the harbour to find the barrel, which had been marked with a cross.

They emptied it in his presence, and he picked up his arm, perfectly preserved in the brine, wrinkled, but free from putre-faction. He wrapped it up in a cloth which he had brought for the purpose and went home.

His wife and children carefully examined father's severed arm, feeling the fingers and removing the grains of salt from the nails; then they sent for the joiner to make a miniature coffin.

Next day the whole crew of the trawler followed the funeral of the severed limb. The two brothers, side by side, headed the procession. The parish sexton carried the coffin under one arm.

The younger Javel gave up the sea. He got a small job at the port, and whenever he talked about the accident later, he would add in a confidential whisper: "If my brother had been willing to cut the trawl rope, of course, I should still have my arm. But with him having's keeping."

THE BRUTE

by Joseph Conrad

The brute of this story is not a man as in de Maupassant's tale but a ship, one of those accursed vessels which bring misfortune to all who sail in them. The folklore of the sea abounds with accounts of such craft and, during his ocean-going days, Joseph Conrad must have heard tell many a tall tale about ill-fated ships and the events that befell their luckless crews. Conrad (1857–1924) has come to be regarded as the finest writer of sea stories in the English language—an extraordinary achievement for a man who knew no English at all until he was nineteen. Conrad's real name was Josef Teodor Korzeniowski and he was Polish by birth. Reading Hugo's *Toilers of the Sea* at an impressionable age is said to have fired him with the ambition to go to sea. At the age of seventeen he left home for Marseilles where he soon realised his ambition by becoming a seaman and then a smuggler in rapid succession. He subsequently served as third mate aboard various ships operating in the Indian Ocean, the setting for some of his best novels including *The Nigger of the Narcissus* (1897), *Lord Jim* (1900) and *The Rescue* (1920). He also spent some time as commander of a river steamer in the Belgian Congo, an experience which inspired his pessimistic short novel, *Heart of Darkness*. In 1896, already a naturalised British subject, he married and settled down in England to devote himself full-time to his writing.

DODGING IN FROM the rain-swept street, I exchanged a smile and a glance with Miss Blank in the bar of the Three Crows. This exchange was effected with extreme propriety. It is a shock to think that, if still alive, Miss Blank must be something over sixty now. How time passes!

Noticing my gaze directed inquiringly at the partition of glass and varnished wood, Miss Blank was good enough to say, encouragingly:

"Only Mr Jermyn and Mr Stonor in the parlour, with another gentleman I've never seen before."

I moved towards the parlour door. A voice discoursing on the other side (it was but a matchboard partition) rose so loudly that the concluding words became quite plain in all their atrocity:

"That fellow Wilmot fairly dashed her brains out, and a good job too!"

This inhuman sentiment, since there was nothing profane or improper in it, failed to do as much as to check the slight yawn Miss Blank was achieving behind her hand. And she remained gazing fixedly at the window-panes, which streamed with rain.

As I opened the parlour door the same voice went on in the same cruel strain:

"I was glad when I heard she got the knock from somebody at last. Sorry enough for poor Wilmot, though. That man and I used to be chums at one time. Of course that was the end of him. A clear case if there ever was one. No way out of it. None at all."

The voice belonged to the gentleman Miss Blank had never seen before. He straddled his long legs on the hearthrug. Jermyn, leaning forward, held his pocket-handkerchief spread out before the grate. He looked back dismally over his shoulder, and as I slipped behind one of the little wooden tables, I nodded to him. On the other side of the fire, imposingly calm and large, sat Mr Stonor, jammed tight into a capacious Windsor arm-chair. There was nothing small about him but his short, white side-whiskers. Yards and yards of extra superfine blue cloth (made up into an overcoat) reposed on a chair by his side. And he must just have brought some liner from sea, because another chair was smothered under his black waterproof, ample as a pall, and made of three fold oiled silk, double-stitched throughout. A man's handbag of the usual size looked like a child's toy on the floor near his feet.

I did not nod to him. He was too big to be nodded to in that parlour. He was a senior Trinity pilot and condescended to take his turn in the cutter only during the summer months. He had been many times in charge of royal yachts in and out of Port Victoria. Besides, it's no use nodding to a monument. And he was like one. He didn't speak, he didn't budge. He just sat there, holding his handsome old head up, immovable, and almost bigger than life. It was extremely fine. Mr Stonor's presence reduced old Jermyn to a mere shabby wisp of a man, and made the talkative stranger in tweeds on the hearthrug look absurdly boyish. The latter must have been a few years over thirty, and was certainly not the sort of individual that gets abashed at the sound of his own voice, because gathering me in, as it were, by a friendly glance, he kept it going without a check:

"I was glad of it," he repeated emphatically. "You may be surprised at it, but then you haven't gone through the experience I've had of her. I can tell you, it was something to remember. Of course, I got off scot free myself—as you can see. She did her best to break up my pluck for me tho'. She jolly near drove as fine a fellow as ever lived into a madhouse. What do you say to that—eh?"

Not an eyelid twitched in Mr Stonor's enormous face. Monumental! The speaker looked straight into my eyes.

"It used to make me sick to think of her going about the world murdering people."

Jermyn approached the handkerchief a little nearer to the grate and groaned. It was simply a habit he had.

"I've seen her once," he declared, with mournful indifference. "She had a house——"

The stranger in tweeds turned to stare down at him surprised.

"She had three houses," he corrected authoritatively. But Jermyn was not to be contradicted.

"She had a house, I say," he repeated, with dismal obstinacy. "A great big, ugly, white thing. You could see it from miles away—sticking up."

"So you could," assented the other readily. "It was old Colchester's notion, though he was always threatening to give her up. He couldn't stand her racket any more, he declared; it was too much of a good thing for him; he would wash his hands of her, if he never got hold of another—and so on. I dare say he would have chucked her, only—it may surprise you—his missus wouldn't hear of it. Funny, eh? But with women, you never know how they will take a thing, and Mrs Colchester, with her moustaches and big eyebrows, set up for being as strong-minded as they make them. She used to walk about in a brown silk dress, with a great gold cable flopping about her bosom. You should have heard her snapping out: 'Rubbish!' or 'Stuff and nonsense!' I daresay she knew when she was well off. They had no children, and had never set up a home anywhere. When in England she just made shift to hang out anyhow in some cheap hotel or boarding-house. I daresay she liked to get back to the comforts she was used to. She knew very well she couldn't gain by any change. And, moreover, Colchester, though a first-rate man, was not what you may call in his first youth, and, perhaps, she may have thought that he wouldn't be able to get hold of another (as he used to say) so easily. Anyhow, for one reason or another, it was 'Rubbish' and 'Stuff and nonsense' for the good lady. I overheard once young Mr Apse himself say to her confidentially: 'I assure you, Mrs Colchester, I am beginning to feel quite unhappy about the name she's getting for herself.' 'Oh,' says she, with her deep little hoarse laugh, 'if one took notice of all the silly talk,' and she showed Apse all her ugly false teeth at once. 'It would take more than that to make me lose my confidence in her, I assure you,' says she."

At this point, without any change of facial expression, Mr Stonor emitted a short sardonic laugh. It was very impressive, but I didn't see the fun. I looked from one to another. The stranger on the hearthrug had an ugly smile.

"And Mr Apse shook both Mrs Colchester's hands, he was so pleased to hear a good word said for their favourite. All these Apses, young and old you know, were perfectly infatuated with that abominable, dangerous——"

"I beg your pardon," I interrupted, for he seemed to be

addressing himself exclusively to me, "but who on earth are you talking about?"

"I am talking of the Apse family," he answered, courteously.

I nearly let out a damn at this. But just then the respected Miss Blank put her head in, and said that the cab was at the door, if Mr Stonor wanted to catch the eleven-three up.

At once the senior pilot arose in his mighty bulk and began to struggle into his coat, with awe-inspiring upheavals. The stranger and I hurried impulsively to his assistance, and directly we laid our hands on him he became perfectly quiescent. We had to raise our arms very high, and to make efforts. It was like caparisoning a docile elephant. With a "Thanks, gentlemen", he dived under and squeezed himself through the door in a great hurry.

We smiled at each other in a friendly way.

"I wonder how he manages to hoist himself up a ship's side-ladder," said the man in tweeds; and poor Jermyn, who was a mere North Sea pilot, without official status or recognition of any sort, pilot only by courtesy, groaned.

"He makes eight hundred a year."

"Are you a sailor?" I asked the stranger, who had gone back to his position on the rug.

"I used to be till a couple of years ago when I got married," answered this communicative individual. "I even went to sea first on that very ship we were speaking of when you came in."

"What ship?" I asked, puzzled. "I never heard you mention a ship."

"I've just told you her name, my dear sir," he replied. "The *Apse Family*. Surely you've heard of the great firm of Apse & Sons, shipowners. They had a pretty big fleet. There was the *Lucy Apse*, and the *Harold Apse*, and *Anne, John, Malcolm, Clara, Juliet*, and so on—no end of *Apses*. Every brother, sister, aunt, cousin, wife—and grandmother too, for all I know—of the firm had a ship named after them. Good, solid, old-fashioned craft they were too, built to carry and to last. None of your new-fangled, labour-saving appliances in them, but plenty of men and plenty of good salt beef and hard tack put aboard—and off you go to fight your way out and home again."

The miserable Jermyn made a sound of approval, which

ounded like a groan of pain. Those were the ships for him. He
pointed out in doleful tones that you couldn't say to labour-
saving appliances: "Jump lively now, my hearties." No labour-
saving appliance would go aloft on a dirty night with the sands
under your lee.

"No," assented the stranger, with a wink at me. "The Apses
didn't believe in them either, apparently. They treated their
people well—as people don't get treated nowadays, and they
were awfully proud of their ships. Nothing ever happened to
them. This last one, the *Apse Family*, was to be like the others,
only she was to be still stronger, still safer, still more roomy
and comfortable. I believe they meant her to last for ever. They
had her built composite—iron, teak-wood, and greenheart, and
her scantling was something fabulous. If ever an order was given
for a ship in a spirit of pride this one was. Everything of the
best. The commodore captain of the employ was to command
her, and they planned the accommodation for him like a house
on shore under a big, tall poop that went nearly to the main
mast. No wonder Mrs Colchester wouldn't let the old man give
her up. Why, it was the best home she ever had in all her
married days. She had a nerve, that woman.

"The fuss that was made while that ship was building! Let's
have this a little stronger, and that a little heavier; and hadn't
that other thing better be changed for something a little thicker.
The builders entered into the spirit of the game, and there
she was, growing into the clumsiest, heaviest ship of her size
right before all their eyes, without anybody becoming aware of
it somehow. She was to be 2,000 tons register, or a little over;
no less on any account. But see what happens. When they came
to measure her she turned out 1,999 tons and a fraction. General
consternation! And they say old Mr Apse was so annoyed,
when they told him, that he took to his bed and died. The old
gentleman had retired from the firm twenty-five years before,
and was ninety-six years old if a day, so his death wasn't,
perhaps, so surprising. Still Mr Lucian Apse was convinced
that his father would have lived to a hundred. So we may put
him at the head of the list. Next comes the poor devil of a
shipwright that brute caught and squashed as she went off the
ways. They called it the launch of a ship, but I've heard people

say that, from the wailing and yelling and scrambling out of the
way, it was more like letting a devil loose upon the river. She
snapped all her checks like pack-thread, and went for the tug
in attendance like a fury. Before anybody could see what she
was up to she sent one of them to the bottom, and laid up
another for three months' repairs. One of her cables parted
and then, suddenly—you couldn't tell why—she let herself be
brought up with the other as quiet as a lamb.

"That's how she was. You could never be sure what she would
be put to next. There are ships difficult to handle, but generally
you can depend on them behaving rationally. With *that* ship
whatever you did with her, you never knew how it would end.
She was a wicked beast. Or, perhaps, she was only just insane."

He uttered this supposition in so earnest a tone that I could
not refrain from smiling. He left off biting his lower lip to
apostrophise me.

"Eh! Why not? Why couldn't there be something in her
build, in her lines corresponding to—What's madness? Only
something just a tiny bit wrong in the make of your brain. Why
shouldn't there be a mad ship—I mean mad in a ship-like way
so that under no circumstances could you be sure she would do
what any other sensible ship would naturally do for you. There
are ships that steer wildly, and ships that can't be quite trusted
always to stay; others want careful watching when running in
a gale; and, again, there may be a ship that will make heavy
weather of it in every little blow. But then you expect her to be
always so. You take it as part of her character, as a ship, just
as you take account of a man's peculiarities of temper when
you deal with him. But with her you couldn't. She was unaccountable. If she wasn't mad, then she was the most evil-
minded, underhand, savage brute that ever went afloat. I've seen
her run in a heavy gale beautifully for two days and on the
third broach to twice in the same afternoon. The first time she
flung the helmsman clean over the wheel, but as she didn't quite
manage to kill him she had another try about three hours
afterwards. She swamped herself fore and aft, burst all the
canvas we had set, scared all hands into a panic, and even
frightened Mrs Colchester down there in these beautiful stern
cabins that she was so proud of. When we mustered the crew

here was one man missing. Swept overboard, of course, without
being either seen or heard, poor devil! and I only wonder more
of us didn't go.

"Always something like that. Always. I heard an old mate
tell Captain Colchester once that it had come to this with him,
that he was afraid to open his mouth to give any sort of order.
He was as much of a terror in harbour as at sea. You could
never be certain what would hold her. On the slightest provoca-
tion she would start snapping ropes, cables, wire hawsers, like
carrots. She was heavy, clumsy, unhappy—but that does not
quite explain that power for mischief she had. You know,
somehow, when I think of her I can't help remembering what
we hear of incurable lunatics breaking loose now and then."

He looked at me inquisitively. But, of course, I couldn't admit
that a ship could be mad.

"In the ports where she was known," he went on, "they
dreaded the sight of her. She thought nothing of knocking away
twenty feet or so of solid stone facing off a quay or wiping off
the end of a wooden wharf. She must have lost miles of chain
and hundreds of tons of anchors in her time. When she fell
aboard some poor offending ship it was the very devil of a job
to haul her off again. And she never got hurt herself—just a few
scratches or so, perhaps. They had wanted to have her strong.
And so she was. Strong enough to ram Polar ice with. And as
she began so she went on. From the day she was launched she
never let a year pass without murdering somebody. I think the
owners got very worried about it. But they were a stiff-necked
generation all these Apses; they wouldn't admit there could be
anything wrong with the *Apse Family*. They wouldn't even
change her name. 'Stuff and nonsense,' as Mrs Colchester used
to say. They ought at least to have shut her up for life in some
dry dock or other, away up the river, and never let her smell
salt water again. I assure you, my dear sir, that she invariably
did kill someone every voyage she made. It was perfectly well
known. She got a name for it, far and wide."

I expressed my surprise that a ship with such a deadly
reputation could ever get a crew.

"Then, you don't know what sailors are, my dear sir. Let me
just show you by an instance. One day in dock at home, while

loafing on the forecastle head, I noticed two respectable salt
come along, one a middle-aged, competent, steady man
evidently, the other a smart, youngish chap. They read the name
on the bows and stopped to look at her. Says the elder man
'*Apse Family*. That's the sanguinary female dog' (I'm putting
in that way) 'of a ship, Jack, that kills a man every voyage.
wouldn't sign in her—not for Joe, I wouldn't.' And the othe
says: 'If she were mine, I'd have her towed on the mud and se
on fire, blamme if I wouldn't.' Then the first man chimes in
'Much do they care! Men are cheap. God knows.' The younge
one spat in the water alongside. 'They won't have me—not fo
double wages.'

"They hung about for some time and then walked up th
dock. Half an hour later I saw them both on our deck lookin
about for the mate, and apparently very anxious to be taken on
And they were."

"How do you account for this?" I asked.

"What would you say?" he retorted. "Recklessness! Th
vanity of boasting in the evening to all their chums: 'We've jus
shipped in that there *Apse Family*. Blow her. She ain't going t
scare us.' Sheer sailor-like perversity! A sort of curiosity. Wel
—a little of all that, no doubt. I put the question to them in th
course of the voyage. The answer of the elderly chap was:

" 'A man can die but once.' The younger assured me in a
mocking tone that he wanted to see 'how she would do it thi
time'. But I tell you what; there was a sort of fascination abou
the brute."

Jermyn, who seemed to have seen every ship in the world
broke in sulkily:

"I saw her once out of this very window towing up the river
a great black ugly thing, going along like a big hearse."

"Something sinister about her looks, wasn't there?" said th
man in tweeds, looking down at old Jermyn with a friendly eye
"I always had a sort of horror of her. She gave me a beastly
shock when I was no more than fourteen, the very first day—
nay, hour—I joined her. Father came up to see me off, and was
to go down to Gravesend with us. I was his second boy to go to
sea. My big brother was already an officer then. We got or
board about eleven in the morning, and found the ship ready

drop out of the basin, stern first. She had not moved three times her own length when, at a little pluck the tug gave her to enter the dock gates, she made one of her rampaging starts, and put such a weight on the check rope—a new six-inch hawser—that forward there they had no chance to ease it round in time, and it parted. I saw the broken end fly up high in the air, and the next moment that brute brought her quarter against the pier-head with a jar that staggered everybody about her decks. She didn't hurt herself. Not she! But one of the boys the mate had sent aloft on the mizzen to do something, came down on the poop deck—thump—right in front of me. He was not much older than myself. We had been grinning at each other only a few minutes before. He must have been handling himself carelessly, not expecting to get such a jerk. I heard his startled cry —Oh!—in a high treble as he felt himself going, and looked up in time to see him go limp all over as he fell. Ough! Poor father was remarkably white about the gills when we shook hands in Gravesend. 'Are you all right?' he says, looking hard at me. 'Yes, father.' 'Quite sure?' 'Yes, father.' 'Well, then, good-bye, my boy.' He told me afterwards that for half a word he would have carried me off home with him there and then. I am the baby of the family—you know," added the man in tweeds, stroking his moustache with an ingenuous smile.

I acknowledged this interesting communication by a sympathetic murmur. He waved his hand carelessly.

"This might have utterly spoiled a chap's nerve for going aloft, you know—utterly. He fell within two feet of me, cracking his head on a mooring-bitt. Never moved. Stone dead. Nice looking little fellow, he was. I had just been thinking we would be great chums. However, that wasn't yet the worst that brute of a ship could do. I served in her three years of my time, and then I got transferred to the *Lucy Apse*, for a year. The sailmaker we had in the *Apse Family* turned up there, too, and I remember him saying to me one evening, after we had been a week at sea: 'Isn't she a meek little ship?' No wonder we thought the *Lucy Apse* a dear, meek, little ship after getting clear of that big rampaging savage brute. It was like heaven. Her officers seemed to me the restfullest lot of them on earth. To me who had known no ship but the *Apse Family*, the *Lucy*

was like a sort of magic craft that did what you wanted her t
do of her own accord. One evening we got caught aback prett
sharply from right ahead. In about ten minutes we had h
full again, sheets aft, tacks down, decks cleared, and the offic
of the watch leaning against the weather rail peacefully.
seemed simply marvellous to me. The other would have stuc
for half an hour in irons, rolling her decks full of wate
knocking the men about—spars cracking, braces snappin
yards taking charge, and a confounded scare going on aft b
cause of her beastly rudder, which she had a way of flappin
about fit to raise your hair on end. I couldn't get over m
wonder for days.

"Well, I finished my last year of apprenticeship in that joll
little ship—she wasn't so little either, but after that other heav
devil she seemed but a plaything to handle. I finished my tim
and passed; and then just as I was thinking of having thre
weeks of real good time on shore I got at breakfast a lette
asking me the earliest day I could be ready to join the *Aps
Family* as third mate. I gave my plate a shove that shot it int
the middle of the table; dad looked up over his paper; mothe
raised her hands in astonishment, and I went out bare-heade
into our bit of garden, where I walked round and round for a
hour.

"When I came in again mother was out of the dining-room
and dad had shifted berth into his big armchair. The letter wa
lying on the mantelpiece.

" 'It's very creditable to you to get the offer, and very kind c
them to make it,' he said. 'And I see also that Charles has bee
appointed chief mate of that ship for one voyage.'

"There was overleaf a PS to that effect in Mr Apse's ow
handwriting, which I had overlooked. Charley was my bi
brother.

" 'I don't like very much to have two of my boys together i
one ship,' father goes on, in his deliberate solemn way. 'And
may tell you that I would not mind writing Mr Apse a letter t
that effect.'

"Dear old dad! He was a wonderful father. What would yo
have done? The mere notion of going back (and as an office
too), to be worried and bothered, and kept on the jump nigh

nd day by that brute, made me feel sick. But she wasn't a ship
ou could afford to fight shy of. Besides, the most genuine
xcuse could not be given without mortally offending Apse &
ons. The firm, and I believe the whole family down to the old
nmarried aunts in Lancashire, had grown desperately touchy
bout that accursed ship's character. This was the case for
nswering 'Ready now' from your very death-bed if you wished
o die in their good grace. And that's precisely what I did
nswer—by wire, to have it over and done with at once.

"The prospect of being shipmates with my big brother
heered me up considerably, though it made me a bit anxious,
oo. Ever since I remember myself as a little chap he had been
ery good to me, and I looked upon him as the finest fellow in
he world. And so he was. No better officer ever walked the
eck of a merchant ship. And that's a fact. He was a fine,
trong, upstanding, sun-tanned young fellow, with his brown
air curling a little, and an eye like a hawk. He was just
plendid. We hadn't seen each other for many years, and even
his time, though he had been in England three weeks already,
e hadn't showed up at home yet, but had spent his spare time
n Surrey somewhere making up to Maggie Colchester, old
Captain Colchester's niece. Her father, a great friend of dad's,
vas in the sugar-broking business, and Charley made a sort of
econd home of their house. I wondered what my big brother
vould think of me. There was a sort of sternness about
Charley's face which never left it, not even when he was larking
n his rather wild fashion.

"He received me with a great shout of laughter. He seemed
o think my joining as an officer the greatest joke in the world.
There was a difference of ten years between us, and I suppose
e remembered me best in pinafores. I was a kid of four when
e first went to sea. It surprised me to find how boisterous he
ould be.

" 'Now we shall see what you are made of,' he cried. And he
eld me off by the shoulders, and punched my ribs, and hustled
ne into his berth. 'Sit down, Ned. I am glad of the chance of
aving you with me. I'll put the finishing touch to you, my
oung officer, providing you're worth the trouble. And, first of

all, get it well into your head that we are not going to let th
brute kill anybody this voyage. We'll stop her racket.'

"I perceived he was in dead earnest about it. He talke
grimly of the ship, and how we must be careful and never allo
this ugly beast to catch us napping with any of her damne
tricks.

"He gave me a regular lecture on special seamanship for th
use of the *Apse Family*; then changing his tone, he began t
talk at large, rattling off the wildest, funniest nonsense, till m
sides ached with laughing. I could see very well he was a b
above himself with high spirits. It couldn't be because of m
coming. Not to that extent. But, of course, I wouldn't hav
dreamt of asking what was the matter. I had a proper respec
for my big brother, I can tell you. But it was all made plai
enough a day or two afterwards, when I heard that Miss Maggi
Colchester was coming for the voyage. Uncle was giving her
sea-trip for the benefit of her health.

"I don't know what could have been wrong with her healtl
She had a beautiful colour, and a deuce of a lot of fair hai
She didn't care a rap for wind, or rain, or spray, or sun, or gree
seas, or anything. She was a blue-eyed, jolly girl of the ver
best sort, but the way she cheeked my big brother used t
frighten me. I always expected it to end in an awful row. How
ever, nothing decisive happened till after we had been in Sydne
for a week. One day, in the men's dinner hour, Charley stick
his head into my cabin. I was stretched out on my back on th
settee, smoking in peace.

" 'Come ashore with me, Ned,' he says, in his curt way.

"I jumped up, of course, and away after him down the gang
way and up George Street. He strode along like a giant, and I a
his elbow, panting. It was confoundedly hot. 'Where on eart
are you rushing me to, Charley?' I made bold to ask.

" 'Here,' he says.

" 'Here' was a jeweller's shop. I couldn't imagine what h
could want there. It seemed a sort of mad freak. He thrus
under my nose three rings, which looked very tiny on his bi
brown palm, growling out—

" 'For Maggie! Which!'

"I got a kind of scare at this. I couldn't make a sound, but ointed at the one that sparkled white and blue. He put it in his waistcoat pocket, paid for it with a lot of sovereigns, and bolted out. When we got on board I was quite out of breath. 'Shake hands, old chap,' I gasped out. He gave me a thump on the back. 'Give what orders you like to the boatswain when the hands turn to,' says he; 'I am off duty this afternoon.'

"Then he vanished from the deck for a while, but presently he came out of the cabin with Maggie, and these two went over the gangway publicly, before all hands, going for a walk together on that awful, blazing, hot day, with clouds of dust flying about. They came back after a few hours looking very staid but didn't seem to have the slightest idea where they had been. Anyway, that's the answer they both made to Mrs Colchester's question at tea-time.

"And didn't she turn on Charley, with her voice like an old night cabman's. 'Rubbish. Don't know where you've been! Stuff and nonsense. You've walked the girl off her legs. Don't do it again.'

"It's surprising how meek Charley could be with that old woman. Only on one occasion he whispered to me, 'I'm jolly glad she isn't Maggie's aunt, except by marriage. That's no sort of relationship.' But I think he let Maggie have too much of her own way. She was hopping all over that ship in her yachting skirt and a red tam-o'-shanter like a bright bird on a dead black tree. The old salts used to grin to themselves when they saw her coming along, and offered to teach her knots or splices. I believe she liked the men, for Charley's sake, I suppose.

"As you may imagine, the diabolic propensities of that cursed ship were never spoken of on board. Not in the cabin, at any rate. Only once on the homeward passage Charley said, incautiously, something about bringing all her crew home this time. Captain Colchester began to look uncomfortable at once, and that silly, hard-bitten old woman flew out at Charley as though he had said something indecent. I was quite confounded myself; as to Maggie, she sat completely mystified, opening her blue eyes very wide. Of course, before she was a day older she wormed it all out of me. She was a very difficult person to lie to.

" 'How awful,' she said, quite solemn. 'So many poor fellows.

I am glad the voyage is nearly over. I won't have a moment'
peace about Charley now.'

"I assured her Charley was all right. It took more than tha
ship knew to get over a seaman like Charley. And she agree
with me.

"Next day we got the tug off Dungeness; and when the tow
rope was fast Charley rubbed his hands and said to me in a
undertone—

" 'We've baffled her, Ned.'

" 'Looks like it,' I said, with a grin at him. It was beautifu
weather, and the sea as smooth as a millpond. We went up th
river without a shadow of trouble except once, when off Hol
Haven, the brute took a sudden sheer and nearly had a barg
anchored just clear of the fairway. But I was aft, looking afte
the steering, and she did not catch me napping that time
Charley came up on the poop, looking very concerned. 'Clos
shave,' says he.

" 'Never mind, Charley,' I answered, cheerily. 'You've tame
her.'

"We were to tow right up to the dock. The river pilot boarde
us below Gravesend, and the first words I heard him say were
'You may just as well take your port anchor inboard at once
Mr Mate.'

"This had been done when I went forward. I saw Maggie o
the forecastle head enjoying the bustle, and I begged her to g
aft, but she took no notice of me, of course. Then Charley, wh
was very busy with the head gear, caught sight of her an
shouted in his biggest voice: 'Get off the forecastle head
Maggie. You're in the way here.' For all answer she made
funny face at him, and I saw poor Charley turn away, hidin
a smile. She was flushed with the excitement of getting hom
again, and her blue eyes seemed to snap electric sparks as sh
looked at the river. A collier brig had gone round just ahead o
us, and our tug had to stop her engines in a hurry to avoi
running into her.

"In a moment, as is usually the case, all the shipping in th
reach seemed to get into a hopeless tangle. A schooner and
ketch got up a small collision all to themselves right in th
middle of the river. It was exciting to watch, and, meantim

ur tug remained stopped. Any other ship than that brute could have been coaxed to keep straight for a couple of minutes —but not she! Her head fell off at once, and she began to drift down, taking her tug along with her. I noticed a cluster of coasters at anchor within a quarter of a mile of us, and I thought I had better speak to the pilot. 'If you let her get amongst that lot,' I said, quietly, 'she will grind some of them to bits before we get her out again.'

" 'Don't I know her!' cries he, stamping his foot in a perfect fury. And he blew with his whistle to make that bothered tug get the ship's head up again as quick as possible. He blew like mad, waving his arm to port, and presently we could see that the tug's engines had been set going ahead. Her paddles churned the water, but it was as if she had been trying to tow a rock— she couldn't get an inch out of that ship. Again the pilot blew his whistle, and waved his arm to port. We could see the tug's paddles turning faster and faster away, broad on our bow.

"For a moment tug and ship hung motionless in a crowd of moving shipping, and then the terrific strain that evil, stony-hearted brute would always put on everything, tore the towing-chock clean out. The tow-rope surged over, snapping the iron stanchions of the head-rail one after another as if they had been sticks of sealing-wax. It was only then I noticed that in order to have a better view over our heads, Maggie had stepped upon the port anchor as it lay flat on the forecastle deck.

"It had been lowered properly into its hardwood beds, but there had been no time to take a turn with it. Anyway, it was quite secure as it was, for going into dock; but I could see directly that the tow-rope would sweep under the fluke in another second. My heart flew up right into my throat, but not before I had time to yell out: 'Jump clear of that anchor!'

"But I hadn't time to shriek out her name. I don't suppose she heard me at all. The first touch of the hawser against the fluke threw her down; she was up on her feet again as quick as light-ning, but she was up on the wrong side. I heard a horrid, scraping sound, and then that anchor, tipping over, rose up like something alive; its great, rough iron arm caught Maggie round the waist, seemed to clasp her close with a dreadful hug, and flung itself with her over and down in a terrific clang of iron,

followed by heavy ringing blows that shook the ship from stern
to stem—because the ring stopper held!"

"How horrible!" I exclaimed.

"I used to dream for years afterwards of anchors catching
hold of girls," said the man in tweeds, a little wildly. He shuddered. "With a most pitiful howl Charley was over after her
almost on the instant. But, Lord! he didn't see as much as a
gleam of her red tam-o'-shanter in the water. Nothing! nothing
whatever! In a moment there were half a dozen boats around
us, and he got pulled into one. I, with the boatswain and the
carpenter, let go the other anchor in a hurry and brought the
ship up somehow. The pilot had gone silly. He walked up and
down the forecastle head wringing his hands and muttering to
himself: 'Killing women, now! Killing women, now!' Not
another word could you get out of him.

"Dusk fell, then a night black as pitch; and peering upon the
river I heard a low, mournful hail, 'Ship, ahoy!' Two Gravesend
watermen came alongside. They had a lantern in their wherry,
and looked up the ship's side, holding on to the ladder without
a word. I saw in the patch of light a lot of loose, fair hair down
there."

He shuddered again.

"After the tide turned poor Maggie's body had floated clear
of one of them big mooring buoys," he explained. "I crept aft,
feeling half-dead and managed to send a rocket up—to let the
other searchers know, on the river. And then I slunk away
forward like a cur, and spent the night sitting on the heel of the
bowsprit so as to be as far as possible out of Charley's way."

"Poor fellow!" I murmured.

"Yes. Poor fellow," he repeated musingly. "That brute
wouldn't let him—not even him—cheat her of her prey. But he
made her fast in dock next morning. He did. We hadn't exchanged a word—not a single look for that matter. I didn't
want to look at him. When the last rope was fast he put his
hands to his head and stood gazing down at his feet as if trying
to remember something. The men waited on the main deck for
the words that end the voyage. Perhaps that is what he was
trying to remember. I spoke for him. 'That'll do, men.'

"I never saw a crew leave a ship so quietly. They sneaked

over the rail one after another, taking care not to bang their sea chests too heavily. They looked our way, but not one had the stomach to come up and offer to shake hands with the mate as is usual.

"I followed him all over the empty ship to and fro, here and there, with no living soul about but the two of us, because the old ship-keeper had locked himself up in the galley—both doors. Suddenly poor Charley mutters, in a crazy voice: 'I'm done here,' and strides down the gangway with me at his heels, up the dock, out at the gate, on towards Tower Hill. He used to take rooms with a decent old landlady in America Square, to be near his work.

"All at once he stops short, turns round, and comes back straight at me. 'Ned,' says he, 'I am going home.' I had the good luck to sight a four-wheeler and got him in just in time. His legs were beginning to give way. In our hall he fell down on a chair, and I'll never forget father's and mother's amazed, perfectly still faces as they stood over him. They couldn't understand what had happened to him till I blubbered out 'Maggie got drowned, yesterday, in the river.'

"Mother let out a little cry. Father looks from him to me, and from me to him, as if comparing our faces—for, upon my soul, Charley did not resemble himself at all. Nobody moved: and the poor fellow raises his big brown hands slowly to his throat, and with one single tug rips everything open—collar, shirt, waistcoat—a perfect wreck and ruin of a man. Father and I got him upstairs somehow, and mother pretty nearly killed herself nursing him through a brain fever."

The man in tweeds nodded at me significantly.

"Ah! there was nothing that could be done with that brute. She had a devil in her."

"Where's your brother?" I asked, expecting to hear he was dead. But he was commanding a smart steamer on the China coast, and never came home now.

Jermyn fetched a heavy sigh, and the handkerchief being now sufficiently dry, put it up tenderly to his red and lamentable nose.

"She was a ravening beast," the man in tweeds started again. "Old Colchester put his foot down and resigned. And would you believe it? Apse & Sons wrote to ask whether he wouldn't reconsider his decision! Anything to save the good name of the *Apse Family*! Old Colchester went to the office then and said that he would take charge again but only to sail her out into the North Sea and scuttle her there. He was nearly off his chump. He used to be darkish iron-grey, but his hair went snow-white in a fortnight. And Mr Lucian Apse (they had known each other as young men) pretended not to notice it. Eh? Here's infatuation if you like! Here's pride for you!

"They jumped at the first man they could get to take her, for fear of the scandal of the *Apse Family* not being able to find a skipper. He was a festive soul, I believe, but he stuck to her grim and hard. Wilmot was his second mate. A harum-scarum fellow, and pretending to a great scorn for all the girls. The fact is he was really timid. But let only one of them do as much as lift her little finger in encouragement, and there was nothing that could hold the beggar. As apprentice, once, he deserted aboard after a petticoat, and would have gone to the dogs then if his skipper hadn't taken the trouble to find him and lug him by the ears out of some house of perdition or other.

"It was said that one of the firm had been heard once to express a hope that this brute of a ship would get lost soon. I can hardly credit the tale, unless it might have been Mr Alfred Apse, whom the family didn't think much of. They had him in the office, but he was considered a bad egg altogether, always flying off to race meetings and coming home drunk. You would have thought that a ship so full of deadly tricks would run herself ashore some day out of sheer cussedness. But not she! She was going to last for ever. She had a nose to keep off the bottom."

Jermyn made a grunt of approval.

"A ship after a pilot's own heart, eh?" jeered the man in tweeds. "Well, Wilmot managed it. He was the man for it, but even he, perhaps, couldn't have done the trick without that green-eyed governess, or nurse, or whatever she was to the children of Mr and Mrs Pamphilius.

"Those people were passengers in her from Port Adelaide to the Cape. Well, the ship went out and anchored outside for the day. The skipper—hospitable soul—had a lot of guests

rom town to a farewell lunch—as usual with him. It was five
n the evening before the last shore boat left the side, and the
weather looked ugly and dark in the gulf. There was no reason
or him to get under way. However, as he had told everybody
ie was going that day, he imagined it was proper to do so
nyhow. But as he had no mind after all these festivities to
ackle the straits in the dark, with a scant wind, he gave orders
o keep the ship under lower topsails and foresail as close as
she would lie, dodging along the land till the morning. Then
ie sought his virtuous couch. The mate was on deck, having
his face washed very clean with hard rain squalls. Wilmot
elieved him at midnight.

"The *Apse Family* had, as you observed, a house on her
poop . . ."

"A big, ugly white thing, sticking up," Jermyn murmured
sadly, at the fire.

"That's it: a companion for the cabin stairs and a sort of
chart-room combined. The rain drove in gusts on the sleepy
Wilmot. The ship was then surging slowly to the southward,
close hauled, with the coast within three miles or so to windward. There was nothing to look out for in that part of the gulf,
and Wilmot went round to dodge the squalls under the lee of
that chart-room, whose door on that side was open. The night
was black, like a barrel of coal-tar. And then he heard a
woman's voice whispering to him.

"That confounded green-eyed girl of the Pamphilius people
had put the kids to bed a long time ago, of course, but
it seems couldn't get to sleep herself. She heard eight bells
struck, and the chief mate come below to turn in. She
waited a bit, then got into her dressing-gown and stole across
the empty saloon and up the stairs into the chart-room. She sat
down on the settee near the open door to cool herself, I daresay.

"I suppose when she whispered to Wilmot it was as if somebody had struck a match in the fellow's brain. I don't know
how it was they had got so very thick. I fancy he had met her
ashore a few times before. I couldn't make it out, because,
when telling the story, Wilmot would break off to swear something awful at every second word. We had met on the quay in
Sydney, and he had an apron of sacking up to his chin, a big

whip in his hand. A wagon-driver. Glad to do anything not to starve. That's what he had come down to.

"However, there he was, with his head inside the door, on the girl's shoulder as likely as not—officer of the watch! The helmsman, on giving his evidence afterwards, said that he shouted several times that the binnacle lamp had gone out. It didn't matter to him, because his orders were to 'sail her close'. 'I thought it funny,' he said, 'that the ship should keep on falling off in squalls, but I luffed her up every time as close as I was able. It was so dark I couldn't see my hand before my face, and the rain came in bucketsful on my head.'

"The truth was that at every squall the wind hauled aft a little, till gradually the ship came to be heading straight for the coast, without a single soul in her being aware of it. Wilmot himself confessed that he had not been near the standard compass for an hour. He might well have confessed! The first thing he knew was the man on the look-out shouting blue murder forward there.

"He tore his neck free, he says, and yelled back at him: 'What do you say?'

" 'I think I hear breakers ahead, sir,' howled the man and came rushing aft with the rest of the watch, in the 'awfullest blinding deluge that ever fell from the sky', Wilmot says. For a second or so he was so scared and bewildered that he could not remember on which side of the gulf the ship was. He wasn't a good officer, but he was a seaman all the same. He pulled himself together in a second, and the right orders sprang to his lips without thinking. They were to hard up with the helm and shiver the main and mizzen topsails.

"It seems that the sails actually fluttered. He couldn't see them, but he heard them rattling and banging above his head. 'No use! She was too slow in going off,' he went on, his dirty face twitching, and the damn'd carter's whip shaking in his hand. 'She seemed to stick fast.' And then the flutter of the canvas above his head ceased. At this critical moment the wind hauled aft again with a gust, filling the sails, and sending the ship with a great sway upon the rocks on her lee bow. She had over-reached herself in her last little game. Her time had come —the hour, the man, the black night, the treacherous gust of

wind—the right woman to put an end to her. The brute deserved nothing better. Strange are the instruments of Providence.
There's a sort of poetical justice——"

The man in tweeds looked hard at me.

"The first ledge she went over stripped the false keel off her.
Rip! The skipper, rushing out of his berth, found a crazy
woman, in a red flannel dressing-gown, flying round and round
the cuddy, screeching like a cockatoo.

"The next bump knocked her clean under the cabin table.
It also started the stern-post and carried away the rudder, and
then that brute ran up a shelving, rocky shore, tearing her
bottom out, till she stopped short, and the foremast dropped
over the bows like a gangway."

"Anybody lost?" I asked.

"No one, unless that fellow Wilmot," answered the gentleman, unknown to Miss Blank, looking round for his cap. "And
his case was worse than drowning for a man. Everybody got
ashore all right. Gale didn't come on till next day, dead from
the west, and broke up that brute in a surprisingly short time.
It was as though she had been rotten at heart." . . . He changed
his tone. "Rain left off. I must get my bike and rush home to
dinner. I live in Herne Bay—came out for a spin this morning."

He nodded at me in a friendly way, and went out with a
swagger.

"Do you know who he is, Jermyn?" I asked.

The North Sea pilot shook his head, dismally. "Fancy losing
a ship in that silly fashion! Oh dear! oh dear!" he groaned in
lugubrious tones, spreading his damp handkerchief again like a
curtain before the glowing grate.

On going out I exchanged a glance and a smile (strictly
proper) with the respectable Miss Blank, barmaid of the Three
Crows.

A PSYCHOLOGICAL SHIPWRECK
by Ambrose Bierce

The disturbing ironies and nightmare themes of Ambrose Bierce's stories led many of his admirers to hail him as the successor to Poe. Bierce (1842–1914) attracted considerable notoriety as a satirical columnist for the press both in the United States and Great Britain. Today he is probably best remembered as the author of "An Occurrence at Owl Creek Bridge", a short story about the American Civil War which has been made into a prize-winning French film.

Always unorthodox and unusual in his behaviour, Bierce bequeathed to the world a mystery as intriguing as anything he wrote. In 1913, at the age of seventy-one, he entered Mexico to report on Pancho Villa's revolutionary war—and vanished from the sight of men. From what little evidence is available, it is generally assumed that he was murdered or executed the following year.

Stories by Ambrose Bierce also appeared in my two previous anthologies, *Beware of the Cat* and *The Hounds of Hell*. Here he turns his attention to the unforeseen hazards of sea voyages —and to a phenomenon as baffling today as when this story was written: telepathic communication.

IN THE SUMMER of 1874 I was in Liverpool, whither I had gone on business for the mercantile house of Bronson & Jarrett, New York. I am William Jarrett; my partner was Zenas Bronson. The firm failed last year, and unable to endure the fall from affluence to poverty he died.

Having finished my business, and feeling the lassitude and exhaustion incident to its dispatch, I felt that a protracted sea voyage would be both agreeable and beneficial, so instead of embarking for my return on one of the many fine passenger steamers I booked for New York on the sailing vessel *Morrow*, upon which I had shipped a large and valuable invoice of the goods I had bought. The *Morrow* was an English ship with, of course, but little accommodation for passengers, of whom there were only myself, a young woman and her servant, who was a middle-aged negress. I thought it singular that a travelling English girl should be so attended, but she afterwards explained to me that the woman had been left with her family by a man and his wife from South Carolina, both of whom had died on the same day at the house of the young lady's father in Devonshire—a circumstance in itself sufficiently uncommon to remain rather distinctly in my memory, even had it not afterwards transpired in conversation with the young lady that the name of the man was William Jarrett, the same as my own. I knew that a branch of my family had settled in South Carolina, but of them and their history I was ignorant.

The *Morrow* sailed from the mouth of the Mersey on the 15th of June, and for several weeks we had fair breezes and unclouded skies. The skipper, an admirable seaman but nothing more, favoured us with very little of his society, except at his table; and the young woman, Miss Janette Harford, and I became very well acquainted. We were, in truth, nearly always together, and being of an introspective turn of mind I often endeavoured to analyse and define the novel feeling with which she inspired me—a secret, subtle, but powerful attraction which constantly impelled me to seek her; but the attempt was hopeless. I could only be sure that at least it was not love. Having assured myself of this and being certain that she was quite as whole-hearted, I ventured one evening (I remember it was on the 3rd of July) as we sat on deck to ask her, laughingly, if she could assist me to resolve my psychological doubt.

For a moment she was silent, with averted face, and I began to fear I had been extremely rude and indelicate; then she fixed her eyes gravely on my own. In an instant my mind was dominated by as strange a fancy as ever entered human consciousness. It seemed as if she were looking at me, not *with*, but *through*, those eyes—from an immeasurable distance behind them—and that a number of other persons, men, women and children, upon whose faces I caught strangely familiar evanescent expressions, clustered about her, struggling with gentle eagerness to look at me through the same orbs. Ship, ocean, sky—all had vanished. I was conscious of nothing but the figures in this extraordinary and fantastic scene. Then all at once darkness fell upon me, and anon from out of it, as to one who grows accustomed by degrees to a dimmer light, my former surroundings of deck and mast and cordage slowly resolved themselves. Miss Harford had closed her eyes and was leaning back in her chair, apparently asleep, the book she had been reading open in her lap. Impelled by surely I cannot say what motive, I glanced at the top of the page; it was a copy of that rare and curious work, *Denneker's Meditations*, and the lady's index finger rested on this passage:

> To sundry it is given to be drawn away, and to be apart from the body for a season; for, as concerning rills which would flow across each other the weaker is borne along by the stronger, so there be certain of kin whose paths intersecting, their souls do bear company, the while their bodies go fore-appointed ways, unknowing.

Miss Harford arose, shuddering; the sun had sunk below the horizon, but it was not cold. There was not a breath of wind; there were no clouds in the sky, yet not a star was visible. A hurried tramping sounded on the deck; the captain, summoned from below, joined the first officer, who stood looking at the barometer. "Good God!" I heard him exclaim.

An hour later the form of Janette Harford, invisible in the darkness and spray, was torn from my grasp by the cruel vortex of the sinking ship, and I fainted in the cordage of the floating mast to which I had lashed myself.

It was by lamplight that I awoke. I lay in a berth amid the familiar surroundings of the state-room of a steamer. On a couch opposite sat a man, half undressed for bed, reading a book. I recognised the face of my friend Gordon Doyle, whom I had met in Liverpool on the day of my embarkation, when he was himself about to sail on the steamer *City of Prague*, on which he had urged me to accompany him.

After some moments I now spoke his name. He simply said, "Well," and turned a leaf in his book without removing his eyes from the page.

"Doyle," I repeated, "did they save *her*?"

He now deigned to look at me and smiled as if amused. He evidently thought me but half awake.

"Her? Whom do you mean?"

"Janette Harford."

His amusement turned to amazement; he stared at me fixedly, saying nothing.

"You will tell me after a while," I continued; "I suppose you will tell me after a while."

A moment later I asked: "What ship is this?"

Doyle stared again. "The steamer *City of Prague*, bound from Liverpool to New York, three weeks out with a broken shaft. Principal passenger, Mr Gordon Doyle; ditto lunatic, Mr William Jarrett. These two distinguished travellers embarked together, but they are about to part, it being the resolute intention of the former to pitch the latter overboard."

I sat bolt upright. "Do you mean to say that I have been for three weeks a passenger on this steamer?"

"Yes, pretty nearly; this is the 3rd of July."

"Have I been ill?"

"Right as a trivet all the time, and punctual at your meals."

"My God! Doyle, there is some mystery here; do have the goodness to be serious. Was I not rescued from the wreck of the ship *Morrow*?"

Doyle changed colour, and approaching me, laid his fingers on my wrist. A moment later, "What do you know of Janette Harford?" he asked very calmly.

"First tell me what *you* know of her?"

Mr Doyle gazed at me for some moments as if thinking what to do, then seating himself again on the couch, said:

"Why should I not? I am engaged to marry Janette Harford, whom I met a year ago in London. Her family, one of the wealthiest in Devonshire, cut up rough about it, and we eloped —are eloping rather, for on the day that you and I walked to the landing stage to go aboard this steamer she and her faithful servant, a negress, passed us, driving to the ship *Morrow*. She would not consent to go in the same vessel with me, and it had been deemed best that she take a sailing vessel in order to avoid observation and lessen the risk of detection. I am now alarmed lest this cursed breaking of our machinery may detain us so long that the *Morrow* will get to New York before us, and the poor girl will not know where to go."

I lay still in my berth—so still I hardly breathed. But the subject was evidently not displeasing to Doyle, and after a short pause he resumed:

"By the way, she is only an adopted daughter of the Harfords. Her mother was killed at their place by being thrown from a horse while hunting, and her father, mad with grief, made away with himself the same day. No one ever claimed the child, and after a reasonable time they adopted her. She has grown up in the belief that she is their daughter."

"Doyle, what book are you reading?"

"Oh, it's called *Denneker's Meditations*. It's a rum lot, Janette gave it to me; she happened to have two copies. Want to see it?"

He tossed me the volume, which opened as it fell. On one of the exposed pages was a marked passage:

To sundry it is given to be drawn away, and to be apart from the body for a season; for, as concerning rills which would flow across each other the weaker is borne along by the stronger, so there be certain of kin whose paths intersecting, their souls do bear company, the while their bodies go fore-appointed ways unknowing.

"She had—she has—a singular taste in reading," I managed to say, mastering my agitation.

"Yes. And now perhaps you will have the kindness to explain how you knew her name and that of the ship she sailed in."

"You talked of her in your sleep," I said.

A week later we were towed into the port of New York. But the *Morrow* was never heard from.

FROM THE DARK WATERS
by David A. Drake

David Drake is without doubt one of the most talented of the younger, upcoming American writers of fantasy and science fiction. After developing an interest in weird fiction at an early age, he became a protégé of the well-known fantasy author and editor, August Derleth, who published two of his first stories in his Arkham House collections, *Travellers by Night* and *Dark Things*. His work now appears regularly in such magazines as *Galaxy, Analog* and *Whispers*.

"From the Dark Waters" takes place in the third century A.D., and forms part of a series of imaginative historical fantasies set against the decline of the Roman Empire. For readers who may wonder, the story was written before *Jaws* . . .

THE BRASSY SEA rocked as a small shark felt the bite of hooks deep in its belly and tried to tear loose. Hlovida was crouched low over her tile oven in the shelter forward, scrunching something in her teeth. "Careful, careful," she cackled in a voice still burred with the German of her early childhood. "One'll fill his belly with you, Dercetus, I can see it."

The Libyan mate, braced ready with a boat pike for the captive his crewmates were hauling aboard, ignored the wizened cook. Sweat beads jewelled his scarred black skin but could not cool him in the breathless air.

"Shut up, old fool," Vettius muttered. With his merchant friend he lay under the awning that stretched from the deckhouse to the broken stump of the mast. The light canvas hung as limp as the jib sail, seeming to trap more heat than it turned. Dama only shrugged moodily and leaned his slight form sideways out of the shadow. The sternpost of their ship, the *Purple Ibis*, curled over the deckhouse in a gentle sweep. It had been too many years since the encaustic paint had been renewed on its bird's-head finial, but it was still a graceful piece of carving. A handsome enough ship, in fact, before the storm. Eighty feet long, it had a three-sided deckhouse aft and a low, roofed shelter in the bow for the cook and her traps. Between mast and bow, a single open hatch gave access to the hold. Forward from the deckhouse ran a low rail, polished by decades of calloused hands. The smooth line broke amidships on the starboard side where raw splinters still gaped . . .

After the first thrashing, the little shark drove straight away from the merchantman. The line and wire leader were heavy but the full shock of the fish would have snapped either. There was no need to wear the shark down, though. A brown-mottled tiger shark struck its lesser kinsman, scalloping out a huge mouthful that cut the hooked beast nearly in half. Its tail lashed briefly in the instant before a dozen other sharks ripped it apart in savage hunger. In the bloody explosion of teeth and fragments, the fishline parted and the sailor holding it stumbled backward.

Dama's face was impassive. His eyes were turned towards the sea, but in his mind it was the dark, pitching surface of the night before.

They were scudding in the bright moonlight, the breeze off the Maureitanian coast nudging them gently towards Massilia and only the helmsman awake. The first gust came as lightning from a clear sky. It heeled the vessel on to her beam-ends. Dama's right hand locked on a stanchion in a reflex developed during years of shepherding cargoes through foul weather. Vettius' massive body hit the slatted wall of the deckhouse, but his long cavalry sword was clear in his hand. The wind slackened momentarily.

The high, wet clouds that piled up over the vineyards of the shore began to flow across the moon. Catfooted crewmen scurried to reef the sail. The ship rocked back sluggishly, logy with the weight of bolted silk in her hold. Then, in the dread silence punctuated only by the captain's frantic orders, the second gust struck. The half-furled sail, a new panel of stout Egyptian linen, blasted out of the hands of the seamen. The full force of the wind snapped at the mast that was as old as the hull, dried and weathered by the sucking heat of forty years. It parted with a crash, taking the captain and three sailors over the side with it.

The merchantman wallowed in the swells like a drunken whore. There was a single chance of saving the seamen clinging to the mast and air-bulged sail. Vettius sheathed his sword as naturally as he had drawn it and wrapped his powerful legs around the deck rail. The rising wind muffled the swish of the lead rope as he spun the loaded end twice around his head. Ignoring storm and the ship's pitching, he arced the rope over the drifting mass of top hamper.

The captain dropped the sheet he held and tugged at the lead. Already the vessel had drifted fifty yards. The floating man's triumphant cry crescendoed horribly as foam and a coloured shadow bloomed in the water around him. The moon glared through the clouds for one last time as the dark sea filled with fins roiling in ghastly delight. The mast trembled among them. Crippled, the PURPLE IBIS continued drifting. Rain began to slash down, but the survivors could still hear the screams from the darkness.

"Another hook," Dercetus ordered in a husky voice. He breathed with his whole body, slowly but in deep, sudden intakes.

The seaman who held the line picked himself up from the deck. He did not look at the mate. For an instant his eyes caught those of the remaining common sailor, a Syrian like himself, before replying in the bad Greek of the sea lanes, "There's no wire for leaders. It's no use."

The mate's left hand, dark and as broad as a wine bowl, took the seaman gently behind the jaw and brought his face around. The pike Dercetus still held added no more to the threat than did the spiked plate on a war elephant's forehead. "There's wire," the mate said. "There's wire enough to string every shark in this sea—and by Moloch! I will."

Vettius chuckled deep in his throat as he watched the seaman slink towards the companionway. "Afraid," he explained conversationally to Dama. "Mithra, I know them. Like the centurion who told me an outpost had already been overrun when I ordered him to relieve it. When he learned he could lead out his section or have me flay him alive—" the big soldier grinned as his finger traced down the scabbard of the cavalry sword—"he led it out. Which was just as well for him."

Dama indicated the mate's broad back with a not-quite-casual thumb. "I know how he feels, with him and the captain as close as they were . . ."

Vettius gestured obscenely with both hands, his smile tolerant but amused.

". . . but this won't bring anybody back. And feeding the sharks around us doesn't make me feel easier, at any rate."

Hlovida shuffled towards the mate from the cooking shelter, hunched as if her bones were on the verge of shattering. Twenty years before, she had been beautiful; time had been cruel. At forty her fine blonde hair had become white and dull, so brittle that the left side of her skull was half naked like an ill-thatched roof. Grey-brown discolorations marked her wrinkled skin and both cheeks bore flat sores. Her clothes were shapeless and filthy, so old that she might have been wearing them when the slavers bought her from a garrison on the Rhastian frontier.

"No, don't do that," she said, her voice breaking in the middle of an attempt to caress. She reached a crooked hand towards the mate's bare shoulder. "I told you, you'll be in a shark's belly soon if you try to hook another. I can see things, now that I've got my beauty back; yes I can."

Dercetus turned suddenly from the pattern of fins and grey shadows streaking the sea. His look of rapt loathing twisted into nausea as he took in the clawed fingers on his arm. Grunting an oath, he jerked away and lurched down the ladder in search of the seaman.

Hlovida's glance brushed the remaining sailor regretfully, then locked on to the passengers. The Cappadocian merchant's blond hair reminded her of her youth, but his stubby body was beneath her addled fancy. Instead, she curtsied under the awning and seated herself at Vettius' side. "Yes, I can see everything," she said, stroking her own cheek. Her voice had an odd rhythm, not wholly distasteful. "The king's coming for poor Dercetus, and he'll take the rest of us too."

Vettius turned his back ostentatiously.

"Ooh!" the woman shrilled, "he's so strong and wise—what do I need with you men?"

"What indeed?" Dama agreed under his breath as the cook rose and flounced to the rail, but her voice jagged on saying, "He's wise, you know? Not like a fish, not even like a man. Down in the deep he lives, and he eats the men the wrecks send to him. Down in the deep, where the seas are as black as he is white . . . but once in a lifetime, in lifetimes, he comes up to take his feed live. He's the king, the king of all the seas."

Dama scowled. "She's mad for men, Dercetus mad for sharks . . . why don't you and I try to pilot this hulk to Circe's island or the Styx, Lucius? Then we could all be mad together."

The ship trembled as something rough-scaled brushed the keel. The merchant broke off his fantasy to call, "Get away from the rail, old woman; there's fish out there that wouldn't make three gulps of you."

Hlovida tittered, irrationally gay again. "Hoo! Not yet. But wait till the king comes. He's bigger than this whole ship, and he'll eat us all, one and one and one and one and one. See how fast he's coming? He's still deep now but rising, rising . . ."

Vettius shook his head. "A shark eighty feet long?" he said with a grimace. "She *is* mad."

"Maybe she means a physeter," Dama suggested idly. "I saw a herd spouting once near Taprobane."

"She's mad," Vettius repeated.

Calloused feet scuffled on the companionway. First the Syrian appeared on deck, then the heavily-muscled mate with a dozen bronze leaders coiled over his arm. "String it," Dercetus ordered the seaman, tossing the wire at his feet; and to the cook, "Give him some pork."

"There's not much . . ." Hlovida suggested doubtfully.

"There'll be enough," Dercetus stated with a short, barking laugh. "As far north as the storm blew us, we'll fetch up on the coast of Spain any day. And maybe I'll boat one of these before he's eaten by his friends—then we'll have meat!"

The cook rummaged barehanded in the deck well where several amphoras were buried to their necks in sand. The gobbet she finally flipped to the sailor was so ripe and blackened that Dama was as glad as not to see it go over the side. Two thick-shanked hooks hid in its heart. A fifteen-foot hammerhead, misshapen and savage even among its present company, slammed the bait and took it straight down. The line hummed.

Dama shook his head and walked to the other rail, divorcing himself from the useless struggle.

"They're as bad as men," Vettius said, amused to watch other killers at work. "As soon as they see one of their own hurt, they're on him. This one doesn't feel the hooks yet. Wait till he does and tries to throw them out—Dercetus won't need the pike to finish any of this pack."

The seaman bracing against the line had fashioned mittens from a hide in the cargo. As the leather dragged on it, the hard linen cord purred and stank. Unexpectedly, the other sharks avoided the hooked hammerhead although their movements changed. Instead of slipping lazily around the becalmed vessel, each began circling its own wake. One leaped, a grisly sight with its jaws spread and a glazed yellow eye glaring at the ship. Something had gone wrong. Even Dercetus, poised at the rail as blank-eyed as the shark, felt that.

The sea was a sheet of hammered bronze. Dama could see deep down below its foamless surface. Miles, it seemed, but that was the distortion. He had never known air to be so still.

"She's rising!" someone called, and the merchant could hear the sailor's quick steps as the man tried to coil the line. It slackened faster than he could pull it in. And something was rising in the liquid depths of Dama's vision, too, a colourless dot quivering in the amber water. It grew, took an indeterminate shape. It was speeding straight up at the ship with the speed of a falling star. An outline formed and flowed with colour: the dirty white of an old shroud.

"Shark!" Dama bawled. He leaped back from the port rail.

Alone of the men on deck, Vettius glanced at the puzzled Cappadocian. The hammerhead was alongside now, strangely quiescent as the Syrian jerked its head out of the water and bent over the rail for another handful of line. "Hold him!" Dercetus ordered sharply. His right arm poised to slam the heavy pike through the shark's brain case.

The sea fountained an enormous cone of pallid white. Jaws

crunched together, their sound muted by the roar of falling water and a glancing impact that rocked the vessel. Ignored in the brittle chaos, the hammerhead arrowed off with the severed leader still trailing from its mouth. The Syrian had locked his calves around the rail. They remained there. Six-inch teeth had sheared off the man's body above his loincloth while his blood sprayed a semicircle of deck behind him.

The huge shark, white except where blood had spattered it, shot out of the sea like a cork bobber released on the bottom. With its dorsal fin still under water, the pointed snout already towered twenty feet above the surface. Dercetus screamed in indecision. He tripped away in fear; then, with the shark still rising, hatred carried him back in a great lunge, jabbing his pike into the great side.

The iron head threw sparks as it scrunched harmlessly across the scales; it was as if the mate had speared a thrusting block of coral. Instead of sliding back into the sea, the shark twisted its body stiffly towards the ship. The rail shattered. Dama dived over the hatch coaming, head first. Dercetus was left nakedly alone amidships when Vettius leaped for his bundled gear in the deckhouse. Letting his useless spear clatter over the side, the big Libyan tried to follow the merchant. His feet skidded on blood and shot him outward towards the rail.

The shark's jaws thudded harmlessly above him but the deck's pitch tipped Dercetus into something worse. Caught between the shark and the planking, he screamed. As the huge beast continued to grind back into the sea, its belly scales rasped the mate to bloody ruin. Face and chest, touched by the serrated hide, were flayed to the bones. Nothing but a car-mine track remained of the right leg below the knee, and the full length of the left fibula was exposed. The sea slapped thunderously, rolling the ship again.

Vettius stripped layers of oil-rich wool from his bow case, ignoring the remaining Syrian frozen open-mouthed beside him. Dercetus made enough noise for two, the soldier thought with detachment. Or a dozen. Well, he couldn't howl for long.

Dama's head, haloed by the sunlight, poked above the deck. "Clear," the bigger man said. "It went back over the side." Dama hopped the rest of the way out of the hatch. His tunic was torn and in his right hand he clasped a hatchet snatched up in the hold.

"Ah," Hlovida crooned softly. She darted to Dercetus' side and began binding tourniquets above the blood spurting from his maimed limbs. Neither Vettius nor the little merchant considered helping her. Each had seen dying men before; also men better off dead. The cook's German-thickened voice buzzed as she worked, saying, "Oh, poor darling. How could you be so reckless when your Hlovida warned you?"

"By the Blood, do fish get that big?" Vettius marvelled to his friend. His hornbow was strung in his hands now. Its fat cord stretched over a yard between ivory tips. Again the sea wove with sharks, their dark sinuosities grimly overshadowed by the pale monster now leading them.

"Isn't he strong, dear one?" Hlovida chortled as she sponged the weakly-protesting Dercetus. "And wise, too. He never comes to the surface when anyone might escape."

The dorsal fin of the white shark was a dozen feet high and all of it was out of the water. Unlike any other shark Vettius had seen, this one was from belly to fins a uniform mouldy hue that made the big soldier think of grave worms. No albino, though, not with its cruel yellow-eyes. More like something which had spent centuries in the depths, which was absurd. It swam stiffly, as if an obelisk with fins.

"It's not for him to be killed by men," the old Marcomann woman concluded cheerfully, "so he'll kill us all soon." Dercetus shrieked as the sponge touched a rib gnawed to the marrow by adamantine scales.

Vettius drew his bow and shot without pausing for conscious aim. The bowstring slapped the inside of his left wrist, leaving a welt because he had not taken time to strap on his bracer. He cursed, less at the pain than the ineffectiveness of his shot. The arrow struck as intended at the root of the high dorsal fin; the narrow iron point may have penetrated, but the transmitted impact shattered the shaft. Vettius nocked another arrow but did not draw the bow. "Now what?" he snarled.

"Now we wait for a breeze to bring us to land," Dama answered, wiping his palms on his tunic before regripping the hatchet.

"Oh, there won't be any wind while he's here," Hlovida said, nodding archly towards the great shark. "*He* rules the sea." She tittered as she dragged the mate towards her shelter.

At midnight the air was silent. Vettius stirred, spat. He and Dama could follow the ripples in the moonlight, spreading faintly until they shivered apart in the track of the circling sharks. The remaining seaman was huddled in the deckhouse. From forward came a faint scraping noise that Dama tried to ignore.

"We have to kill that fish," Vettius said flatly, his back to the mast and his stubbled jaw cradled between his knees.

The merchant grinned and spread his hands, palms down. "Sure, and I'd like a chance to study the carcase. Don't know how we'll get it aboard, but if you can kill something that big, you can figure that out too . . ."

"Well, we can't just wait here and watch it," the soldier growled irritably. "You saw what it did to him and the other." Vettius' spade-broad hand gestured forward.

"I didn't say we should get too near the rail," protested Dama more seriously, "but we're sure to strike land soon."

"How do we know?" Vettius demanded. He slapped his bow against his thigh for emphasis, setting the waxed cord singing. "What if that bitch is right again and we'll never see land so long as that thing dogs us?"

Dama let out a sceptical hiss.

"Anyway, I want to kill it," the bigger man admitted sheepishly. "It's out there laughing at us and . . . I want to end it."

Dama laughed out loud. "Well, there's a fine reason to risk our lives. But if neither spears nor arrows do the job, what do we do?"

"Um," the soldier grunted. "Well, I've got a notion about arrows, enough of them in the right places. Now if you're willing . . ."

The sun had merged sea and sky so that the *Purple Ibis* seemed to float within a bronze drum. The perpendicular rays exposed every dreadful line of the white shark. It cruised just as it had all the morning and the previous day. More sharks followed it than before. As far down as Dama's eyes could peer into the clear, golden water, nothing swam but sharks. He tossed the pork-baited line over the side. The fat meat floated a dozen feet from the ship, rocking slightly from the unbalanced weight of the leader. None of the smaller sharks left their grim formation.

The great white shark sank smoothly, the tip of its dorsal fin leaving a narrow track of foam before it, too, dipped below the surface. The shrinking torpedo shape continued to circle down into the lucid depths for as long as it was visible.

"He's gone," the soldier announced tensely, peering over the port rail. Dama licked his lips. He leaned over the rail, but his weight was balanced on the balls of his feet.

Vettius half-drew his bow. Three more arrows poked out of his left hand, each point gripped between a pair of fingers. He remembered how his friend had described the first appearance of the shark, a growing dot far down in the water. Now he saw it himself—

"Ready!" Vettius called. He drew the arrow to the head but still looked over his shoulder back into the sea. "Ready, ready —NOW!"

Dama porpoised, flinging himself down the companionway. He was still in the air when the white shark burst upward, a corpse-coloured volcano. Its gullet was pale pink, a cathedral of flesh arched darkly on either side by five gill slits. Washed clean by the sea, its saw-edged teeth winked in the sun.

Vettius slapped his first arrow into the centre of the rising belly. If the great fish noticed, its actions gave no sign. Curving its body like a fifty-ton boar tusk, the shark arced over the high stern of the *Ibis*. Deck stringers cracked under the awesome impact. Vettius dropped his weapons and thrust himself backward reflexively as the white bulk hurtled towards him. He had expected to fire three, perhaps all four of his readied arrows, but it had not occurred to him that the fish might throw itself aboard. Ferocity had guided it, that or something else not to be considered at the instant.

Two-thirds of the shark's length lay on the deck, the snout a pace short of Hlovida's shelter. The enormous tail threshed out of the water and slashed across the deckhouse from starboard to port. Light wood exploded into splinters that fanned the sea.

With them pitched the screaming sailor, bloodied by the tearing impact but all too conscious of the shapes arrowing towards where he must land. Water choked his cry; then a column of bloody froth spurted high into the air.

The ship wallowed. Forward of the mast stump, where the deck sloped nearest the sea, there was almost no freeboard left. The shark's body loomed over Vettius, a scaly, deadly surge that reached the port rail just as he cleared it. The soldier's biceps knotted hugely as they took the shock of his full weight on the rail. He hung there, his hobnailed boots skittering in the water as the ship rolled. A corner of his mind doubted any of the other sharks would leave the water to strike, but the overburdened vessel was perilously near foundering.

There was a mighty splash to starboard and the ship yawed violently to port as the shark dropped back into the sea. Vettius went under to the throat. As the ship righted itself, he used his momentum to spring out of the sea and back on to the deck. Behind him, teeth clashed.

The fish had left only shambles behind it. The mast stump was gone, broken off flush with the planking. The beast's flailing body had sheared away almost everything from the stern forward: bitts, deckhouse, railings, and the steering oar. At least the jib sail had survived, though it hung limp as Tiberius' prick. Mithra, unless there came a breeze . . .

Dama climbed on deck with a questioning eyebrow cocked. "I hit him," Vettius said morosely. He glanced around for his bow. "For all the good it did. Look at him there."

The sharks were all circling again. There was nothing else on the sea or in it.

"I told you you'd never kill him," the blurred voice said. The soldier's face went grey beneath his wiry black hair and eyebrows. He turned to the cook.

Dama touched the big man's arm. "We're not sharks," he said quietly.

Blissfully ignorant of how close she had come to death, Ilovida prattled on, "You'll starve, you know. There's nothing left but a little grain and enough oil to coat the jar." She giggled. "All the meat's gone, over the side, lost—and you'll not be fishing more, will you?"

In three jumps, both men were under the shelter and jerking the stoppers from amphoras. Dercetus' left leg was stuck to the neck of one jar. The black ichor oozing through the bandage cracked as Dama eased the mate aside, and he screamed himself awake. The amphora held less than a peck of wheat. The meat containers sloshed with stinking brine, nothing else.

"Did they hurt you, dearest?" Hlovida cooed as she ran her speckled hands down Dercetus' face. She had wrapped the mate mummy-fashion in what had been one or more layers of her own garments. It would not have helped for them to start clean, Dama thought grimly, considering the way Dercetus leaked where his skin was gone.

"The bitch hid the rest of the grain on her," Vettius suggested huskily. His great hands closed on the cook's shoulders and threw her back on the deck. Insanely, the woman began to scream, "Oh! Oh! You'll rape me for my beauty!"

Dama jerked loose her sash. A paper-wrapped packet hidden somewhere within the Marcomann's clothing thumped the deck and skittered down a broken plank. The Cappadocian's hand speared it before it could slip into the hold. "Castor and Pollux, she *has* got something!" he cried.

Through a chorus of sobs, Hlovida shrieked, "No, you won' take my beauty?"

Vettius back-handed her into silence.

The blond merchant peeled away two layers of scrap papyrus while his friend watched anxiously. Inside lay a large, flat crystal. It was clear in the centre, translucently white around the chipped edges. Part of one side had been scraped concave by a sharp instrument. "Rock salt?" Vettius queried. He ignored the cook groaning softly behind him.

"I don't . . .," Dama muttered. He touched a loose granule to his tongue. It tasted faintly metallic and had a gritty, insoluble texture. The merchant spat it out, spat again to clear the saliva from his mouth. "Poison!" he said. "There's enough arsenic here to wipe out a city."

His tongue touched his lips as another thought occurred to him. "What does a cook do with poison, old woman?"

Hlovida was on her knees and snuffling. "He wouldn't look at me because I wasn't pretty any more," she mumbled. "

aved some of the money each time I bought supplies—"

"Stole it, she means," Vettius interjected sardonically, but the merchant hushed him swiftly.

"My sisters, they used to use it to make men look at them. So white, such white skins they had. Oh!" she concluded with a wail, "nobody would look at me any more!"

"*Dis*," the Cappadocian whispered, "no wonder her mind's gone."

"Don't take it, will you?" Hlovida begged. A gnarled, poison-blotched hand crept towards the crystal.

Vettius' great paw caught it first, tossed it in the air. "We've got a better use for it," he stated flatly.

"Umm," Dama agreed, "but he may not take it. He's . . . that is, it isn't . . . well, it doesn't act like a shark."

"It'll take the bait we offer it," Vettius promised with a stark grin. "And that's all we have, isn't it?"

Dama followed the big soldier's eyes forward. "Yes," he admitted, "I guess it is." He checked the edge of his hatchet.

Knocking Hlovida down wasn't enough. Vettius finally tied the screaming woman to the rail before he could return to Dama in the forward shelter. For a man as near death as he was, Dercetus fought like a demon. It took all the soldier's strength to hold him down while Dama smashed through the bone at mid-thigh, just beneath the new tourniquet. The merchant drained his grisly trophy over the side, watching the blood dilute outward in semicircles.

A brown-mottled tiger shark broke momentarily from the pack, then rejoined it without noticeable interchange with any of the other sharks. The white shark rolled so that its left eye glared at the ship through the air; then it dived away more swiftly than before. The others—the sea was rotten with sharks —went wild in leaping and corkscrews but did not approach the *Purple Ibis.*

"Quick," the merchant requested. Vettius' dagger ripped a deep channel into the thigh muscle and he inserted the crystal. Two quick twists of rag and a knot closed the flesh back over the poison. Dama grunted and threw the leg overboard.

"Should have the pike ready," he said.

"What for?" the soldier queried with a chuckle. "Think he'll
fool with us any more if this doesn't work?"

The great shark shot skyward with all its rigid power. The
mate's leg was there and then gone, and spray fountained as the
fish bellied back into the sea. The white shadow slipped beneath the ship. Wood rasped, then splintered tremulously as
the keel tore away. The whole leaping, gasping pack of killers
was approaching the vessel from all sides. Perhaps they sensed
as both men did that the ship could break up at any moment.

Dama swore. "Even that wasn't enough poison," he said.
"Look—it knows something's wrong but it's not about to roll
belly up."

The white shark paused in its assault on the hull and shook
itself side to side. It did not appear seriously disordered and
the trembling slackened to an end. "You'll never kill him!"
Hlovida shrieked from where she was bound. She lashed her
head so violently that some of the brittle hair snapped and
floated into the sea. "Men can't kill him!"

Vettius grimaced and started for the cook. Dama again
caught his arm. "Let her rave, Lucius."

"Raving or not, she's been right too often," the soldier
growled. "I don't want her finding more of that to say. It
comes true."

Before he could act, the shark slid back towards the ship
through foam-muddled water. "Watch it!" Dama called, but
Vettius had already seen the danger. One tail flick, a second,
and the shark was on them. But instead of another graceful
leap to bring its body down shatteringly on weakened timbers,
the sleek movements dissolved into a spasm working forward
from the tail. The shark's nose bumped the ship almost gently
and the beast backed off. It vomited hugely into the sea:
Dercetus' leg already bleached white by stomach acid, and a
less identifiable lump that must have been the sailor.

"He'll come out of it now," Dama said bleakly. He had seen
enough men poisoned to know that the survivors were the ones
who turned their stomachs out quickly. A glance overboard
gave him the dizzy feeling that he could step off the rail and
run across the backs of the sharks. A big hammerhead, the
bronze glint of a leader trailing back from its mouth, nuzzled

he ejecta avidly. Seared again by the poison, the white shark lurched forward uncontrolled and snouted its T-headed relative. The lesser shark turned lazily. Its jaws opened incredibly wide, so wide they appeared to dislocate in the instant before they slammed closed on the white shark's belly.

"God of Calvary," Dama breathed, his lips forming words unspoken since his childhood. His fingers gouged bruises in Vettius' rigid arm. "Lord of the meek, be with us now!"

The huge fish arched into a flat bow, ripping loose the slaty hammerhead. A bloody gobbet of flesh had torn away. Scales proof against Man's weapons crunched apart under jaw muscles with thirty tons of rending power.

The rest of the pack went mad.

The sea blasted apart in a fury of blood and froth. The other sharks ringed the great white like doles about a wounded tiger. Twisting mightily, the white shark broke away in a dive. Already a score of platter-sized gaps in its hide streamed red into the sea. But there was time in the depths for wounds to scar; for reflection, perhaps, if a shark's mind could reflect . . .

Poison-riddled muscles spasmed again, shattering the smooth thrust for sanctuary. The rest was carnage. When the enormous tail flipped a small blue through the air broken-backed, the nearest of the pack bolted the new victim. The others continued to squirm toward the wounded white with deadly intent. The great fish did not die easily, but nothing could have survived that thrashing chaos. Logy with arsenic, ever more tattered by its maddened kin, the shark hurled itself from the carmine water in a convulsive arc. As it fell back, Dama caught its eye. It was glazed and empty.

"There's a cloud south of us," Dama said at last. "Maybe we're due for some wind."

Vettius continued to scan the bloody water about the ship. It had suddenly been drained of life. Dercetus moaned, out of sight forward.

"Rest easy, darling," Hlovida cackled grossly. "I'll never leave you."

SEA CURSE

by Robert E. Howard

As far as I have been able to discover, Robert Ervin Howard (1906–1936) never went to sea. He spent the whole of his brief but productive life in and around Cross Plains, a small village in Texas. Fortunately, his imagination roamed far beyond his physical surroundings enabling him to chronicle the exploits of such splendid, far-flung adventurers as Conan of Cimmeria, King Kull of Atlantis and Cormac Mac Art, a Gaelic pirate of Arthurian times. As with his friend and correspondent, H. P. Lovecraft, Howard and his work are far better known and appreciated today than in his own lifetime. His Conan stories especially have become popular throughout the world, spawning many imitations. "Sea Curse" is an unusual story from Howard's typewriter in that it is uncharacteristically set in recent times and not in some ancient mythical land of his own imagining. The influence of Jack London may be detected here and there but the dark, sombre element of the supernatural is unmistakably Howard . . .

And some return by the failing light
And some in the waking dream,
For she hears the heels of the dripping ghosts
That ride the rough roofbeam.

—Kipling

THEY WERE THE brawlers and braggarts, the loud boasters and hard drinkers of Faring town, John Kulrek and his crony Lie-lip Canool. Many a time have I, a tousled-haired lad, stolen to the tavern door to listen to their curses, their profane arguments and wild sea songs; half fearful and half in admiration of these wild rovers. Aye, all the people of Faring own gazed on them with fear and admiration, for they were not like the rest of the Faring men; they were not content to ply their trade along the coasts and among the shark-teeth shoals. No yawls, no skiffs for them! They fared far, farther than any other man in the village, for they shipped on the great sailing-ships that went out on the white tides to brave the restless grey ocean and make ports in strange land.

Ah, I mind it was swift times in the little sea-coast village of Faring when John Kulrek came home, with the furtive Lie-lip at his side, swaggering down the gang-plank, in his tarry sea-clothes, and the broad leather belt that held his ever-ready dagger; shouting condescending greeting to some favoured acquaintance, kissing some maiden who ventured too near; then up the street, roaring some scarcely decent song of the sea. How the cringers and the idlers, the hangers-on, would swarm about the two desperate heroes, flattering and smirking, guffawing hilariously at each nasty jest. For to the tavern loafers and to some of the weaker among the straight-forward villagers, these men with their wild talk and their brutal deeds, their tales of the Seven Seas and the far countries, these men, I say, were valiant knights, nature's noblemen who dared to be men of blood and brawn.

And all feared them, so that when a man was beaten or a woman insulted, the villagers muttered—and did nothing. And so when Moll Farrell's niece was put to shame by John Kulrek, none dared even to put into words what all thought. Moll had never married, and she and the girl lived alone in a little hut down close to the beach, so close that in high tide the waves came almost to the door.

The people of the village accounted old Moll something of a witch, and she was a grim, gaunt old dame who had little to say to anyone. But she minded her own business, and eked out a slim living by gathering clams, and picking up bits of driftwood.

The girl was a pretty, foolish little thing, vain and easily befooled, else she had never yielded to the shark-like blandishments of John Kulrek.

I mind the day was a cold winter day with a sharp breeze

out of the east when the old dame came into the village stree
shrieking that the girl had vanished. All scattered over th
beach and back among the bleak inland hills to search for he
—all save John Kulrek and his cronies who sat in the taver
dicing and toping. All the while beyond the shoals, we hear
the never-ceasing droning of the heaving, restless grey monste
and in the dim light of the ghostly dawn Moll Farrell's gi
came home.

The tides bore her gently across the wet sands and laid he
almost at her own door. Virgin-white she was, and her arm
were folded across her still bosom; calm was her face, and th
grey tides sighed about her slender limbs. Moll Farrell's eye
were stones, yet she stood above her dead girl and spoke n
word till John Kulrek and his crony came reeling down fro
the tavern, their drinking-jacks still in their hands. Drunk wa
John Kulrek, and the people gave back for him, murder in the
souls; so he came and laughed at Moll Farrell across the bod
of her girl.

"Zounds!" swore John Kulrek; "the wench has drowne
herself, Lie-lip!"

Lie-lip laughed, with the twist of his thin mouth. He alwa
hated Moll Farrell, for it was she that had given him the nam
of Lie-lip.

Then John Kulrek lifted his drinking-jack, swaying on h
uncertain legs. "A health to the wench's ghost!" he bellowe
while all stood aghast.

Then Moll Farrell spoke, and the words broke from her in
scream which sent ripples of cold up and down the spines
the throng.

"The curse of the Foul Fiend upon you, John Kulrek!" sh
screamed. "The curse of God rest upon your vile soul throug
out eternity! May you gaze on sights that shall sear the ey
of you and scorch the soul of you! May you die a bloody dea
and writhe in hell's flames for a million and a million ar
yet a million years! I curse you by sea and by land, t
earth and by air, by the demons of the swamplands, th
fiends of the forest and the goblins of the hills! Ar
you"—her lean finger stabbed Lie-lip Canool and he start
backward, his face paling—"you shall be the death of Jol

Kulrek and he shall be the death of you! You shall bring John Kulrek to the doors of hell and John Kulrek shall bring you to the gallows-tree! I set the seal of death upon your brow, John Kulrek! You shall live in terror and die in horror far out upon the cold grey sea! But the sea that took the soul of innocence to her bosom shall not take you, but shall fling forth your vile carcass to the sands! Aye, John Kulrek"—and she spoke with such a terrible intensity that the drunken mockery on the man's face changed to one of swinish stupidity—"the sea roars for the victim it will not keep! There is snow upon the hills, John Kulrek, and ere it melts your corpse will lie at my feet. And I shall spit upon it and be content."

Kulrek and his crony sailed at dawn for a long voyage, and Moll went back to her hut and her clam gathering. She seemed to grow leaner and more grim than ever and her eyes smouldered with a light not sane. The days glided by and people whispered among themselves that Moll's days were numbered, for she faded to a ghost of a woman; but she went her way, refusing all aid.

That was a short, cold summer and the snow on the barren inland hills never melted; a thing very unusual, which caused much comment among the villagers. At dusk and at dawn Moll would come up on the beach, gaze up at the snow which glittered on the hills, then out to sea with a fierce intensity in her gaze.

Then the days grew shorter, the nights longer and darker, and the cold grey tides came sweeping along the bleak strands, bearing the rain and sleet of the sharp east breezes.

And upon a bleak day a trading-vessel sailed into the bay and anchored. And all the idlers and the wastrels flocked to the wharfs, for that was the ship upon which John Kulrek and Lie-lip Canool had sailed. Down the gang-plank came Lie-lip, more furtive than ever, but John Kulrek was not there.

To shouted queries, Canool shook his head. "Kulrek deserted ship at a port of Sumatra," said he. "He had a row with the skipper, lads; wanted me to desert, too, but no! I had to see you fine lads again, eh boys?"

Almost cringing was Lie-lip Canool, and suddenly he recoiled

as Moll Farrell came through the throng. A moment they stood
eyeing each other; then Moll's grim lips bent in a terrible smile

"There's blood on your hand, Canool!" she lashed out sud
denly—so suddenly that Lie-lip started and rubbed his right
hand across his left sleeve.

"Stand aside, witch!" he snarled in sudden anger, striding
through the crowd which gave back for him. His admirer
followed him to the tavern.

Now, I mind that the next day was even colder; grey fog
came drifting out of the east and veiled the sea and the beaches
There would be no sailing that day, and so all the villager
were in their snug houses or matching tales at the tavern. So
came that Joe, my friend, a lad of my own age, and I, wer
the ones who saw the first of the strange thing that happened.

Being harum-scarum lads of no wisdom, we were sitting in
small rowboat, floating at the end of the wharfs, each shivering
and wishing the other would suggest leaving, there being n
reason whatever for our being there, save that it was a goo
place to build air-castles undisturbed.

Suddenly Joe raised his hand. "Say," he said, "d'ye hear
Who can be out on the bay upon a day like this?"

"Nobody. What d'ye hear?"

"Oars. Or I'm a lubber. Listen."

There was no seeing anything in that fog, and I heard nothing
Yet Joe swore he did, and suddenly his face assumed a strang
look.

"Somebody rowing out there, I tell you! The bay is aliv
with oars from the sound! A score of boats at the least! Y
dolt, can ye not hear?"

Then, as I shook my head, he leaped and began to und
the painter.

"I'm off to see. Name me liar if the bay is not full of boat
all together like a close fleet. Are you with me?"

Yes, I was with him, though I heard nothing. Then out in th
greyness we went, and the fog closed behind and before so tha
we drifted in a vague world of smoke, seeing naught and hear
ing naught. We were lost in no time, and I cursed Joe fo
leading us upon a wild goose chase that was like to end wit

our being swept out to sea. I thought of Moll Farrell's girl and shuddered.

How long we drifted I know not. Minutes faded into hours, hours into centuries. Still Joe swore he heard the oars, now close at hand, now far away, and for hours we followed them, steering our course towards the sound, as the noise grew or receded. This I later thought of, and could not understand.

Then, when my hands were so numb that I could no longer hold the oar, and the forerunning drowsiness of cold and exhaustion was stealing over me, bleak white stars broke through the fog which glided suddenly away, fading like a ghost of smoke, and we found ourselves afloat just outside the mouth of the bay. The waters lay smooth as a pond, all dark green and silver in the starlight, and the cold came crisper than ever. I was swinging the boat about, to put back into the bay, when Joe gave a shout, and for the first time I heard the clack of oarlocks. I glanced over my shoulder and my blood went cold.

A great beaked prow loomed above us, a weird, unfamiliar shape against the stars, and as I caught my breath, sheered sharply and swept by us, with a curious swishing I never heard any other craft make. Joe screamed and backed oars frantically, and the boat walled out of the way just in time; for though the prow missed us, still otherwise we had died. For from the sides of the ship stood long oars, bank upon bank which swept her along. Though I had never seen such a craft, I knew her for a galley. But what was she doing upon our coasts? They said, the far-farers, that such ships were still in use among the heathens of Barbary; but it was many a long, heaving mile to Barbary, and even so she did not resemble the ships described by those who had sailed far.

We started in pursuit, and this was strange, for though the waters broke about her prow, and she seemed fairly to fly through the waves, yet she was making little speed, and it was no time before we caught up with her. Making our painter fast to a chain far back beyond the reach of the swishing oars, we hailed those on deck. But there came no answer, and at last, conquering our fears, we clambered up the chain and found ourselves upon the strangest deck man has trod for many a long, roaring century.

Joe muttered fearsomely. "Look how old it seems! Almost ready to fall to pieces. Why, 'tis fairly rotten!"

There was no one on deck, no one at the long sweep with which the craft was steered. We stole to the hold and looked down the stair. Then and there, if ever men were on the verge of insanity, it was we. For there were rowers there, it is true; they sat upon the rowers' benches and drove the creaking oars through the grey waters. *And they that rowed were skeletons!*

Shrieking, we plunged across the deck, to fling ourselves into the sea. But at the rail I tripped upon something and fell headlong, and as I lay, I saw a thing which vanquished my fear of the horrors below for an instant. The thing upon which I had tripped was a human body, and in the dim grey light that was beginning to steal across the eastern waves I saw a dagger hilt standing up between his shoulders. Joe was at the rail, urging me to haste, and together we slid down the chain and cut the painter.

Then we stood off into the bay. Straight on kept the grim galley, and we followed, slowly, wondering. She seemed to be heading straight for the beach beside the wharfs, and as we approached, we saw the wharfs thronged with people. They had missed us, no doubt, and now they stood, there in the early dawn light, struck dumb by the apparition which had come up out of the night and the grim ocean.

Straight on swept the galley, her oars a-swish; then ere she reached the shallow water—crash!—a terrific reverberation shook the bay. Before our eyes the grim craft seemed to melt away; then she vanished, and the green waters seethed where she had ridden, but there floated no driftwood there, nor did there ever float any ashore. Aye, something floated ashore, but it was grim driftwood!

We made the landing amid a hum of excited conversation that stopped suddenly. Moll Farrell stood before her hut, limned gauntly against the ghostly dawn, her lean hand pointing seaward. And across the sighing wet sands, borne by the grey tide, something came floating; something that the waves dropped at Moll Farrell's feet. And there looked up at us, as we crowded about, a pair of unseeing eyes set in a still, white face. John Kulrek had come home.

Still and grim he lay, rocked by the tide, and as he lurched sideways, all saw the dagger hilt that stood from his back— the dagger all of us had seen a thousand times at the belt of Lie-lip Canool.

"Aye, I killed him!" came Canool's shriek, as he writhed and grovelled before our gaze. "At sea on a still night in a drunken brawl I slew him and hurled him overboard! And from the far seas he has followed me"—his voice sank to a hideous whisper—"because—of—the—curse—the—sea—would —not—keep—his—body!"

And the wretch sank down, trembling, the shadow of the gallows already in his eyes.

"Aye!" Strong, deep and exultant was Moll Farrell's voice. "From the hell of lost craft Satan sent a ship of bygone ages! A ship red with gore and stained with the memory of horrid crimes! None other would bear such a vile carcass! The sea has taken vengeance and has given me mine. See now, how I spit upon the face of John Kulrek."

And with a ghastly laugh, she pitched forward, the blood starting to her lips. And the sun came up across the restless sea.

FISHHEAD

by Irvin S. Cobb

For much of his working life, Irvin Shrewsbury Cobb (1876–1944) was a newspaper editor. He did not write his first short story until the age of thirty-seven—and he then went on to become one of America's favourite humourists with over sixty books to his credit. Later, towards the end of his life, Cobb embarked on yet another career and became an actor in films. His books include *Back Home* (1912), *Paths of Glory* (1915), *The Life of the Party* (1919), *The Shark Doctor and Other Stories* (1923) and *Exit Laughing* (1941). The following story, which is not at all humorous, is from a collection entitled *The Escape of Mr Trimm* (1914). H. P. Lovecraft, a professed admirer of Cobb's occasional excursions into the macabre, called it "banefully effective". I think you will agree.

I T G O E S P A S T the powers of my pen to try to describe Reelfoot Lake for you so that you, reading this, will get the picture of it in your mind as I have it in mine. For Reelfoot Lake is like no other lake that I know anything about. It is an afterthought of Creation.

The rest of this continent was made and had dried in the sun for thousands of years—for millions of years for all I know —before Reelfoot came to be. It's the newest big thing in nature on this hemisphere probably, for it was formed by the great earthquake of 1811, just a little more than a hundred years ago. That earthquake of 1811 surely altered the face of the earth on the then far frontier of this country. It changed the course of rivers, it converted hills into what are now the sunk lands of three states, and it turned the solid ground to jelly and made it roll in waves like the sea. And in the midst of the retching of the land and the vomiting of the waters it depressed to varying depths a section of the earth crust sixty miles long, taking it down—trees, hills, hollows and all; and a crack broke through to the Mississippi River so that for three days the river ran up stream, filling the hole.

The result was the largest lake south of the Ohio, lying mostly in Tennessee, but extending up across what is now the Kentucky line, and taking its name from a fancied resemblance in its outline to the splay, reeled foot of a cornfield Negro. Niggerwool Swamp, not so far away, may have got its name from the same man who christened Reelfoot; at least so it sounds.

Reelfoot is, and has always been, a lake of mystery. In places it is bottomless. Other places the skeletons of the cypress trees that went down when the earth sank still stand upright, so that if the sun shines from the right quarter and the water is less muddy than common, a man peering face downward into its depths sees, or thinks he sees, down below him the bare top-limbs upstretching like drowned men's fingers, all coated with the mud of years and bandaged with pennons of the green lake slime. In still other places the lake is shallow for long stretches, no deeper than breast deep to a man, but dangerous because of the weed growths and the sunken drifts which entangle a swimmer's limbs. Its banks are mainly mud, its waters are muddied too, being a rich coffee colour in the spring and a copperish yellow in the summer, and the trees along its shore are mud coloured clear up to their lower limbs after the spring floods, when the dried sediment covers their trunks with a thick, scrofulous-looking coat.

There are stretches of unbroken woodland around it and slashes where the cypress knees rise countlessly like headstones and footstones for the dead snags that rot in the soft ooze. There are deadenings with the lowland corn growing high and rank below and the bleached, fire-blackened girdled trees rising above, barren of leaf and limb. There are long, dismal flats where in the spring the clotted frog-spawn clings like patches of white mucus among the weed stalks and at night the turtles crawl out to lay clutches of perfectly round, white eggs with tough, rubbery shells in the sand. There are bayous leading off to nowhere and sloughs that wind aimlessly, like great, blind worms, to finally join the big river that rolls its semi-liquid torrents a few miles to the westward.

So Reelfoot lies there, flat in the bottoms, freezing lightly in the winter, steaming torridly in the summer, swollen in the spring when the woods have turned a vivid green and the buffalo gnats by the million and the billion fill the flooded hollows with their pestilential buzzing, and in the fall ringed about gloriously with all the colours which the first frost brings —gold of hickory, yellow-russet of sycamore, red of dogwood and ash and purple-black of sweet-gum.

But the Reelfoot country has its uses. It is the best game and fish country, natural or artificial, that is left in the South today. In their appointed seasons the duck and the geese flock in, and even semi-tropical birds, like the brown pelican and the Florida snake-bird, have been known to come there to nest. Pigs, gone back to wildness, range the ridges, each razor-backed drove captained by a gaunt, savage, slab-sided old boar. By night the bull frogs, inconceivably big and tremendously vocal, bellow under the banks.

It is a wonderful place for fish—bass and crappie and perch and the snouted buffalo fish. How these edible sorts live to spawn and how their spawn in turn live to spawn again is a marvel, seeing how many of the big fish-eating cannibal fish there are in Reelfoot. Here, bigger than anywhere else, you find the garfish, all bones and appetite and horny plates, with a snout like an alligator, the nearest link, naturalists say, between the animal life of today and the animal life of the Reptilian Period. The shovel-nose cat, really a deformed kind of freshwater sturgeon, with a great fan-shaped membranous plate jutting out from his nose like a bowsprit, jumps all day in the quiet places with mighty splashing sounds, as though a horse had fallen into the water. On every stranded log the huge snapping turtles lie on sunny days in groups of four and six, baking their shells black in the sun, with their little snaky heads raised watchfully, ready to slip noiselessy off at the first sound of oars grating in the row-locks.

But the biggest of them all are the catfish. These are monstrous creatures, these catfish of Reelfoot—scaleless, slick things, with corpsy, dead eyes and poisonous fins like javelins and long whiskers dangling from the sides of their cavernous heads. Six and seven feet long they grow to be and to weigh two hundred pounds or more, and they have mouths wide enough to take in a man's foot or a man's fist and strong enough to break any hook save the strongest and greedy enough to eat anything, living or dead or putrid, that the horny jaws can master. Oh, but they are wicked things, and they tell wicked tales of them down there. They call them man-eaters and compare them, in certain of their habits, to sharks.

Fishhead was of a piece with this setting. He fitted into it as an acorn fits its cup. All his life he had lived on Reelfoot, always in the one place, at the mouth of a certain slough. He had been born there, of a Negro father and a half-breed Indian mother, both of them now dead, and the story was that before his birth his mother was frightened by one of the big fish, so that the child came into the world most hideously marked. Anyhow, Fishhead was a human monstrosity, the veritable embodiment of nightmare. He had the body of a man—a short, stocky, sinewy body—but his face was as near to being the face of a great fish as any face could be and yet retain some trace of human aspect. His skull sloped back so abruptly that he could hardly be said to have a forehead at all; his chin slanted off right into nothing. His eyes were small and round with shallow, glazed, pale-yellow pupils, and they were set wide apart in his head and they were unwinking and staring, like a fish's eyes. His nose was no more than a pair of tiny slits in the middle of the yellow mask. His mouth was the worst of all. It was the awful mouth of a catfish, lipless and almost inconceivably wide, stretching from side to side. Also when Fishhead became a man grown his likeness to a fish increased, for the hair upon his face grew out into two tightly kinked, slender pendants that dropped down either side of the mouth like the beards of a fish.

If he had any other name than Fishhead, none excepting he knew it. As Fishhead he was known and as Fishhead he answered. Because he knew the waters and the woods of Reelfoot better than any other man there, he was valued as a guide by the city men who came every year to hunt or fish; but there were few such jobs that Fishhead would take. Mainly he kept to himself, tending his corn patch, netting the lake, trapping a little and in season pot hunting for the city markets. His neighbours, ague-bitten whites and malaria-proof Negroes alike, left him to himself. Indeed for the most part they had a superstitious fear of him. So he lived alone, with no kith nor kin, nor even a friend, shunning his kind and shunned by them.

His cabin stood just below the state line, where Mud Slough runs into the lake. It was a shack of logs, the only human habitation for four miles up or down. Behind it the thick timber came shouldering right up to the edge of Fishhead's small truck patch, enclosing it in thick shade except when the sun stood just overhead. He cooked his food in a primitive fashion, outdoors, over a hole in the soggy earth or upon the rusted red ruin of an old cook stove, and he drank the saffron water of the lake out of a dipper made of a gourd, faring and fending for himself, a master hand at skiff and net, competent with duck gun and fish spear, yet a creature of affliction and loneliness, part savage, almost amphibious, set apart from his fellows, silent and suspicious.

In front of his cabin jutted out a long fallen cottonwood trunk, lying half in and half out of the water, its top side burnt by the sun and worn by the friction of Fishhead's bare feet until it showed countless patterns of tiny scrolled lines, its under side black and rotted and lapped at unceasingly by little waves like tiny licking tongues. Its farther end reached deep water. And it was a part of Fishhead, for no matter how far his fishing and trapping might take him in the daytime, sunset would find him back there, his boat drawn up on the bank and he on the outer end of this log. From a distance men had seen him there many times, sometimes squatted, motionless as the big turtles that would crawl upon its dipping tip in his absence, sometimes erect and vigilant like a creek crane, his misshapen yellow form outlined against the yellow sun, the yellow water, the yellow banks—all of them yellow together.

If the Reelfooters shunned Fishhead by day they feared him by night and avoided him as a plague, dreading even the chance of a casual meeting. For there were ugly stories about

Fishhead—stories which all the Negroes and some of the whites believed. They said that a cry which had been heard just before dusk and just after, skittering across the darkened waters, was his calling cry to the big cats, and at his bidding they came trooping in, and that in their company he swam in the lake on moonlight nights, sporting with them, diving with them, even feeding with them on what manner of unclean things they fed. The cry had been heard many times, that much was certain, and it was certain also that the big fish were noticeably thick at the mouth of Fishhead's slough. No native Reelfooter, white or black, would willingly wet a leg or an arm there.

Here Fishhead had lived and here he was going to die. The Baxters were going to kill him, and this day in mid-summer was to be the time of the killing. The two Baxters—Jake and Joel—were coming in their dugout to do it. This murder had been a long time in the making. The Baxters had to brew their hate over a slow fire for months before it reached the pitch of action. They were poor whites, poor in everything—repute and worldly goods and standing—a pair of fever-ridden squatters who lived on whisky and tobacco when they could get it, and on fish and cornbread when they couldn't.

The feud itself was of months' standing. Meeting Fishhead one day in the spring on the spindly scaffolding of the skiff landing at Walnut Log, and being themselves far overtaken in liquor and vainglorious with bogus alcoholic substitute for courage, the brothers had accused him, wantonly and without proof, of running their trot-line and stripping it of the hooked catch—an unforgivable sin among the water dwellers and the shanty boaters of the South. Seeing that he bore this accusation in silence, only eyeing them steadfastly, they had been emboldened then to slap his face, whereupon he turned and gave them both the beating of their lives—bloodying their noses and bruising their lips with hard blows against their front teeth, and finally leaving them, mauled and prone, in the dirt. Moreover, in the onlookers a sense of the everlasting fitness of things had triumphed over race prejudice and allowed them—two free-born, sovereign whites—to be licked by a Negro.

Therefore, they were going to get the Negro. The whole thing had been planned out amply. They were going to kill him on his log at sundown. There would be no witnesses to see it, no retribution to follow after it. The very ease of the undertaking made them forget even their inborn fear of the place of Fishhead's habitation.

For more than an hour now they had been coming from their shack across a deeply indented arm of the lake. Their dugout, fashioned by fire and adz and draw-knife from the bole of a gum tree, moved through the water as noiselessly as a swimming mallard, leaving behind it a long, wavy trail on the stilled waters. Jake, the better oarsman, sat flat in the stern of the round-bottomed craft, paddling with quick, splashless strokes. Joel, the better shot, was squatted forward. There was a heavy, rusted duck gun between his knees.

Though their spying upon the victim had made them certain sure he would not be about the shore for hours, a doubled sense of caution led them to hug closely the weedy banks. They slid along the shore like shadows, moving so swiftly and in such silence that the watchful mud turtles barely turned their snaky heads as they passed. So, a full hour before the time, they came slipping around the mouth of the slough and made for a natural ambuscade which the mixed breed had left within a stone's jerk of his cabin to his own undoing.

Where the slough's flow joined deeper water a partly uprooted tree was stretched, prone from shore, at the top still thick and green with leaves that drew nourishment from the earth in which the half-uncovered roots yet held, and twined about with an exuberance of trumpet vines and wild fox-grapes. All about was a huddle of drift—last year's cornstalks, shreddy strips of bark, chunks of rotted weed, all the riffle and dunnage of a quiet eddy. Straight into this green clump glided the dugout and swung, broadside on, against the protecting trunk of the tree, hidden from the inner side by the intervening curtains of rank growth, just as the Baxters had intended it should be hidden, when days before in their scouting they marked this masked place of waiting and included it, then and there, in the scope of their plans.

There had been no hitch or mishap. No one had been abroad in the late afternoon to mark their movements—and in a little while Fishhead ought to be due. Jake's woodman's eye followed the downward swing of the sun speculatively. The shadows, thrown shoreward, lengthened and slithered on the small ripples. The small noises of the day died out; the small noises of the coming night began to multiply. The green-bodied flies went away and big mosquitoes, with speckled grey legs, came to take the places of the flies. The sleepy lake sucked at the mud banks with small mouthing sounds as though it found the taste of the raw mud agreeable. A monster crawfish, big as a chicken lobster, crawled out of the top of his dried mud chimney and perched himself there, an armoured sentinel on the watchtower. Bull bats began to flitter back and forth above the tops of the trees. A pudgy muskrat, swimming with head up, was moved to sidle off briskly as he met a cotton-mouth moccasin snake, so fat and swollen with summer poison that it looked almost like a legless lizard as it moved along the surface of the water in a series of slow torpid s's. Directly above the head of either of the waiting assassins a compact little swarm of midges hung, holding to a sort of kite-shaped formation.

A little more time passed and Fishhead came out of the woods at the back, walking swiftly, with a sack over his shoulder. For a few seconds his deformities showed in the clearing, then the black inside of the cabin swallowed him up. By now the sun was almost down. Only the red nub of it showed above the timber line across the lake, and the shadows lay inland a long way. Out beyond, the big cats were stirring, and the great smacking sounds as their twisting bodies leaped clear and fell back in the water came shoreward in a chorus.

But the two brothers in their green covert gave heed to nothing except the one thing upon which their hearts were set and their nerves tensed. Joel gently shoved his gun-barrels across the log, cuddling the stock to his shoulder and slipping two fingers caressingly back and forth upon the triggers. Jake held the narrow dugout steady by a grip upon a fox-grape tendril.

A little wait and then the finish came. Fishhead emerged from the cabin door and came down the narrow footpath to the water and out upon the water on his log. He was barefooted and bareheaded, his cotton shirt open down the front to show his yellow neck and breast, his dungaree trousers held about his waist by a twisted tow string. His broad splay feet, with the prehensile toes outspread, gripped the polished curve of the log as he moved along its swaying, dipping surface until he came to its outer end and stood there erect, his chest filling, his chinless face lifted up and something of mastership and dominion in his poise. And then—his eye caught what another's eyes might have missed—the round, twin ends of the gun barrels, the fixed gleams of Joel's eyes, aimed at him through the green tracery.

In that swift passage of time, too swift almost to be measured by seconds, realisation flashed all through him, and he threw his head still higher and opened wide his shapeless trap of a mouth, and out across the lake he sent skittering and rolling his cry. And in his cry was the laugh of a loon, and the croaking bellow of a frog, and the bay of a hound, all the compounded night noises of the lake. And in it, too, was a farewell and a defiance and an appeal. The heavy roar of the duck gun came.

At twenty yards the double charge tore the throat out of him. He came down, face forward, upon the log and clung there, his trunk twisting distortedly, his legs twitching and kicking like the legs of a speared frog, his shoulders hunching and lifting spasmodically as the life ran out of him all in one swift coursing flow. His head canted up between the heaving shoulders, his eyes looked full on the staring face of his murderer, and then the blood came out of his mouth and Fishhead, in death still as much fish as man, slid flopping, head first, off the end of the log and sank, face downward, slowly, his limbs all extended out. One after another a string of big bubbles came up to burst in the middle of a widening reddish stain on the coffee-coloured water.

The brothers watched this, held by the horror of the thing they had done, and the cranky dugout, tipped far over by the recoil of the gun, took water steadily across its gunwale; and now there was a sudden stroke from below upon its careening bottom and it went over and they were in the lake. But shore was only twenty feet away, the trunk of the uprooted tree only five. Joel, still holding fast to his hot gun, made for the log, gaining it with one stroke. He threw his free arm over it and clung there, treading water, as he shook his eyes free. Something gripped him—some great, sinewy, unseen thing gripped him fast by the thigh, crushing down on his flesh.

He uttered no cry, but his eyes popped out and his mouth set in a square shape of agony, and his fingers gripped into the bark of the tree like grapples. He was pulled down and down, by steady jerks, not rapidly but steadily, so steadily, and as he went his fingernails tore four little white strips in the tree bark. His mouth went under, next his popping eyes. Then his erect hair, and finally his clawing, clutching hand, and that was the end of him.

Jake's fate was harder still, for he lived longer—long enough to see Joel's finish. He saw it through the water that ran down his face, and with a great surge of his whole body he literally flung himself across the log and jerked his legs up high into the air to save them. He flung himself too far, though, for his face and chest hit the water on the far side. And out of this water rose the head of a great fish, with the lake slime of years on its flat, black head, its whiskers bristling, its corpsy eyes alight. Its horny jaws closed and clamped in the front of Jake's flannel shirt. His hand struck out wildly and was speared on a poisoned fin, and unlike Joel, he went from sight with a great yell and a whirling and a churning of the water that made the cornstalks circle on the edges of a small whirlpool.

But the whirlpool soon thinned away into widening rings of ripples and the cornstalks quit circling and became still again, and only the multiplying night noises sounded about the mouth of the slough.

The bodies of all three came ashore on the same day near the same place. Except for the gaping gunshot wound where the neck met the chest, Fishhead's body was unmarked. But the bodies of the two Baxters were so marred and mauled that the Reelfooters buried them together on the bank without ever knowing which might be Jake's and which might be Joel's.

DAGON

by H. P. Lovecraft

During his own lifetime the work of the great American fantasy writer, H. P. Lovecraft (1890–1937), was relegated to the pulp magazines such as *Weird Tales* and *Marvel Tales*. Only after his death did his stories achieve the hardback publication they deserved, thanks largely to the efforts of an enthusiastic band of Lovecraft devotees led by August Derleth. Lovecraft's literary reputation is now firmly established and, forty years after his death, his work is more popular than he could ever have imagined, paperback sales of his collected short stories running into millions.

Lovecraft appears to have had a pronounced aversion to the sea and the life-forms dwelling within it. It is said that he could not bear to eat, or even to contemplate, seafood of any kind. After having read this story, others may be inclined to share his aversion.

I AM WRITING this under an appreciable mental strain, since by tonight I shall be no more. Penniless, and at the end of my supply of the drug which alone makes life endurable, I can bear the torture no longer; and shall cast myself from this garret window into the squalid street below. Do not think from my slavery to morphine that I am a weakling or a degenerate. When you have read these hastily scrawled pages you may guess, though never fully realise, why it is that I must have forgetfulness or death.

It was in one of the most open and least frequented parts of the broad Pacific that the packet of which I was super-cargo fell a victim to the German sea-raider. The great war was then at its very beginning, and the ocean forces of the Hun had not com pletely sunk to their later degradation; so that our vessel was made a legitimate prize, whilst we of her crew were treated with all the fairness and consideration due us as naval prisoners. So liberal, indeed, was the discipline of our captors, that five days after we were taken I managed to escape alone in a small boat with water and provisions for a good length of time.

When I finally found myself adrift and free, I had but little idea of my surroundings. Never a competent navigator, I could only guess vaguely by the sun and stars that I was somewhat south of the equator. Of the longitude I knew nothing, and no island or coastline was in sight. The weather kept fair, and for uncounted days I drifted aimlessly beneath the scorching sun; waiting either for some passing ship, or to be cast on the shores of some habitable land. But neither ship nor land appeared, and I began to despair in my solitude upon the heaving vastness of unbroken blue.

The change happened whilst I slept. Its details I shall never know; for my slumber, though troubled and dream-infested, was continuous. When at last I awaked, it was to discover myself half sucked into a slimy expanse of hellish black mire which extended about me in monotonous undulations as far as I could see, and in which my boat lay grounded some distance away.

Though one might well imagine that my first sensation would be of wonder at so prodigious and unexpected a transformation of scenery, I was in reality more horrified than astonished; for there was in the air and in the rotting soil a sinister quality which chilled me to the very core. The region was putrid with the carcasses of decaying fish, and of other less describable things which I saw protruding from the nasty mud of the unending plain. Perhaps I should not hope to convey in mere words the unutterable hideousness that can dwell in absolute silence and barren immensity. There was nothing within hearing, and nothing in sight save a vast reach of black slime; yet the very completeness of the stillness and the homogeneity of the landscape oppressed me with a nauseating fear.

The sun was blazing down from a sky which seemed to me almost black in its cloudless cruelty; as though reflecting the inky marsh beneath my feet. As I crawled into the stranded boat I realised that only one theory could explain my position.

Through some unprecedented volcanic upheaval, a portion of the ocean floor must have been thrown to the surface, exposing regions which for innumerable millions of years had lain hidden under unfathomable watery depths. So great was the extent of the new land which had risen beneath me, that I could not detect the faintest noise of the surging ocean, strain my ears as I might. Nor were there any sea-fowl to prey upon the dead things.

For several hours I sat thinking or brooding in the boat, which lay upon its side and afforded a slight shade as the sun moved across the heavens. As the day progressed, the ground lost some of its stickiness, and seemed likely to dry sufficiently for travelling purposes in a short time. That night I slept but little, and the next day I made for myself a pack containing food and water, preparatory to an overland journey in search of the vanished sea and possible rescue.

On the third morning I found the soil dry enough to walk upon with ease. The odour of the fish was maddening; but I was too much concerned with graver things to mind so slight an evil, and set out boldly for an unknown goal. All day I forged steadily westward, guided by a far-away hummock which rose higher than any other elevation on the rolling desert. That night I encamped, and on the following day still travelled towards the hummock, though that object seemed scarcely nearer than when I had first espied it. By the fourth evening I attained the base of the mound, which turned out to be much higher than it had appeared from a distance; an intervening valley setting it out in sharper relief from the general surface. Too weary to ascend, I slept in the shadow of the hill.

I know not why my dreams were so wild that night; but ere the waning and fantastically gibbous moon had risen far above the eastern plain, I was awake in a cold perspiration, determined to sleep no more. Such visions as I had experienced were too much for me to endure again. And in the glow of the moon I saw how unwise I had been to travel by day. Without the glare of the parching sun, my journey would have cost me less energy; indeed, I now felt quite able to perform the ascent which had deterred me at sunset. Picking up my pack, I started for the crest of the eminence.

I have said that the unbroken monotony of the rolling plain was a source of vague horror to me; but I think my horror was greater when I gained the summit of the mound and looked down the other side into an immeasurable pit or canyon, whose black recesses the moon had not yet soared high enough to illumine. I felt myself on the edge of the world; peering over the rim into a fathomless chaos of eternal night. Through my terror ran curious reminiscences of *Paradise Lost*, and Satan's hideous climb through the unfashioned realms of darkness.

As the moon climbed higher in the sky, I began to see that the slopes of the valley were not quite so perpendicular as I had imagined. Ledges and outcroppings of rock afforded fairly easy footholds for a descent, whilst after a drop of a few hundred feet, the declivity became very gradual. Urged on by an impulse which I cannot definitely analyse, I scrambled with difficulty down the rocks and stood on the gentler slope beneath, gazing into the Stygian deeps where no light had yet penetrated.

All at once my attention was captured by a vast and singular object on the opposite slope, which rose steeply about a hundred yards ahead of me; an object that gleamed whitely in the newly bestowed rays of the ascending moon. That it was merely a gigantic piece of stone, I soon assured myself; but I was conscious of a distinct impression that its contours and position were not altogether the work of Nature. A closer scrutiny filled me with sensations I cannot express; for despite its enormous magnitude, and its position in an abyss which had yawned at the bottom of the sea since the world was young, I perceived beyond a doubt that the strange object was a well-shaped monolith whose massive bulk had known the workmanship and perhaps the worship of living and thinking creatures.

Dazed and frightened, yet not without a certain thrill of the scientist's or archaeologist's delight, I examined my surroundings more closely. The moon, now near the zenith, shone weirdly and vividly above the towering steeps that hemmed in the chasm, and revealed the fact that a far-flung body of water flowed at the bottom, winding out of sight in both directions, and almost lapping my feet as I stood on the slope. Across the chasm, the wavelets washed the base of the Cyclopean monolith, on whose surface I could now trace both inscriptions and crude hieroglyphics unknown to me, and unlike anything I had ever seen in books, consisting for the most part of conventional aquatic symbols such as fishes, eels, octopi, crustaceans, molluscs, whales and the like. Several characters obviously represented marine things which are unknown to the modern world, but whose decomposing forms I had observed on the ocean-risen plain.

It was the pictorial carving, however, that did most to hold me spellbound. Plainly visible across the intervening water on account of their enormous size was an array of bas-reliefs whose objects would have excited the envy of a Doré. I think that these things were supposed to depict men—at least, a certain sort of men; though the creatures were shown disporting like fishes in the waters of some marine grotto, or paying homage at some monolithic shrine which appeared to be under the waves as well. Of their faces and forms I dare not speak in detail; for the mere remembrance makes me grow faint. Grotesque beyond the imagination of a Poe or a Bulwer, they were damnably human in general outline despite webbed hands and feet, shockingly wide and flabby lips, glassy, bulging eyes, and other features less pleasant to recall. Curiously enough, they seemed to have been chiselled badly out of proportion with their scenic background; for one of the creatures was shown in the act of killing a whale represented as but little larger than himself. I remarked, as I say, their grotesqueness and strange size; but in a moment decided that they were merely the imaginary gods of some primitive fishing or seafaring tribe; some tribe whose last descendant had perished eras before the first ancestor of the Piltdown or Neanderthal Man was born. Awestruck at this unexpected glimpse into a past musing conception of the most daring anthropologist, I stood musing while the moon cast queer reflections on the silent channel before me.

Then suddenly I saw it. With only a slight churning to mark its rise to the surface, the thing slid into view above the dark waters. Vast, Polyphemus-like, and loathsome, it darted like a stupendous monster of nightmare to the monolith, about which it flung its gigantic scaly arms, the while it bowed its hideous head and gave vent to certain measured sounds. I think I went mad then.

Of my frantic ascent of the slope and cliff, and of my deliri-

ous journey back to the stranded boat, I remember little. I
believe I sang a great deal, and laughed oddly when I was unable to sing. I have indistinct recollections of a great storm some
time after I reached the boat; at any rate, I know that I heard
peals of thunder and other tones which Nature utters only in
her wildest moods.

When I came out of the shadows I was in a San Francisco
hospital; brought thither by the captain of the American ship
which had picked up my boat in mid-ocean. In my delirium I
had said much, but found that my words had been given scant
attention. Of any land upheaval in the Pacific, my rescuers knew
nothing; nor did I deem it necessary to insist upon a thing which
I knew they could not believe. Once I sought out a celebrated
ethnologist, and amused him with peculiar questions regarding
the ancient Philistine legend of Dagon, the Fish-God; but soon
perceiving that he was hopelessly conventional, I did not press
my inquiries.

It is at night, especially when the moon is gibbous and
waning, that I see the thing. I tried morphine; but the drug has
given only transient surcease, and has drawn me into its clutches
as a hopeless slave. So now I am to end it all, having written a
full account for the information for the contemptuous amusement of my fellow-men. Often I ask myself if it could not all
have been a pure phantasm—a mere freak of fever as I lay sun-
stricken and raving in the open boat after my escape from the
German man-of-war. This I ask myself, but ever does there
come before me a hideously vivid vision in reply. I cannot think
of the deep sea without shuddering at the nameless things that
may at this very moment be crawling and floundering on its
slimy bed, worshipping their ancient stone idols and carving
their own detestable likenesses on submarine obelisks of water-
soaked granite. I dream of a day when they may rise above the
billows to drag down in their reeking talons the remnants of
puny, war-exhausted mankind—of a day when the land shall
sink, and the dark ocean floor shall ascend amidst universal
pandemonium.

The end is near. I hear a noise at the door, as of some
immense slippery body lumbering against it. It shall not find
me. God, *that hand*! The window! The window!

FIRE IN THE GALLEY STOVE
by Captain William Outerson

The disappearance of the crew of the brigantine, *Marie Celeste*, which was discovered abandoned and adrift in 1873 is one of the most famous of all sea mysteries and one which continues to invite speculation even today. In a story called "J. Habakuk Jephson's Statement", Sir Arthur Conan Doyle deduced that the missing crew had been the victims of a Negro uprising. Others have made a more convincing case for smuggling or piracy being the cause of the crew's hasty and inexplicable evacuation of the ship. "Fire in the Galley Stove" is not specifically about the *Marie Celeste* but the chilling events which overtake the *Unicorn* offer a solution to the mystery as plausible as any other so far offered.

The story brings to mind certain lines of Coleridge's *The Ancient Mariner*:

> The very deep did rot: O Christ!
> That this should ever be!
> Yea, slimy things did crawl with legs
> Upon the slimy sea . . .

T H E S H I P *Unicorn* loitered to the westward, running large with a gentle breeze from the south. In the light of the brilliant moon her decks gleamed whitely; aloft, sly shadows played among her sails and spars. Overside, the quiet sea murmured as she passed.

Mister Mergam stood on the weather side of the poop, staring sourly ahead and seeing though not perceiving the beauty of the night. His keen ears caught the various sounds of ship and

ea and wind, and his trained mind recognised them automatic-
lly, especially the soft thud of the rudder as the sea touched
, now on one side and now on the other. It was a simple
ound, near and familiar, relentless as fate and sounding a note
f caution, obscurely ominous, as if the voice of the helm
ttempted to warn him against any lack of vigilance. In this
articular morning watch it gave him that impression, not
ecause he was feeling down and defeated, since he had felt
hat way for years, but owing to his mood of sour rebellion,
vhich had now reached a climax. He hated the empty plains of
1e sea and the narrow rounds of sailing-ship duties, but had to
ndure them because he could not make a living ashore.

Through all his years of roving, even on nights like this, he
ad remained blind to the beauty of the sea, and now his feel-
1g towards it had settled into weary hatred. He knew its effects
f blended colour, its wide gradations of sound and action, the
ireless charm of a sailing ship's effortless movement, the quality
f silent distance and the wonder of the skies. Dimly at times,
1 moments of rare emotion, he had caught a glimpse of the
1ystic hand that beckons beyond the horizon and felt for a
ttle while the fated urge of the wanderer. But that was in the
eginning, long ago when he had first gone to sea, and he had
orgotten it.

The lee side of the deck, to starboard, abounded in shadows
ast by the moon. Under the main sail a dark blotch extended
rom the half deck to the main hatch, and a bright space lay
etween that and the forward house. Observing this with his
ustomary dull disinterest in details not requiring action, he
vatched the shadow thrown by the foot of the main sail, back-
1g and filling in the languid breeze. Raising his eyes from the
eck to the sail, he suddenly stiffened and gazed unseeing in
:ont of him as he felt an unusual movement of the hull, a
trange shaking that startled him because it was outside of all
is former experience. The whole ship, hull and spars and
igging, trembled eerily, and all the gear aloft made a weird
latter. He had never known any ship to move like this, and as
e stood wondering what had caused it the skipper came
urriedly from the companion and halted beside him.

"What was that?" he demanded nervously.

"I don't know, sir," Mister Mergam answered. "I've never felt anything like it until now, so I wouldn't know what it was."

"You don't know!" exclaimed the skipper. "You're here on deck in charge of the ship and something scrapes along her side—a derelict, more than likely—and you don't know what it was! You don't know." The skipper waved his hands helplessly. "Why don't you know? Didn't you see anything? Invisible things don't shake a ship like that. It must have been something big enough to be seen. Were you asleep?"

"No, sir, I wasn't asleep. I was wider awake than you are now, attending to my job, and I saw nothing. There was nothing to be seen. The lookout didn't see anything, or he would've reported it, and the man at the wheel didn't see anything either."

"The man at the wheel," the skipper repeated unpleasantly. "How do you know he didn't see anything? It isn't his job to see things and report them. He's here to steer the ship, not to keep lookout."

The mate turned away sullenly and approached the man at the wheel.

"Did you see what shook her a minute ago, Thomson?" he inquired.

"No, sir," Thompson answered. "I didn't see nothin'. I looked astern after she stopped shakin' an' there wasn't nothin' in sight."

"You heard what he said, sir," Mister Mergam remarked to the skipper in a tone of meagre triumph. "There was nothing in sight."

"Aye, I heard him," Captain Garton returned impatiently. "What do you suppose it could have been? Possibly a submerged derelict?"

"No, sir, I don't think so. It wasn't the sort of shock any kind of derelict would give. I've been in collision with a derelict and it was something entirely different. This was strong, but soft and trembly. A derelict would grind and scrape along her side and make enough noise to wake the dead."

"I suppose you're right," the skipper admitted unwillingly. He moved away from the mate and stood with his hands on the poop rail staring at the sea ahead, a tall man, gaunt and

rascible from chronic dyspepsia due to overeating and lack
of exercise, tired of life and hating everybody, including himself. His excessively bright eyes wandered fretfully along the
deck on the weather side, which was lit by the moon except
for an edge of shadow here and there, and he glanced at the
leech of the main sail. Something attracted his attention then,
and he looked over on the port bow. A startled exclamation
broke from him and he threw up his arm in swift apprehension,
pointing urgently.

"Hey, Mister Mergam!" he cried. "What's that?"

The mate looked in the direction indicated by the captain's
finger and noted a lifting of the skyline, an effect he had often
observed while approaching a high coast from the sea, though
this was not quite so well defined. He stared in silence and
without understanding, disregarding the impatient questions of
the captain until he arrived at the conclusion that the elevation
ahead was a great wave approaching the ship at high speed.
In the moonlight he could see its steep unbroken slope shining
like bright metal and rushing towards them, and he was disturbed by the thought that it might sweep the decks clean.

"It's a big wave, sir," he said at last in faint excitement.

"Yes, it is," the skipper agreed. "It couldn't be anything else.
And it explains the shaking of the ship a few minutes ago.
There's been an upheaval of the sea bottom, a submarine earth-
quake, and when the sea bottom shook, the sea shook with it.
The sea floor hereabouts has risen nearly two thousand feet
during the past twenty years."

"Tidal wave on the port bow, sir," the lookout reported
elatedly. He had been uncertain what name to give it, or
whether to make any report about it, since waves of any size
are not usually reported aboard ships at sea. They take them as
they come.

"Aye, aye," replied Mister Mergam. "Close all ports forrid."

They could see the forms of men moving about on their bare
feet as they carried out this order, scattering silently and passing
among the shadows from the sails on the fore mast. The ports
were closed in a little while, and the men thought they ought to
shut all the doors, but before they could begin to do this the
big wave rolled up like the side of a mountain.

The skipper and the mate watched it come, not expecting any particular trouble from it, whatever its size, since ships are buil to ride the seas in all weathers and conditions, and the wave approaching from a favourable direction, about two points on the weather bow. As it drew nearer and revealed its enormou size, its smooth crest towering loftily above the level of the sea the two officers began to feel doubtful. They could hardly expect the ship to ride dry over such a mass of water as that so abruptly sloped and moving so swiftly.

When it reached the bows of the *Unicorn*, she gave a mighty heave and lifted her head in a gallant effort to climb the watery height, but she could not rise swiftly enough. Halfway up, her bowsprit and cutwater drove into it, and it broke over her coming down on the decks with a solid crash that seemed to beat her under the sea. It swept over the forecastle head and rolled along the main deck in an avalanche, burying the houses far under the foaming against the masts as high as the foot of the courses. Rolling over the poop a fathom deep, it submerged the skipper, the mate, and the man at the wheel. They held on grimly, and in a few seconds the wave passed on.

The water sluiced off the decks into the calm sea, and soon all was normal again, save that the galley fire was black out the morning coffee was ruined, and all the pots and pans were adrift in eighteen inches of salt water. Both forecastles were flooded, because the watch on deck, having been given barel enough time to close the ports, had not been able to shut the doors, and the watch below came spluttering out, cursing the other blokes for not having sense enough to do such thing without waiting for orders.

"Call yourselves sailors," they sneered malevolently. "You ain't got sense enough to tighten your belts when your pant are slippin' down. Nurses is what you need." They raved bac and forth till somebody struck out and the forward deck became a tumbled scene of fighting sailors, cursing and mauling each other but inflicting no serious injuries. Like a pack of sportiv demons in the shadows of the moon they rolled about the mai deck as far aft as the main hatch, locked in fierce embraces of sound and fury.

The skipper and the mate stood on the poop watching the

rawl, and a light came into Mister Mergam's eye. Extracting a
heavy teakwood belaying pin from the taffrail, he swung it
gently up and down, almost lovingly, holding it loosely in his
right hand.

"I'd better put a stop to that," he suggested to the skipper.

"No," said Captain Garton. "They won't hurt each other too
much, and a little exercise will do them good. They've had it
too easy this passage."

Mister Mergam seemed disappointed by this decision, but
he obediently replaced the pin in the rail and continued to watch
the waning battle on the forward deck.

Before long, the rage of the men abated and they separated
two by two. Returning to their respective forecastles, they found
that the water had drained out through the scupper holes, so
the starboard watch lit their pipes and turned in to smoke while
falling asleep. In the galley the cook cursed tidal waves and
everything else as he gathered up his pots and pans and relit
the fire in the stove after cleaning out the mess of sodden coals.
It was now half-past four, and the morning coffee—the most
welcome event of the day to seafaring men—was due at two
bells, therefore he must hurry. He would have a fresh brew
ready in time if it could be done.

The skipper felt better after witnessing the fight between the
watches, and he smiled for the first time in weeks as he listened
to the reeking obscenities of the cook. There was something
reckless and defiant in his piercing blasphemies that pleased the
old man, who suffered a great deal from indigestion. But he
soon became aware of the chill from his wet clothing and
turned towards the companion with a sigh.

"Keep a sharp lookout, Mister," he said to the mate as he
started down to the cabin. "We don't want any more tidal
waves."

"Very good, sir," Mister Mergam replied, swearing under his
breath. The skipper's remark seemed to imply that he was to
blame for tidal waves.

"Damned old fool," he muttered. "He didn't even know the
difference between a collision with a derelict and an earthquake
shock."

WOT * *

In the port forecastle the men of the watch were changing into dry dungarees and discussing after their fashion the events of the morning.

"That was a big sea," said one.

"Aye, it was, but I've seen bigger off the Horn," old Charlie declared.

"You never seen a bigger one anywheres, Charlie. You must of dreamt it."

"This old hooker is full of bad luck."

"So she is. She ain't had a lucky day since we left port."

"When d'ya think coffee will be ready?"

"Ask the cook. Mebbe he knows."

"I give Snooky in the sta'bo'd watch a coupla black eyes."

"Take a squint at yer own."

"The skipper's crazy."

"Naw, he ain't crazy. He's sick. He oughta stay ashore."

"Say! Did ya feel that? What the hell was that?"

On the quiet poop Mister Mergam stood with feet apart, glancing listlessly at the sky line from time to time, casting his eyes aloft at the towering sails, surveying the deck, and watching the play of shadows born of the moon. The colour of the sea had changed, and it no longer gleamed with the purple blue of deep water. As they were not within two hundred miles of the Grand Bank he surmised that the disturbance on the sea bottom had sent up clouds of ooze that imparted a dull hue to the water. While considering this, turning it over in his mind with slow interest, he felt the ship quiver again to a sudden shock, altogether different from the first. It felt as if a floating body, soft and enormously heavy, had come to rest against the bottom of the ship, and he went swiftly to the taffrail to peer intently over the side. At the same time he noticed the men of the watch running silently to the main rail forward, where they also stared down at the sea. Evidently they had felt the shock. He had just finished his casual observance of them when the skipper erupted on the poop again, very much annoyed.

"What was that, Mister Mergam?" he demanded in his usual exasperated tone. "That was no earthquake shock. Something hit her that time—you can't deny it. Something actual and material struck against her bottom."

"Yes, sir, I'm not denying it. Something certainly hit her then, and I'm looking to see what it was, but there's nothing in sight."

"Nothing in sight," the skipper repeated. "Nothing in sight. What in the name of all the mysteries is happening to this ship, anyhow? All sorts of things going on, and nobody knows anything about it!"

There came another soft, heavy shock, followed by others at short intervals.

"My God!" the skipper whispered, staring fearfully down at the muddy sea. More and more of the things, a whole crowd of them, monsters of some horrible sort, clamped along her keel, driven up from the bottom of the sea by the disturbance down there! "What are they? Can you tell me that, Mister Mergam?"

"No, sir, I can't," the mate replied uneasily.

They stared at each other in the light of the sinking moon, two perturbed and bewildered men suspecting some lurking danger.

"The wheel's jammed, sir!" cried Thomson. "I can't move ."

The skipper and the mate turned and stared at the man, watching his strenuous but unavailing efforts to move the wheel.

"She's lost headway, sir," said Mister Mergam, looking over the side again. "She's standing still."

"You're quite right," the captain agreed in a different tone of voice, low and troubled. "These big brutes clinging to her bottom have stopped her, and one of them has clamped itself across the rudder. Whatever they are down there, they're keeping out of sight. Ah! There's another. That one struck forrid under the bows. There must be a lot of them."

The man at the wheel, peering at the timepiece in the binacle, saw that it was five o'clock and made two bells. Forward on the forecastle head, the man on lookout struck the ship's bell twice, two measured strokes that boomed and lingered about the shadowy decks. Placid now, and smoking a short clay pipe as black as ebony, the cook, who had flaming red hair and hailed from Glasgow, thrust his head through the galley doorway and asked what the hell was wrong now. The men strung

along the rail told him they didn't bloody well know what wa
wrong, but if he would hurry with the coffee they would te
him as soon as they found out.

"If there's anither tidal wave comin', give us a shout so's
can close the doorrs and the porrts," the cook requested.

"How about coffee?" they inquired, turning from the ra
to observe him with the bantering regard that sailors bestow o
sea cooks.

"It'll be ready in aboot ten meenits," he promised them.

In a little less time than that he beat with a ladle on th
bottom of an empty pan, making a racket that might have bee
heard or felt by the beasts along the keel, and the men left th
rail to fetch their hook-pots from the forecastle. They wer
puzzled and a trifle scared and had little to say to each othe
though they had chattered enough when those queer shock
had been felt. Some of them thought whales had rubbed thei
backs against the hull, but others argued that this would no
have stopped the ship's headway. There must be a lot of bi
soft beasts hanging on to her, scared up from the depths by th
earthquake down there that had caused the tidal wave, or th
ship wouldn't be standing still the way she was.

In silence they went one by one to the galley door and waite
in line for their pots of coffee. Charlie was first. He stood at th
door holding his hook-pot inside, to be filled with a ladleful o
the stuff the cook called coffee, dipped from a boiler on th
stove.

The skipper and the mate still waited at the taffrail for a sigh
of the things from the deep, and the long inaction had begu
to affect their nerves.

"If we could only see them, and find out what they are,"
muttered the captain, "we might be able to decide on som
plan of action. But how can we fight against invisible things o
unknown nature!" He paced back and forth along a shor
path between the taffrail and the standard binnacle, frownin
impatiently, clenching and opening his hands nervously.

Mister Mergam had glanced forward at the sound of th
cook's gong, and he watched the men as they came out of th
forecastle and went to the galley door to await their turn fo

offee. The first man in line received his coffee and started for
ie fore hatch, where he intended to sit while drinking it, and
e did not see the long slender tentacle that quirted over the
iil above his head and waved here and there seeking what he
iight find.

It found old Charlie as he reached the fore hatch, concealed
om his watchmates by the corner of the forward house,
rapped itself round his neck with a strangling hold that pre-
ented him from uttering a sound, and dragged him violently
ver the rail.

The next man, following with his coffee, saw Charlie at the
iil, striking madly at the tentacle with his hook-pot, and a
artled yell attracted the attention of the others. They spun
ound and saw old Charlie going over the side in a headlong
ive with his waving hook-pot, but were too late to notice the
eadly tentacle round his neck. They rushed to the rail and
ared down at the dull water, but the man who had seen the
ntacle held back. He knew the sort of beast it belonged to.

Men may sail the seas for a lifetime and seldom, if ever, come
 contact with the nightmare monsters that inhabit the caves
nd cliffs of the ocean floor. Gazing down at the slightly muddy
ater, the men of the *Unicorn* saw a squirming mass of inter-
oven tentacles resembling enormous snakes, immensely thick
nd long and tapering at their free ends to the size of a man's
umb. It was a foul sight, an obscene growth from the dark
laces of the world, where incessant hunger is the driving force.
t one place, down near the bulge of the hull, appeared a
aring gorgon face with great lidless eyes and a huge parrot
eak that moved slightly, opening and shutting as though it had
ist crunched and swallowed a meal of warm flesh. In its neigh-
ourhood the water was stained a reddish hue, possibly with
lood from the veins of old Charlie. There were many of those
eepsea devils under the ship, ravenously hungry and now
ware that there was food on her decks in the form of puny
odies that could be had for the taking.

Suddenly the men of the watch saw the air above the rail
live with tentacles. They swayed uncertainly for a second or
wo in order to feel the position of their prey, then lashed out
ith swift aim at the horrified men. Whipping round them, they

tightened their hold to a vice-like grip that no human strengt
could break, though a sharp knife could slice them in two
properly used. The men were panic-stricken and struck wildl
with sheath knives and hook-pots, but failed in their excitemer
to cut themselves adrift and went over the rail screaming. Th
boatswain, carpenter, and sailmaker jumped up from the mai
hatch and rushed across the deck to rescue the few survivors c
the watch, but half a dozen tentacles seized them and jerke
them over the side, striking futile blows.

When the first tentacle came over the rail and fastened itse
on Charlie, the steward was ambling forward to the galley fc
the cabin coffee. On seeing the man dragged violently over th
rail the steward stopped and stared in amazement, trying t
imagine what had happened to the sailor and thinking tha
perhaps he had become suddenly insane. The reeling gait c
old Charlie, however, his struggles and the manner in which h
went over the rail, convinced the steward that something ha
hold of him. His smooth-shaven face, round and placid, becam
puckered with anxiety and he stared in growing consternatio
at the struggle that developed between the men of the watch an
the tapering tentacles that whipped over the rail in dozen
While he stood watching this primitive contest, a tentacle flun
itself round his portly waist and dragged him down before h
whimper could rise to a scream of terror.

The cook with the flaming hair came out of the galley wit
a carving knife and tried to run aft to the poop, but was caugh
He slashed off the tentacle but was seized by others and dragge
over, the severed tentacle clinging round his body. The men c
the starboard watch tumbled out raving with drawn knives i
ready hands. They had to divide forces to protect themselve
on both sides, as the tentacles were now swaying above eac
rail from forecastle to poop. Though they fought with fury an
some skill they had small chance to win against such desperat
odds. Some of them jumped into the rigging to get out of reac
by climbing aloft, but the men who tried that exposed them
selves to the beasts lurking below and were snatched awa
immediately. There were too many tentacles to be cut, an
even when they were slashed clean through they continued t

ling round a man's body. They had suction cups on their under
sides and rings of sharp claws within these.

"There's the answer," said the mate to the skipper when the
battle began after the death of old Charlie "The things sticking
to the bottom are giant octopuses. They're the biggest things in
the sea, except for the whales, and only the sperm whale can
tackle them. He feeds on them, and sometimes they feed on
him, if they can hold him down till he drowns. I'll get a knife
and give the men a hand."

"Better do that than stand here telling me things I already
know," the skipper retorted sharply. "There's men dying forrid
here."

The mate hurried to the companion on the way to his room
for a hunting knife he kept there—a beautiful weapon hitherto
useless, with an eight-inch blade as sharp as a razor. The
octopus which had folded itself over the stern and jammed the
rudder, aware that its companions were obtaining food from
the top of this rock-like mass they were clinging to, flung two
tentacles over the taffrail and waved one of them in Mister
Mergam's direction.

"Look out, sir!" The man at the wheel screamed a warning.

Mister Mergam was just about to descend the companionway
when he heard this cry, and he threw a swift glance over his
shoulder, saw the thing flicking towards him, and tried to jump
down the companionway. He was too late. The tentacle wrapped
itself round his chest and tightened. He strained against it,
uttering a faint grunt, and braced himself with hands and feet
against the hatch.

"Bring a knife, sir, and cut me loose," he implored the captain, who stared at him in horror and rushed away for a knife,
going down the poop ladder to the door leading to the cabin
from the main deck.

The other tentacle found the man at the wheel and caught
him round the waist, binding one arm to his side but leaving
the other free. It was the rule aboard the *Unicorn* that no seaman should wear a knife while standing his trick at the wheel,
therefore Thomson carried none. He knew that human strength
would not prevail against the power of these tentacles, though

they could be cut, and he waited for the return of the skippe
with the knife. Meantime, he made a sudden jerk and dragge
the tentacle a couple of feet towards him, wrapped two turns c
it round a spoke of the wheel, and held it fast there. It require
desperate strength to do that with one hand, and he succeede
only because he was an exceptionally powerful man. Now th
octopus could not drag him over the side without breaking th
spoke, which was teakwood and very tough.

The mate had nothing but his hands, and these could nc
serve him. A sharp axe was hung on the bulkhead a few step
below him in the companionway, and he made supreme effort
to go down there against the pull of the beast to secure th
weapon. His efforts were unsuccessful, for the octopus refuse
to slack up and tightened its grip till he groaned with the pai
of it.

Though the skipper had not been gone more than a fe
seconds, Mister Mergam thought he would never come bac
and cried in a gasping voice for him to hurry. Captain Garto
shouted that he could not find the knife in the mate's cabin an
was bringing the axe from the bulkhead. He was coming rigl
up.

"For God's sake, hurry!" the mate entreated. "The brute
crushing me."

The skipper wrenched the axe out of the slings and staggere
up the companionway to cut Mister Mergam free, but as h
reached him the mate was dragged violently away from th
hatch. Captain Garton followed in urgent pursuit. Dashing o
on deck, he made a swift step towards the unfortunate mat
and swung up the axe for a severing stroke, but before the blac
fell Mister Mergam was whipped with a crash against the taf
rail and went down over the side.

The man at the wheel found it difficult to hold against th
pull of the octopus, even with a double turn of the tentacl
round the spoke. He was gasping and purple in the face, an
the harder he strove against it the tighter the tentacle wa
drawn. He was rapidly becoming exhausted. After peering ov
the side for a few precious moments to see what became of h
lost mate, the skipper drew back from the rail horrified an
trembling. He was not a strong man. Turning towards th

wheel, he noted the perilous plight of the man there, and stumbled across the deck intending to sever the tentacle where it was wrapped round the spoke. In his condition of quaking repulsion he could hardly lift the axe and stood for seconds trying to swing it above his head.

The octopus jamming the rudder eased its pressure down there, and the wheel spun round under the pull of the tentacle, which slipped off the spoke. Thomson was hurtled across the poop and over the side, crashing against the skipper and knocking him down. The axe fell from Captain Garton's hands, and he rose staggering to pick it up. As he seized it he saw another tentacle whipping over the rail towards him, and in a surge of blind fury he swung the axe, which left his hands and went flashing into the sea. He swooned when the tentacle gripped him, and the octopus drew him down.

Cowering on the forecastle head, the man on lookout saw the last of the crew go down to feed the octopuses, and his mind roved in every direction searching for a means of saving his life. Up to the present no tentacles had come up over the head rail, and he stood absolutely still, hoping that they would not find him.

But in this he was disappointed. One of them came up and waved about, drawing nearer every second. Out of his mind with terror, he sprang to the rail and saw in the water below the appalling face of an octopus. Taking his knife by the blade, he threw it with miraculous aim and saw it sink out of sight in the eye of the beast, which went into a tremendous flurry. Looking aft, the man saw that there were few tentacles now waving over the main deck, and he crept down the ladder to look for a knife. Stealing along the port side, he searched eagerly but could not find one, returned along the starboard side and met the same result. All the men had gone down fighting with the knives in their hands, and the hook-pots. Reaching the fore hatch, he decided to enter the forecastle and shut the door. The ports were already closed. But he was just a moment too late. They got him.

A little while later a pod of sperm whales came up to blow not far from the *Unicorn*; and the octopuses, feeling the near presence of their deadly enemies went away from there and returned to the deep places.

The ship *Merivale*, heading eastward some days out of New York, sighted a ship with all sail set. She was observed to behave in an erratic manner and appeared to be abandoned since there was nobody at the wheel or about the decks. In the gentle breeze that was blowing shortly after sunrise the strange vessel bore away to the west, came up in the wind with all her canvas flapping, paid off slowly, and bore away again, repeating this endlessly. The skipper and the second mate of the *Merivale* watched her queer behaviour from the poop, and, as no answer was made to their signals, a boat was sent off to the stranger to investigate.

The boat pulled alongside the *Unicorn*, and the second mate was boosted to the rail. They hove up the boat's painter, which he made fast, and scrambled up beside him. Except for some stains of coffee on the fore deck, which had not completely dried, the decks were clear and shipshape. In the cabin the second mate noted that the table was set for coffee, but the dishes had not been used. He scratched his head in complete bewilderment. All the boats were in the chocks, their covers untouched, and there was no sign of disease or mutiny. As he stood pondering the mysterious situation, one of his men came aft and halted in front of him.

"They ain't been gone very long. sir," he reported. "The fire's still fresh in the galley stove."

THE SLAVER
by John Russell

The son of Charles Russell, an American novelist and explorer, John Russell (1885–1956) wrote chiefly about life afloat and ashore in the Pacific—which led to him being labelled the "Kipling of the South Seas". He was the author of over six hundred short stories and several novels. His best-known works include *The Red Mark and Other Stories* (1919), *In Dark Places* (1923), *Where the Pavement Ends* (1928), *Cops 'n Robbers* (1930) and *The Lost God and Other Adventure Stories* (1947). During the First World War he was in charge of U.S. Government propaganda for Great Britain and achieved the amiable distinction of being nearly ejected from the House of Commons for "vociferous laughter". His presence seems to have been better appreciated in Samoa where, as with Robert Louis Stevenson before him, he was made an honorary chieftain of the islanders in recognition of his talents as a storyteller.

SHE HAD LEARNED her trade before the American War. And again before the Brazilian emancipation of '71 she had drifted back to the same hateful traffic until driven by stress of weather or British cruisers to try the West Coast, where she took refuge with her last cargo among the mangrove swamps of the Guayas. So the legend ran. It was certain that she was very old, and had served many unsavoury masters; as a smuggler, a river pirate, and a convict hulk. Her last owner was a Babahoyo planter, who patched her up as a cacao barge, drank himself to death in her cabin one night, and left her to rot at his rotting wharf. Since that she had been shunned, for ships are like folks, their ill-repute grows sinister with age.

And ships are like folks, too, in that they move through wide courses with the fatality of drama—each following a destiny to an appointed end, edifying, pitiful, or disastrous ...

Her ribs were oak, but her heart was evil. No man can check her far wanderings, nor the lawless ladings she bore, but she knew Porto Bango and Mana and Palmas and the shames of Amelia Island, and the slave depôts of Barataria and San Paulo. Stranded in the slime of the bayou, she seemed to have reached her proper berth at last, given up for ever to solitude and tropic decay.

Until another day came when they burst her cerements and put forth into the world again on a final venture, and this was the curious manner of it:

Early one rainy season occurred the famous gold discovery on the western shoulders of Chimborazo, where a sheep herder lost his flock and found riches in the sudden spate of a mountain stream. It was a find trumpeted with high hopes, and, before it dwindled, it drew to Ecuador some scores of those rovers on the outskirts that seek, that eternally and hungrily have sought, the fat chance and the easy profit.

Early in April the first consignment of gold-dust was ready for transport from the diggings to the coast. It came down through the foothills on mule-back, through the upper waters of the Babahoyo by canoe, and at the head of navigation was transported to a little stern-wheel river steamer under guard for the run to Guayaquil ... It never reached Guayaquil, and the river steamer was never seen again, nor any of the crew, nor the guard. But four of the passengers—men who had passed that way as prospectors a month before, and were then returning empty-handed, continued their journey down the Babahoyo to the Guayas. And the gold-dust went with them.

Under a tinted twilight when the narrow lane of sky and its mirrored image showed like strips of mother-of-pearl between massed banks of foliage, the peace of the bayou was troubled. A small canoe might have been observed to thread the passage towards the old cacao wharf. Those aboard of it were under some urgency, and indeed the craft was ready to swamp with

them; they had to bail as they paddled. At a bend they came
in sudden sight of the little schooner, standing stark across
their course.

"Did I lie or didn't I—tell me that?" demanded a voice that
broke hoarsely. An active, squab-armed figure leapt from the
bow of the canoe into the channels of the *Jorguina*, and held
a hand to steady the next below.

"Yes—but will she float?" mumbled the other. "She sets like
a dead log."

"I promised you a ship. Ain't you satisfied?"

A third man, tall and angular, scrambled past them both,
and bounced aboard like a thing on wires.

"All serene, Brewer, my son," he hiccuped. "A ship—with
a deck. A quarter deck would you say? Faith, it's whole and
dry at least, which is better than being three-quarters drowned
in a leaky coffin.

> "Oh, a life on the ocean wave:
>   A home on the rolling deep——"

He danced a step.

"Merry!" he sang, and collapsed against the rail.

The second began to complain in husky exasperation.

"Another dam' fool tha's no sort o' use! Say, you think I'm
goin' to hoist all d' swag alone? An' d' canoe, she be sunk in a
minute!" The little craft spun, and ducked under his clumsy
feet.

"Easy all, Chrispim," said the first more quietly. "I'll give
you a lift."

Between them they emptied the canoe, shifting sacks and
bundles to the schooner's deck, until the dusk overtook them
there, a knot of shadowy invaders.

"Where's that blame' lantern?" demanded Brewer suddenly.
"And where's George?" he added.

No trace of George, who seemed to have been mislaid.

> "Oh, once he was his mother's pride,
>   And his brave fa-ther's hope and joy,
>   But now where is that orphing boy?"

sang the tall man.

"George!" they bawled in chorus, and the jungle gave them back the word until an illuminating sentence floated up. "Drunk, an' asleep down there!"

"Let 'im sink," advised Chrispim bitterly, but Brewer climbed down again and rescued a limp and dripping form.

"Let him sink," it muttered. "Let *me* sink. I'd—I'd rather sink. I shot two of 'em swimming away, and they made bubbles —red bubbles in the water . . . Are you sure we sunk 'em all?"

"You sit down and shake yourself together," growled Brewer. "One drink, mind—no more."

Chrispim struck a light and the lantern threw them into a ring. They were a scraggy lot, types, all more or less recognisable, of the tramp. Much romance is woven about such men without much improving the model, which is generally sordid and abject, given to lesser outlawry at home and in outlandish parts to cadging on consuls and to selling the repute and authority of their white skins. In stained and tattered drill, variously booted, belted, and armed, these four achieved a certain swagger. But it was only achieved, and their flushed faces and wide gestures betrayed the kind of heartening they had had for a job beyond their natural compass.

Only Brewer, their leader, came nearest the tough breed of buccaneer times. He had been a Key West wrecker, a poacher among the Pearl Islands, an engineer in the Colombian Navy— drifter and ne'er-do-well. Ruddy skin and strong white teeth, an open and bold expression, gave him an appearance of genial force until it was seen that his eyes were too full and too far apart, his features thickened by the stamp of abnormality. Such as he was, he supplied the drive and the imagination for this exploit, and straightway he had found a handspike and set to making busy clatter at the pump.

"She'll do," he hailed. "Dig into this now, you lads. We'll have her afloat in an hour!"

The others made no move, and presently he came back to stand over them, gathering each eye with his own menacing blue sparkle.

"Look here; if any of you has a fancy to settle down in this country, he can move ashore. Only he's got to choose quick.

D'y' think that river craft ain't goin' to be missed tomorrow at Guayaquil, and a reg'lar bees-nest of saddle-coloured police-men turned loose to hunt all hands?"

"Me—I'm done," said Chrispim sulkily.

"We're all done," echoed the tall man. He called himself Charlie Dibdin, "Singing Charlie", but as he was apt on occasion and quite solemnly to substitute Sullivan or even Tom Moore, the name was hardly an identification. A bone-built clotheshorse of a man with a stringy yellow moustache and grid-ironed face, he contrived just now to appear half sober after a fashion of his own.

"Perhaps you don't know how done we are," he pleaded. "It's been—it's been a hefty day's work." He wiped his mouth with a dirty, clawlike hand that shook. "We'd sooner rest a bit."

"And the whole crowd of us as good as standin' on the drop this minute," was Brewer's comment, made without heat. "Or maybe it won't be hanging," he added. "They use the garrotte in some places still, don't they—the iron collar that drives a spike through the back of your neck?... Or a mud wall and a firin' squad."

The others stirred uneasily.

"Wha's the use to pump tha' dam' river in an out again?" demanded Chrispim. "The ship is rotten."

"And I tell you the ship is sound as a dollar—rebuilt only three years ago. I know; I heard all about her at Babahoyo. She's been tended to and kep' part dry. That pump's in first-class order. Will y' help?"

"Tell George," suggested Chrispim; but George sitting apart, stupid with fever and exhaustion, paid no heed. He was the youngest of them, scarcely more than a boy, and he had apparently given up altogether.

Brewer considered them one by one, the poor material with which he had to work. In their brief partnership they had had no show-down yet, no test of dominance. He went about it without unnecessary violence.

"I give you a minute or so to make up your minds, and then *I'll* help the crew of y' to shore!"

They stared up at him where he stood smiling a little with

the pump-bar fisted, his revolver bulging at his hip. After all they had been through that day it seemed monstrous to them that he should be so vigorous, so determined; that nothing should have touched this stocky, arch-chested rogue—not rum nor weariness nor horror.

"Oh?" snarled Chrispim rousing. "And what would we be doing?"

"You can take your shares of the dust; they're all correct in the leather bags," said Brewer amiably. "This is no strong-arm play. Only I know when I'm lucky, and tonight is my get-away, understand? It's a great summer resort hereabouts, isn't it? You'd like it, Charlie, without your rum. And George—he'd be comfortable hidin' in a swamp. There's an old plantation back somewhere. Vacant, they tell me, except for devils and night walkers and such." He swung round on the stout one. "You wouldn't be at all lonesome, Chris."

He struck at tautened nerves, particularly with an eye to Chrispim. This follower was capable of trouble, but Brewer had the measure of him—a scullion by his trade, a Porto Santo Portuguese, dull and malignant, who had lost among galleys and waterfront kitchens almost the last trace of his origin save a streak of the gross island superstition.

"Devils?" he stammered.

"Forest devils, the natives say. It looks a proper home for 'em among these queer places—what?"

They saw only the dim archways of the trees opening on black vaults about them, but while they looked they harkened. Hard-bitten gang as they might be, certain cries still tingled in their ears, certain warnings of pursuit they must henceforth dread to hear. Since the welter and hot excitement of their crime this was the first pause. Silence spread like a pall, but slowly their guilty attention overbore it until they caught a multiple whispering beyond.

There was no wind, the flame of their rude lantern stood straight as a nail, yet a chill air came and passed as if a great black wing had brushed them. The night was empty and yet astir with crawling and creeping and flitting things. The wilderness pressed it with strange sounds and scents. They shrank from it—even the cynical Brewer himself—from its unguessed possibilities.

And the same shrinking fed their isolation; they were thrown back upon the schooner. She was their one chance. They were aware of the solid bulk of her under them, her hewn planks and timbers, the work of men's hands. They felt grateful towards this friendly accomplice who offered herself for their very need in the midst of such perils.

George scrambled to his feet.

"For any sakes, what are we doing here?" he cried, swaying. "Let's get out of this hole. They're after us; they're bound to be after us; and it's—it's awful here—so deathly—and alive, too! We got to run—run—keep running!.... Let's get away. Let's get out!"

Dibdin nodded with a drunken man's sudden gravity.

"George, I believe you're right. It does seem a bit crowded for pleasure; besides, doocid unhealthy. And as for devils, d'y' see"—he reached for the rum gourd—"I got enough of my own."

So at the last they were all waiting for Chrispim. He stayed half-kneeling, but there was no defiance about him now; it had dropped from him with his grip from the haft of his knife. Under his breath he called some forgotten saint, and his face, turned upward in the splash of yellow lantern light, was awed and stricken. And following his gaze, they could see what he saw—the stubby foretop of the vessel lined sharp against the fading sky. It made a sign above them there to speed their voyage, an omen—like a cross, as it might have been—or like the frame of a gallows, if they cared to take it so.

"*Sagrada Familia!*" he mumbled. "If only we don' carry none o' them devils alon' wit' us!"

No man saw her go. At midnight the weather broke with seasonable tropic rains. About that hour the *Jorguina* must have passed Guayaquil, hugging the Duran shore. Some scraps of canvas quickened her pace on the wet and rising gusts; she fled like a ragged wraith, slipping down the roadstead where a few hazy lights still showed. It was close on dawn before she found another inlet among the mangroves where she could lie up in hiding, and her crew, drenched and stupefied, could fall asleep on her sopping deck . . .

Brewer awoke to find the sun standing high, glowing through the jungle like the hot spot in a crown sheet. With genial impulse, he kicked the others into consciousness and indulged a moment of pride—quite pardonable. Everything had shaped according to his plan, it seemed. The worst of their dangers were now behind them. They owned a light little craft, and they knew whom to thank for that. Their supplies, looted from the river steamer they had sunk, were good for a week. As soon as they cleared the river mouth, he proposed to navigate the coasts towards Colombia.

"And if I can't buy anything we need in them parts, from a governor to an alibi," he concluded, "I've forgot how to spell me name!"

Thus far exultation carried him before he marked that the rest were not responding. They sat with haggard faces, listless, silent.

Brewer laughed without sympathy.

"Gentlemen o' leisure," he observed, "ain't you beginnin' pretty early? Look here, I'll name your trouble You ain't up to this kind of a game. I seen that at the diggings, but I had to take you for lack of better, and I tell you straight, you get no pamperin' on any ship with me! It don't go—understand? Once we're through, you can snivel all you like, but till we are —you jump. Get that?"

They roused themselves languidly, but when they sat to breakfast on the hatch a little later he sprang a bombshell.

"Say, who th' hell's the funny bloke around here?" he began gruffly. "Where's George!"

"Faith, have you lost that youngster again?" inquired Dibdin. "Why don't you tie him up?"

"I'll tie him fast enough if he had a hand in this," declared Brewer; and as they blinked he added: "One of them bags of gold-dust is gone!"

Here was a word to jolt them out of lethargy.

"I left 'em atop of the transom there last night—four of 'em, in plain sight. You can see for yourselves—only three left! And, by jiminy, if you lads been playin' any tricks among you——"

Chrispim rose like a prodded buffalo.

"Ah, tha's right! You come holler to us because tha' dam' boy run away. Didn' I tell you two, three, twenty time he is no good? Only let *me* catch 'im!"

"I'll let you do nothin'," snapped Brewer. "And where would he run to, I'd like to know? It's a cinch he can't ha' gone very far."

In fact, he had gone no farther than the tiny mildewed cabin, where presently they tracked him down and found him stretched in the one bunk.

"Well!"

George raised a lustreless gaze.

"I'm sick," he murmured.

"Is tha' so?" growled Chrispim. "I wonder——"

But they wondered still more when they came to paw about the bunk. George had no gold-dust with him, seemed not even to understand their angry questioning. They were left to regard each other across the fact. Nothing else could have split their confederacy wider.

"Chris, where'd you sleep?" challenged Brewer.

"Me? Ri' here in d' doorway. What? Don' you say I done it!"

"Charlie——"

"Come off it. I slept beside Chris."

"Whoever he is," scowled Brewer, "I can tell him flat this little joke won't do him any good."

"Whoever he is," echoed Dibdin.

Brewer turned upon him.

"Are you gettin' at me?... You don't think if I wanted to be crooked with you chaps I couldn't do better than that?"

"Yes, but d' gold is gone," Chrispim intervened.

It was, undeniably—a leather sack like a plump sausage, weighing some thirty pounds and worth possibly ten thousand dollars.

"A blame' queer thing if we can't find it on this coffin of a schooner."

So they started their search of the *Jorguina*. She had been pretty well stripped of small gear; they made quick work of

her bare cabin. In the forward bulkhead a low open panel gave
entrance down a pair of steps on the hold. They stood peering
into that obscure cavern, dank and ill-smelling, floored with
rotted remnants of planking and roofed in black shadow. On
either side they descried a narrow shelf running the length like
a continuous bunk, and Brewer rattled a set of rusty shackles
bolted to a beam.

"Slave quarters. See that? They used to pack 'em in spoon
fashion, by layers."

"Do you mean—niggers?"

"I heard so in Babahoyo. She's been a tough bird in her time,
this old ship." Brewer's tone became grimly speculative. "How
many black souls must ha' passed out through this panel?
Wastage, hey? Starved or diseased or cut up with whips to keep
the others quiet. Quite a merry little hell down here—what?
They used to howl, I guess—they mostly will. 'Member how
that stoker on the steamer yelled when you caught him through
the ribs, Charlie? He was a Negro. And the one Chris got
jumpin' from the pilot-house?... What's bitin' you now?"
Dibdin had drawn back from the foul exhalation of the bilge.
"Lost your nerve?"

"You can search the darned ship for all o' me," said Charlie
irritably. "And stow your gab, can't you?"

Brewer stood aside for Chrispim, but the flabby fellow,
without Dibdin's distaste, showed no heightened anxiety about
entering.

"You go?" he offered.

Brewer himself shook his head with a twisted hint of a smile.

"I'm just as willin' to leave it to anybody else. So we're even
all again, and take your choice of the crook. None of us seems
to care if he never sees the place—or anythin' in it."

They climbed back to the deck and hunted forward. The main
hatch, drifted with dead vegetation, had plainly not been disturbed for years. And when they came to the tiny hood to the
foc's'le, the only remaining spot for a possible hiding-place,
they found its doors barred fast without latch or key. Whereat
Brewer, with a stray freak of fantasy that now and then caught
him, was moved to knock.

"Hello, below!" he called.

A hollow reverberation under their feet was the answer that drove home the mystery upon them, and while they turned aft again they had each an odd impulse to go tiptoe, with roving glance. And again, and rather differently, they were aware of the vessel as an entity, as a presence, with the curious air of personality that houses and ships long deserted can take, somehow suspect and doubtful. She had secrets. She had known men like them and crimes like theirs in her wicked past—had outlived them all. Beneath her scars and tatters they sensed something malevolent, a spirit persisting in the memory of old wrongs, still uncancelled, unsatisfied.

"Well," said Brewer at length, as they stood by the transom, "I guess we'll every one take his own share to keep by him, won't we? Too bad George should ha' dropped his bit, ain't it?"

"Careless of him, I call it," said Dibdin.

They settled the incident on that basis.

The second night gave them some hours of starlight, by which they made all speed with a pair of clumsy sweeps, so that dawn saw them crossing the river bar thirty-five miles below Guayaquil. They had passed few craft, and those only at a distance, and when Brewer laid his course to avoid Puna Island and the deep water port they could count themselves well clear of any pursuit. Before they slept again they were comfortably headed to open sea.

The second day Charlie Dibdin awoke a poorer man by some ten thousand dollars.

There was a possibly humorous aspect to the fact. He first became aware of it at the foot of the cabin stairs, where he had slid to rest, following sundry convivial visits to the bottle. His treasure, as he quite remembered, had been safely in his possession at the time; since when it had evaporated seemingly. But the wrath of that gaunt derelict, with his shaking hands and burned-out eyes, was no piece of pleasantry.

"Sing about it," advised Chrispim, grinning like an ape. "It don' sound so good w'en you talk."

Dibdin cursed him in a spurt of acid fury until Brewer cut across and drew the fire.

"Will *you* make me quit? Will you check me?" Even then

Dibdin had a manner with him, a military set to his thin shoulders. "Do you hear me say my gold is stolen—the price of my wading in this ruddy mess? Faith, there'll be more than a word to it before the pair of you rob me so easy!"

But here Chrispim set up a diversion. It developed that the Portuguese kept an unaccountable commodity about him which he called his honour, and which he now considered to have been abraded. This thief would not be called a thief; he came lurching to the assault. The other drew out to meet him. Weapons glittered in the sun—

"—Or banked," Brewer was repeating. He had tripped them both on a long roll of the ship as the neatest way of enforcing attention. "Stolen or *banked*, I tell you. You're a rude little man, Charlie . . . Here's your dust back. And now apologise and cool off."

Dibdin stared at the bag that had been thrust into his hands. "This isn't mine!"

"No," said Brewer, sneering, "it's mine; but we aim to pay across the counter if you're going to raise such a holler. This is no time for scrappin'. I'm satisfied to keep the bank with all deposits, you see. Why, you poor, blame' fools, how would you guess anybody could get away with anything out here?"

They had only to blink over the rail to know what he meant. The coast was no more than a line in the east; the *Jorguina* swung to the broad rhythm of the Pacific. Quite docilely, almost stealthily, as if a lashed helm and some shreds of rig were all the favours she could have asked, she had borne them into big waters. Their world had narrowed to her single hull.

It was a world where strange things happened.

Charlie and the Portuguese, discovering a community of interest, agreed to stand watch and watch between them in the cabin that night. To make it less tedious, they broached from stock a second store of rum.

"There's a sweet little cherub that sits up aloft
To keep watch for the life of poor Jack."

So Dibdin melodiously declared; but there could have been little watching done, for at daybreak the two came stumbling out in a furious tangle—their two remaining bags had disappeared with the rest!

The wind had freshened; they found Brewer already at the wheel, oddly subdued and constrained, a set-faced figure in the morning light. He took the news very quietly.

"Gone, is it? Well, that makes a clean sweep—what?"

"Yes, and I want somebody smashed for it!" cried Dibdin, swinging to a stay, white-faced, trembling.

"Take your pick and name your pleasure," returned Brewer, in curt abstraction.

"Is that all you can say?"

"Why, no—I can say that gold is still aboard this ship. Where else would it be? I ain't worryin'. As to who's been stackin' it up for us I dunno', and I wish him joy of the amusement until this blasted voyage is over and time comes to collect."

"Somebody did it."

"Somebody," agreed Brewer. "Maybe it was Chris here; he looks guilty. Or you yourself, Charlie. Maybe it was me. Maybe," he added, "it was somebody—or somethin'—else."

"George!" Chrispim put in hastily.

"Where is George," demanded Dibdin, "anyway?"

"A question," answered Brewer, with one of his twisted smiles. "But you needn't fret. Wherever he is he hasn't taken the dust with him."

And when they went below to investigate, the others felt quite reassured on that point—for George was dead.

He was dead in rather a remarkable way. Stretched in the one bunk, from which, apparently, he had never risen, he resembled a thing of wax somewhat melted and run together, or a mummy partly dried. He had shrunken so that he was scarcely to be recognised. And over his bare chest, his limbs and neck, even his face, appeared a rash of small red spots—a stippling of the skin like the prints of bloody finger-tips. Except for those marks his flesh was absolutely colourless...

They were huddled aft a little later.

"You knew of this?" asked Dibdin, when he could speak.

Brewer nodded.

"I saw him."

"W-what is it?" Dibdin held out his arm and exhibited three

red spots above the wrist. On inspection they showed like light bruises, the kind that might be made with a vaccination lancet or in shaving too close with a sharp razor, as if the skin had been scraped to the capillaries. "I'm covered with it and so is Chris. And we can't—by Jove, we can hardly stand, Brewer!"

In fact, with the shock of this awakening their weakness of the first morning had increased upon them. Their legs bent like bad pipe stems; the pith had gone from their bodies.

"George had fever," suggested Brewer.

" 'Tisn't fever. 'Tisn't anything I ever heard of. I'm—I'm all of a sop and a quake."

"Fright——"

"Will fright roar in your ears and m-m-make dots dance in the sun? And press on you like lead, as if you'd been bed-rid for months? Brewer, I ask you, what *is* it?"

"I don't know," admitted Brewer. He seemed to gird himself, straddling there by a wheel, to brace against acknowledged chagrin—a creature of compacted vicious will and energy. "I don't know, and be hanged to you!" he blurted out in an angry flush. "Some blame' thing's gone wrong with this job of ours, and who'll deny it? Well, it was a dam' nasty job from the start. I never reckoned to put it through without trouble—some kind of trouble. But you can bet I reckoned to put it through. We got to last four days more before we make a port. You hear that—you two? Four days before we can land anywhere but a wilderness. That's all I know or want to know now. Because the job is goin' to go through just the same!"

He delivered it as an ultimatum, and Dibdin turned for comfort to the other.

"Chris——"

The Portuguese sat crouched against the rail, sunk in flabby passivity. He had no cheer for any one, but he had a word that summed up the terror between pattering tag-ends of prayer.

"It's them devils we brought alon' wit' us. . . . D' ship is a devil ship, an' that's all about it!"

And so it came to seem in the dreary hours that followed. Favourable winds were the rule; they had seldom to do more than to steer by the sun or a glimpse of the coast. The old slaver held steadily on her course, bearing those men with their burden of guilt and fear, and mutual distrust, to some destination that grew dimmer and more remote as they yearned for it. Their anxieties were so baffling, so much a part of the gloom and mystery that surrounded her. They came to hate her like a living thing, a malicious harpy of the sea who had put herself in their path, had lured and trapped them as her prey...

One result of the tension was another search below. Singing Charlie Dibdin kept off the rum. Perhaps his thoughts ran clearer. Along about noon he managed to force the foc's'le entrance, and, while a strong sunlight flooded the hatchway, to venture through the parts unexplored. He saw only what they had seen before, bare boards and filth underfoot and massed shadows above, fore and aft.

"Been changin' your bank?" challenged Brewer on his return.

"I had a notion I might find *yours*," retorted Dibdin. "You seemed so very clever in scaring us away."

"Maybe I wanted to stand you off," suggested Brewer, with a glint of teeth, "so you wouldn't be in no hurry to look in the right place."

"That's just what I thought! Faith, I don't know but it's just what I think! And this bally mystification, do you imagine I can't see how it backs your hand? If you meant to do us, it would be strategy to break us up—to beat us in detail."

"You're smart, Charlie," admired Brewer. "I won't say you ain't smart. Military gent, hey?... Maybe I started this blame' disease, too?"

"Maybe you did! You haven't caught it!"

"Only a touch, I figger—a few spots on my ankles the night we slept up the river. I'm feeling quite hunky, thanks."

"There it is, you see—you are holding best! But, look here, Brewer—look out, I say! You'll never live to rob us!"

"Right back at you. Either you or Chris. I don't know which, and I don't care. And with all your thinkin', did you think how I could ha' slipped you your finish while you was all asleep? If I wanted to do you down, what would I miss a chance like that for? You ain't no use that I can see, and I'm blamed if you're ornamental!"

But they proved of use towards evening, when the wind

failed, and, in spite of their wretchedness, he insisted on driving with the oars again—making a poor knot, or thereabouts.

"Four days is what I said, and four days goes," he told them. "We got to get on! Would you want to extend this floatin' picnic any longer?"

That night they lost the second member of their crew.

It came about through Chrispim's dread of the dark and a sudden fancy he took that he would not be left without the lantern. Brewer, arguing a still possible pursuit, would allow no lights on deck. So the Portuguese occupied the cabin alone, for Dibdin had had enough of it, and its late tenant had been dispossessed. The result was disturbing . . .

Some time towards morning the two on deck, keeping an uneasy watch by the stars, were wrenched from their doze by the bubble and yell of a man in a nightmare and by sounds of a frantic struggle below. A moment later Chrispim burst out, flailing with the darkened lantern, clawing as if to free himself from an invisible adversary. He slammed the little double doors behind him and fell against them. When the others ran to pick him up his hands and face were covered with blood.

"Don't go down there!" he screamed. "*Sagrada*—don't touch tha' hatch. Keep'm fast—keep'm fast!"

And that was very nearly all they learned from him.

His hurts seemed slight enough; a fresh outbreak of the plague of red spots, with such scratches as he might have inflicted himself. He showed no signs of any illness they could identify. By all appearance the fellow had been literally frightened to death. He lapsed into delirium, wherein he found his native tongue again, and lay babbling until the dawn. Only a little before he died he gave them a glimpse of the vengeance that had found him down there in the cabin.

They gathered that he had slept, that while he slept his lantern had gone out, and that in his dream he had lived over the action of their crime, their murders on the river steamer. But the phantasm had shifted so that he had seemed to share the agony of his last victim, the Negro shot and drowned from the pilot-house of the boat they had looted. He had felt himself sinking and weakening in the grip of a monstrous assailant, and had awakened at last in darkness to a vivid persistence of the illusion.

"He was all over me!" he gasped. "I fight wit' him, *so*! I twis', I turn. No good. He pulls me down, down—heavy. I faint; I holler, an' then—I wake. And *he is there*! Somet'ing—some dam' t'ing is there, I tell you; all live an' hangin' on me. All—all over me! ... D'devils! ... D'devil's!"

There was little light conversation aboard the *Jorguina* that morning, but when the two survivors had done their graveyard task, had freed themselves of an intolerable presence by sending the Portuguese to join George astern, they considered each other for a space.

Dibdin was in a bad way. Brewer, with a face like a skull, had reserves more nearly adequate.

"I guess we'll take that tip about keepin' all hatches fast, won't we?" he drawled. "I reckon we got no particular use for anythin' that happens to be locked up inside this old hooker—at this time, hey?"

Charlie's gesture, if not surrender, was tribute.

"The treasure? Good heaven, are you still able to keep up that game? I'm—I'm wondering how we're ever going to sleep again on the cursed craft! ... 'For in that sleep'," he added under his breath, " ' 'what dreams may come!' "

Thereafter he crawled away forward. His instinct was to hide; he made himself a shelter among the rubbish by the foc's'le, where he took his share of food and stayed. Whether he slept or not was no knowing. But Brewer—of the buccaneer breed—Brewer never closed an eye throughout the rest of their ordeal. It became the story of the endurance of that indomitable man.

He had called for four more days.

Their start from the bayou had been made on a Friday; George's death fixed a date at Monday. From Tuesday night until late Thursday afternoon he remained at the wheel.

The *Jorguina* sailed on. The weather continued fair; the sea, a ring where none intruded, wherein they hung enchanted save for heave and send, the crush of foam alongside, the continuous small voices of hull and rigging. She sailed on, but Brewer took no chances. Issue was joined at last between the man and the ship; the one stolidly watchful and masterful, the other nursing a malign and mysterious power under her battened hatches—each, as it might have seemed, biding a secret purpose and a moment of reckoning.

Towards evening of Thursday, when the sun had filled the great bowl of the sky with a crimson flood, they raised far over to eastward a certain headland like the shadow of a knotted fist. At sight of it Brewer threw off the drowsiness that bowed him and became instantly alert. Various vocal rumours earlier in the day had indicated that Singing Charlie was consoling himself with the rum again, but Brewer had not seen him for hours. Peering along the deck and under the sails, he failed to place him now. Though puzzled for a time, he presently lashed the helm, left his post, and, moving pad-foot here and there, began his preparations.

From their looted stock he selected all weapons, ammunition, bags of biscuit and cassava meal, utensils—such as might be useful in a rough country. These he bore aft from the transom and the main hatch to the taffrail, where he stacked them. Once or twice he paused to sniff curiously at the air, detecting an ususual quality, a haziness. He even looked for signs of storm, and swept the placid horizon before he stopped to cast loose a rope just under his hand.

"Brewer——!"

Charlie Dibdin had fallen away to the frame of a man. Clinging there beside the main mast, he was like some rickety toy that sags on its strings, a ghastly white and spotted apparition. But the rum had been his servant for once; rum, or emotion, had rallied him to the strangest nervous elation.

"Brewer!" he cried. "I've found—I've found out——"

Brewer made an abrupt movement.

"——what's wrong with the ship!" Dibdin went on between a gulp and a giggle. "I've been down below again. Inside. Through the foc's'le. I meant to sink her, she haunted me so!" He showed a smoking torch of tarred oakum. "Faith I meant to sink her and the whole cursed outfit. And I started to before I saw—I saw——"

He stopped, open-mouthed. The stack of supplies by the taffrail had caught his glance, and from that it quickened on Brewer.

"I say, you weren't going to skip?"

"I mean to," said Brewer.

Swift suspicion struck a very different note from Singing Charlie.

"Without *me*?"

The other nodded.

"And the—the bank? By Jove, you'd never go without it; never tell me you would. You *were* doing us, after all! . . . You've got the gold, too?"

"It's just here," said Brewer amiably, "where it's been right along—fattened up from time to time."

He held up the loosened bight of rope and pointed below and astern—at an inconspicuous canoe littered with rubbish which had been trailing behind the schooner from the start, to which none of his companions had ever given a thought.

This was Mr Brewer's little triumph. After the unexpected strain his success had cost him, he could have wished it this way. It was such a climax as the abnormal conceit of the criminal savours with greatest zest, the dramatic gesture of the double-cross. He savoured it, and none the less when the hammer of Dibdin's revolver clicked twice—thrice.

"That's all," he said, grinning sideways. "I never did have no use for you chaps; I thought I'd show you up a bit while I was cornerin' the dust. I was goin' to take you along till you worked the craft hereabouts for me and then let you kill each other off, y'see. It would ha' been fun, only this blame' old schooner begun cuttin' in with her blame' plague spots and her ghosts of dead niggers——"

He drew the canoe alongside and, mounting the rail, began to make fast to a stay: a stout and vigorous figure blotted black against the west, too much interested in self-appreciation to notice the ominous haze that had been thickening about the *Jorguina*'s deck.

Dibdin had sunk upon the transom, in a state of apparent collapse, staring at him.

"Go on," Brewer jeered, "you and what you found! I've beat the old ship with all her tricks, and I've beat you for the stake—forty thousand dollars' worth. Kind of slick, hey? Kind of easy—what? . . . As easy as pickin' cartridges from the gun of a military gent when he's drunk!"

"Yes," said Dibdin, "it's a fair do!"

With the word his right hand dipped back over his shoulder and shot forward. Something like a great dragon-fly flashed at the target offered by the squab-armed silhouette. It struck in the side of the throat—Chrispim's knife . . .

Brewer's start almost threw him backward, and as he caught at the stay to save himself, the towline slipped from his grasp. With violent effort he recovered, drew his revolver, and emptied it into Dibdin on the transom, point-blank.

Then he tried to retrieve the canoe. The schooner had moved ahead—he missed it. The gap widened. He fumbled at his wound; with an oath whipped out his kerchief and wrapped it about his neck, ran aft, and lowered himself and found the little canoe with his feet.

Meanwhile, the writhing form on the transom had struggled to the after-break. Just as Brewer bobbed up overside from the canoe and climbed clumsily aboard again with the towrope, Dibdin reached the bolted cabin doors and threw them open.

A great pent cloud of smoke and heat burst out from below, and through it and with it another and a darker cloud, a cloud that broke into countless flitting and skimming units— ravenous, predatory, loathsome . . .

When Brewer staggered to his feet once more he was covered with a furry, living mantle of little winged, reddish creatures that clung and bit and rose and settled again as fast as he plucked them off; bewildered and blindly clustering assailants with tiny razor teeth and sucking mouths, famishing from their long fast, driven from their dwelling in the dark corners of the ship—her devils . . .

"In the land of far Peru—eru—eru,
    Where that lovely orchid grew—and grew—and grew:
    And the vampire bats flew——"

So Dibdin sang, and laughed as he sang, dying on the deck while Brewer fought his terrible and hopeless fight with fast-

ebbing strength, rose shrieking, floundered towards the rail, and
fell again.

> "And the vampire bats flew
> Through that vapour so blue,
> In the land—of—far——"

And the old slaver sailed on. Tongues of flame burst from
her hatches, wrapped about her masts; the smoke of her burning spread wide over the empty sea. As if to free herself of a
final evil, she left behind her a little canoe that drifted in her
wake with its cargo of tainted gold. Herself, she sailed on,
dwindling through the blood-red sunset to the finish of her last
commission and the clearing of her account.

THE SINKING SHIP

by Robert Louis Stevenson

Robert Louis Stevenson (1850–1894) is best remembered as the author of the immortal pirate yarn, *Treasure Island* (1883), and of an equally immortal classic of the macabre, *The Strange Case of Doctor Jekyll and Mister Hyde* (1888). Here, he combines his understanding of seafaring men with a penchant for terror in a fable wherein British *sang-froid* is taken to its ultimate extreme . . .

"SIR," SAID THE first lieutenant, bursting into the captain's cabin, "the ship is going down."

"Very well, Mr Spoker," said the captain; "but that is no reason for going about half-shaved. Exercise your mind a moment, Mr Spoker, and you will see that to the philosophic eye there is nothing new in our position: the ship (if she is to go down at all) may be said to have been going down since she was launched."

"She is settling fast," said the first lieutenant, as he returned from shaving.

"Fast, Mr Spoker?" asked the captain. "The expression is a strange one, for time (if you will think of it) is only relative."

"Sir," said the lieutenant, "I think it is scarcely worth while to embark in such a discussion when we shall all be in Davy Jones's Locker in ten minutes."

"By parity of reasoning," returned the captain gently, "it would never be worth while to begin any inquiry of importance; the odds are always overwhelming that we must die before we shall have brought it to an end. You have not considered, Mr Spoker, the situation of man," said the captain, smiling and shaking his head.

"I am much more engaged in considering the position of the
ship," said Mr Spoker.

"Spoken like a good officer," replied the captain, laying his
hand on the lieutenant's shoulder.

On deck they found the men had broken into the spirit-room,
and were fast getting drunk.

"My men," said the captain, "there is no sense in this. The
ship is going down, you will tell me, in ten minutes: well, and
what then? To the philosophic eye there is nothing new in our
position. All our lives long, we may have been about to break
a blood-vessel or to be struck by lightning, not merely in ten
minutes, but in ten seconds; and that has not prevented us from
eating dinner, no, nor from putting money in the savings bank.
I assure you, with my hand on my heart, I fail to comprehend
your attitude."

The men were already too far gone to pay much heed.

"This is a very painful sight, Mr Spoker," said the captain.

"And yet to the philosophic eye, or whatever it is," replied
the first lieutenant, "they may be said to have been getting
drunk since they came aboard."

"I do not know if you always follow my thought, Mr Spoker,"
returned the captain gently. "But let us proceed."

In the powder magazine they found an old salt smoking his
pipe.

"Good God," cried the captain, "what are you about?"

"Well, sir," said the old salt, apologetically, "they told me as
he were going down."

"And suppose she were?" said the captain. "To the philosophic eye, there would be nothing new in our position. Life,
my old shipmate, life, at any moment and in any view, is as
dangerous as a sinking ship; and yet it is man's handsome
fashion to carry umbrellas, to wear indiarubber overshoes, to
begin vast works, and to conduct himself in every way as if he
might hope to be eternal. And for my own poor part I should
despise the man who, even on board a sinking ship, should
omit to take a pill or to wind up his watch. That, my friend,
would not be the human attitude."

"I beg pardon, sir," said Mr Spoker. "But what is precisely

the difference between shaving in a sinking ship and smokin
in a powder magazine?"

"Or doing anything at all in any conceivable circumstances?
cried the captain. "Perfectly conclusive; give me a cigar!"

Two minutes afterwards the ship blew up with a gloriou
detonation.

MORE NEWS FROM THE "HOMEBIRD"

by William Hope Hodgson

I N T H E A U G U S T of 1902, Captain Bateman, of the chooner *Agnes*, picked up a small barrel, upon which was painted a half obliterated word; which finally, he succeeded in deciphering as "Homebird", the name of a full-rigged ship, which left London in the November of 1873, and from thenceforth was heard of no more by any man.

Captain Bateman opened the barrel, and discovered a packet of manuscript, wrapped in oilskin. This, on examination, proved o be an account of the losing of the *Homebird* amid the desolate wastes of the Sargasso sea. The papers were written by one, Arthur Samuel Philips, a passenger in the ship; and, from hem, Captain Bateman was enabled to gather that the ship, mastless, lay in the very heart of the dreaded Sargasso; and that all of the crew had been lost—some in the storm which drove hem thither, and some in attempts to free the ship from the weed, which locked them in on all sides.

Only Mr Philips and the captain's daughter had been left alive, and they two, the dying captain had married. To them had been born a daughter, and the papers ended with a brief but touching allusion to their fear that, eventually, they must un short of food.

There is need to say but little more. The account was copied into most of the papers of the day, and caused widespread comment. There was even some talk of fitting out a rescue expedition; but this fell through, owing chiefly to lack of knowledge of the whereabouts of th ship in all the vastness of the immense Sargasso Sea. And so, gradually, the matter has slipped into the background of the public's memory.

Now, however, interest will be once more excited in the lonesome fate of this lost trio; for a second barrel, identical, it would seem, with that found by Captain Bateman, has been picked up by a Mr Bolton, of Baltimore, master of a small brig, engaged in the South American coast-trade. In this barrel was enclosed a further message from Mr Philips—the fifth that he has sent abroad to the world; but the second, third and fourth, up to this time, have not been discovered.

This "fifth message" contains a vital and striking account of their lives during the year 1879, and stands unique as a document informed with human lonesomeness and longing. I have seen it, and read it through, with the most intense and painful interest. The writing, though faint, is very legible; and the whole manuscript bears the impress of the same hand and mind that wrote the piteous account of the losing of the *Homebird*, of which I have already made mention, and with which, no doubt, many are well acquainted.

In closing this little explanatory note, I am stimulated to wonder whether, somewhere, at some time, those three missing messages ever shall be found. And then there may be others. What stories of human, strenuous fighting with Fate may they not contain. We can but wait and wonder. Nothing more may we ever learn; for what is this one little tragedy among the uncounted millions that the silence of the sea holds so remorselessly. And yet, again, news may come to us out of the Unknown—out of the lonesome silences of the dread Sargasso Sea —the loneliest and the most inaccessible place of all the lonesome and inaccessible places of this earth.

And so I say, let us wait.

W. H. H.

THE FIFTH MESSAGE

"This is the fifth message that I have sent abroad over the loathsome surface of this vast Weed-World, praying that it may come to the open sea, ere the lifting power of my fire-balloon be gone, and yet, if it come there—the which I could now doubt—how shall I be the better for it! Yet write I must, or go mad, and so I choose to write, though feeling as I write that no living creature, save it be the giant octopi that live in the weed about me, will ever see the thing I write.

"My first message I sent out on Christmas Eve, 1875, and since then, each eve of the birth of Christ has seen a message to skywards upon the winds, towards the open sea. It is as though this approaching time, of festivity and the meeting of parted loved ones, overwhelms me, and drives away the half apathetic peace that has been mine through spaces of these years of lonesomeness; so that I seclude myself from my wife and the little one, and with ink, pen, and paper, try to ease my heart of the pent emotions that seem at times to threaten to burst it.

"It is now six completed years since the Weed-World claimed us from the World of the Living—six years away from our mothers and sisters of the human and living world—It has been six years of living in a grave! And there are all the years ahead! Oh! My God! My God! I dare not think upon them! I must control myself——

"And then there is the little one, she is nearly four and a half now, and growing wonderfully, out among these wilds. Four and a half years, and the little woman has never seen a human face besides ours—think of it! And yet, if she lives four and forty years, she will never see another ... Four and forty years! It is foolishness to trouble about such a space of time; for the future, for us, ends in ten years—eleven at the most. Our food will last no longer than that ... My wife does not know; for it seems to me a wicked thing to add unnecessarily to her punishment. She does but know that we must waste no ounce of food-stuff, and for the rest she imagines that the most of the cargo is of an edible nature. Perhaps, I have nurtured this belief. If anything happened to me, the food would last a few extra years; but my wife would have to imagine it an accident, else would each bite she took sicken her.

"I have thought often and long upon this matter, yet I fear to leave them; for who knows but that their lives might at any time depend upon my strength, more pitifully, perhaps, than upon the food which they must come at last to lack. No, I must not bring upon them, and myself, a *near* and *certain*

calamity, to defer one that, though it seems to have but littl
less certainty, is yet at a further distance.

"Until lately, nothing has happened to us in the past fou
years, if I except the adventures that attended my mad attemp
to cut a way through the surrounding weed to freedom, an
from which it pleased God that I and those with me should b
preserved.[1] Yet, in the latter part of this year, an adventur
much touched with grimness, came to us most unexpectedly, i
a fashion quite unthought of—an adventure that has brough
into our lives a fresh and more active peril; for now I hav
learned that the weed holds other terrors besides that of th
giant octopi.

"Indeed, I have grown to believe this world of desolatio
capable of holding *any* horror, as well it might. Think of it-
an interminable stretch of dank, brown loneliness in all direc
tions, to the distant horizon; a place where monsters of the dee
and the weed have undisputed reign; where never an enem
may fall upon them; but from which they may strike with suc
den deadliness! No human can ever bring an engine of destruc
tion to bear upon them, and the humans whose fate it is t
have sight of them, do so only from the decks of lonesom
derelicts, whence they stare lonely with fear, and withou
ability to harm.

"I cannot describe it, nor can any hope ever to imagine it
When the wind falls, a vast silence holds us girt, from horizo
to horizon, yet it is a silence through which one seems to fee
the pulse of hidden things all about us, watching and waiting-
waiting and watching; waiting but for the chance to reac
forth a huge and sudden death-grapple.... It is no use!
cannot bring it home to any; nor shall I be better able t
convey the frightening sounds of the wind, sweeping acros
these vast, quaking plains—the shrill whispering of the wee
fronds, under the stirring of the winds. To hear it from beyon
our canvas screen, is like listening to the uncounted dead of th
mighty Sargasso wailing their own requiems. Or again, m
fancy, diseased with much loneliness and brooding, likens it t

[1] This is evidently a reference to something which Mr Philips ha
set forth in an earlier message—one of the three lost messages.-
W. H. H.

ιe advancing rustle of armies of the great monsters that are
lways about us—waiting.

"And so to the coming of this new terror:—

"It was in the latter end of October that we first had know-
dge of it—a tapping in the night time against the side of
ιe vessel, below the water-line; a noise that came distinct,
et with a ghostly strangeness in the quietness of the night. It
'as on a Monday night when first I heard it. I was down in the
ιzarette, overhauling our stores, and suddenly I heard it—
ιp—tap—tap—against the outside of the vessel upon the star-
oard side, and below the water-line. I stood for a while listen-
ιg; but could not discover what it was that should come a-
ιpping against our side, away out here in this lonesome world
f weed and slime. And then, as I stood there listening, the
ιpping ceased, and so I waited, wondering, and with a hateful
:nse of fear, weakening my manhood, and taking the courage
ιt of my heart . . .

"Abruptly, it recommenced; but now upon the opposite side
f the vessel, and as it continued, I fell into a little sweat; for
seemed to me that some foul thing out in the night was tap-
ing for admittance. Tap—tap—tap—it went, and continued,
ιd there I stood listening, and so gripped about with frightened
ιoughts, that I seemed without power to stir myself; for the
ιell of the Weed-World, and the fear bred of its hidden terrors
ιd the weight and dreeness of its loneliness have entered into
ιy marrow, so that I could, then and now, believe in the likeli-
ood of matters which, ashore and in the midst of my fellows,
might laugh at in contempt. It is the dire lonesomeness of
ιis strange world into which I have entered, that serves so
) take the heart out of a man.

"And so, as I have said, I stood there listening, and full of
ightened, but undefined, thoughts; and all the while the tap-
ing continued, sometimes with a regular insistence, and anon
'ith a quick spasmodic tap, tap, tap-a-tap, as though some
'hing, having intelligence, signalled to me.

"Presently, however, I shook off something of the foolish
ight that had taken me, and moved over to the place from
'hich the tapping seemed to sound. Coming near to it, I bent
ιy head down, close to the side of the vessel, and listened.

Thus, I heard the noises with greater plainness, and could di
tinguish easily, now, that something knocked with a hard obje
upon the outside of the ship, as though someone had been stri
ing her iron side with a small hammer.

"Then, even as I listened, came a thunderous blow close
my ear, so loud and astonishing, that I leaped sideways
sheer fright. Directly afterwards there came a second hea
blow, and then a third, as though someone had struck the ship
side with a heavy sledge-hammer, and after that, a space
silence, in which I heard my wife's voice at the trap of th
lazarette, calling down to me to know what had happened
cause so great a noise.

" 'Hush, my dear!' I whispered; for it seemed to me that th
thing outside might hear her; though this could not have bee
possible, and I do but mention it as showing how the nois
had set me off my natural balance.

"At my whispered command, my wife turned her abo
and came down the ladder into the semi-darkness of the plac

" 'What is it, Arthur?' she asked, coming across to me, an
slipping her hand between my arm and side.

"As though in reply to her query, there came against th
outside of the ship, a fourth tremendous blow, filling the who
of the lazarette with a dull thunder.

"My wife gave out a frightened cry, and sprang away fro
me; but the next instant, she was back, and gripping hard at m
arm.

" 'What is it, Arthur? What is it?' she asked me; her voic
though no more than a frightened whisper, easily heard in th
succeeding silence.

" 'I don't know, Mary,' I replied, trying to speak in a lev
tone. 'It's——'

" 'There's something again,' she interrupted, as the min
tapping noises recommenced.

"For about a minute, we stood silent, listening to thos
eerie taps. Then my wife turned to me:—

" 'Is it anything dangerous, Arthur—tell me? I promise yo
I shall be brave.'

" 'I can't possibly say, Mary,' I answered. 'I can't say; b
I'm going up on deck to listen . . . Perhaps,' I paused a momer

to think; but a fifth tremendous blow against the ship's side, drove whatever I was going to say, clean from me, and I could do no more than stand there, frightened and bewildered, listening for further sounds. After a short pause, there came a sixth blow. Then my wife caught me by the arm, and commenced to drag me towards the ladder.

" 'Come up out of this dark place, Arthur,' she said. 'I shall be ill if we stay here any longer. Perhaps the—the thing outside can hear us, and it may stop if we go upstairs.'

"By this, my wife was all of a shake, and I but little better, so that I was glad to follow her up the ladder. At the top, we paused for a while to listen, bending down over the open hatchway. A space of, maybe, some five minutes passed away in silence; then there commenced again the tapping noises, the sounds coming clearly up to us where we crouched. Presently, they ceased once more, and after that, though we listened for a further space of some ten minutes, they were not repeated. Neither were there any more of the great bangs.

"In a little, I led my wife away from the hatch, to a seat in the saloon; for the hatch is situated under the saloon table. After that, I returned to the opening, and replaced the cover. Then I went into our cabin—the one which had been the Captain's, her father—and brought from there a revolver, of which we have several. This, I loaded with care, and afterwards placed in my side pocket.

"Having done this, I fetched from the pantry, where I have made it my use to keep such things at hand, a bull's-eye lantern, the same having been used on dark nights when clearing up the ropes from the decks. This, I lit, and afterwards turned the dark-slide to cover the light. Next, I slipped off my boots; and then, as an afterthought, I reached down one of the long-handled American axes from the rack about the mizzen mast—these being keen and very formidable weapons.

"After that, I had to calm my wife and assure her that I would run no unnecessary risks, if, indeed, there were any risks to run; though, as may be imagined, I could not say what new peril might not be upon us. And then, picking up the lantern, I made my way silently on stockinged feet, up the companion-way. I had reached the top, and was just stepping out on to the deck, when something caught my arm. I turned swiftly, and perceived that my wife had followed me up the steps, and from the shaking of her hand upon my arm, I gathered that she was very much agitated.

" 'Oh, my dear, my dear, don't go! don't go!' she whispered, eagerly. 'Wait until it is daylight. Stay below tonight. You don't know what may be about in this horrible place.'

"I put the lantern and the axe upon the deck beside the companion; then bent towards the opening, and took her into my arms, soothing her, and stroking her hair; yet with ever an alert glance to and fro along the indistinct decks. Presently, she was more like her usual self, and listened to my reasoning, that she would do better to stay below, and so, in a little, left me, having made me promise afresh that I would be very wary of danger.

"When she had gone, I picked up the lantern and the axe, and made my way cautiously to the side of the vessel. Here, I paused and listened very carefully, being just above that spot upon the port side where I had heard the greater part of the tapping, and all of the heavy bangs; yet, though I listened, as I have said, with much attention, there was no repetition of the sounds.

"Presently, I rose and made my way forrard to the break of the poop. Here, bending over the rail which ran across, I listened, peering along the dim main decks; but could neither see nor hear anything; not that, indeed, I had any reason for expecting to see or hear aught unusual *aboard* of the vessel; for all of the noises had come from over the side, and, more than that, from beneath the water-line. Yet in the state of mind in which I was, I had less use for reason than fancy; for that strange thudding and tapping, out here in the midst of this world of loneliness, had set me vaguely imagining unknowable terrors, stealing upon me from every shadow that lay upon the dimly-seen decks.

"Then, as still I listened, hesitating to go down on to the main deck, yet too dissatisfied with the result of my peerings, to cease from my search, I heard, faint yet clear in the stillness of the night, the tapping noises recommence.

"I took my weight from off the rail, and listened; but I

could no longer hear them, and at that, I leant forward again over the rail, and peered down on to the main deck. Immediately, the sounds came once more to me, and I knew now, that they were borne to me by the medium of the rail, which conducted them to me through the iron stanchions by which it is fixed to the vessel.

"At that, I turned and went aft along the poop deck, moving very warily and with quietness. I stopped over the place where first I had heard the louder noises, and stooped, putting my ear against the rail. Here, the sounds came to me with great distinctness.

"For a little, I listened; then stood up, and slid away that part of the tarred-canvas screen whch covers the port opening through which we dump our refuse; they being made here for convenience, one upon each side of the vessel. This, I did very silently; then, leaning forward through the opening, I peered down into the dimness of the weed. Even as I did so, I heard plainly below me a heavy thud, muffled and dull by reason of the intervening water, against the iron side of the ship. It seemed to me that there was some disturbance amid the dark, shadowy masses of the weed. Then I had opened the dark-slide of my lantern, and sent a clear beam of light down into the blackness. For a brief instant, I thought I perceived a multitude of things moving. Yet, beyond that they were oval in shape, and showed white through the weed fronds, I had no clear conception of anything; for with the flash of the light, they vanished, and there lay beneath me only the dark, brown masses of the weed—demurely quiet.

"But an impression they did leave upon my over excited imagination—an impression that might have been due to morbidity, bred of too much loneliness; but nevertheless it seemed to me that I had seen momentarily a multitude of dead white faces, upturned towards me among the meshes of the weed.

"For a little, I leant there, staring down at the circle of illumined weed; yet with my thoughts in such a turmoil of frightened doubts and conjectures, that my physical eyes did but poor work, compared with the orb that looks inward. And through all the chaos of my mind there rose up weird and creepy memories—ghouls, the un-dead. There seemed nothing improbable, in that moment, in associating the terms with the fears that were besetting me. For no man may dare to say what terrors this world holds, until he has become lost to his brother men, amid the unspeakable desolation of the vast and slimy weed-plains of the Sargasso Sea.

"And then, as I leaned there, so foolishly exposing myself to those dangers which I had learnt did truly exist, my eyes caught and subconsciously noted the strange and subtle undulation which always foretells the approach of one of the giant octopi. Instantly, I leapt back, and whipped the tarred-canvas cover across the opening, and so stood alone there in the night, glancing frightenedly before and behind me, the beam from my lamp casting wavering splashes of light to and fro about the decks. And all the time, I was listening—listening; for it seemed to me that some Terror was brooding in the night, that might come upon us at any moment and in some unimagined form.

"Then, across the silence, stole a whisper, and I turned swiftly towards the companionway. My wife was there, and she reached out her arms to me, begging me to come below into safety. As the light from my lantern flashed upon her, I saw that she had a revolver in her right hand, and at that, I asked her what she had it for; whereupon she informed me that she had been watching over me, through the whole of the time that I had been on deck, save for the little while that it had taken her to get and load the weapon.

"At that, as may be imagined, I went and embraced her very heartily, kissing her for the love that had prompted her actions; and then, after that, we spoke a little together in low tones—she asking that I should come down and fasten up the companion-doors, and I demurring, telling her that I felt too unsettled to sleep; but would rather keep watch about the poop for a while longer.

"Then, even as we discussed the matter, I motioned to her for quietness. In the succeeding silence, she heard it, as well as I, a slow—tap! tap! tap! coming steadily along the dark main decks. I felt a swift vile fear, and my wife's hold upon me became very tense, despite that she trembled a little. I released her grip from my arm, and made to go towards the break of the poop; but she was after me instantly, praying me at least to stay where I was if I would not go below.

"Upon that, I bade her very sternly to release me, and go down into the cabin; though all the while I loved her for her very solicitude. But she disobeyed me, asserting very stoutly, though in a whisper, that if I went into danger, she would go with me; and at that I hesitated; but decided, after a moment, to go no further than the break of the poop, and not to venture on the main deck.

"I went very silently to the break, and my wife followed me. From the rail across the break, I shone the light of the lantern; but could neither see nor hear anything; for the tapping noise had ceased. Then it recommenced, seeming to have come near to the port side of the stump of the main mast. I turned the lantern towards it, and, for one brief instant, it seemed to me that I saw something pale, just beyond the brightness of my light. At that, I raised my pistol and fired, and my wife did the same, though without any telling on my part. The noise of the double explosion went very loud and hollow sounding along the decks, and after the echoes had died away, we both of us thought we heard the tapping going away forrard again.

"After that, we stayed awhile, listening and watching; but all was quiet, and, presently, I consented to go below and bar up the companion, as my wife desired; for, indeed, there was much sense in her plea of the futility of my staying up upon the decks.

"The night passed quietly enough, and on the following morning, I made a very careful inspection of the vessel, examining the decks, the weed outside of the ship, and the sides of her. After that, I removed the hatches, and went down into the holds; but could nowhere find anything of an unusual nature.

"That night, just as we were making an end of our supper, we heard three tremendous blows given against the starboard side of the ship, whereat, I sprang to my feet, seized and lit the dark-lantern, which I had kept handy, and ran quickly and silently up on to the deck. My pistol, I had already in my pocket, and as I had soft slippers upon my feet, I needed not to pause to remove my footgear. In the companionway, I had left the axe, and this I seized as I went up the steps.

"Reaching the deck, I moved over quietly to the side, and slid back the canvas door; then I leant out and opened the slide of the lantern, letting its light play upon the weed in the direction from which the bangs had seemed to proceed; but nowhere could I perceive anything out of the ordinary, the weed seeming undisturbed. And so, after a little, I drew in my head, and slid-to the door in the canvas screen; for it was but wanton folly to stand long exposed to any of the giant octopi that might chance to be prowling near, beneath the curtain of the weed.

"From then, until midnight, I stayed upon the poop, talking much in a quiet voice to my wife, who had followed me up into the companion. At times, we could hear the knocking, sometimes against one side of the ship, and again upon the other. And, between the louder knocks, and accompanying them, would sound the minor tap, tap, tap-a-tap, that I had first heard.

"About midnight, feeling that I could do nothing, and no harm appearing to result to us from the unseen things that seemed to be encircling us, my wife and I made our way below to rest, securely barring the companion-doors behind us.

"It would be, I should imagine, about two o'clock in the morning, that I was aroused from a somewhat troubled sleep, by the agonised screaming of our great boar, away forrard. I leant up upon my elbow, and listened, and so grew speedily wide awake. I sat up, and slid from my bunk to the floor. My wife, as I could tell from her breathing, was sleeping peacefully, so that I was able to draw on a few clothes without disturbing her.

"Then, having lit the dark-lantern, and turned the slide over the light, I took the axe in my other hand, and hastened towards the door that gives out of the forrard end of the saloon, on to the main deck, beneath the shelter of the break of the poop. This door, I had locked before turning-in, and now, very noiselessly, I unlocked it, and turned the handle, opening the door with much caution. I peered out along the dim stretch of the main deck; but could see nothing; then I turned on the slide of the lamp, and let the light play along the decks; but still nothing unusual was revealed to me.

"Away forrard, the shrieking of the pig had been succeeded by an absolute silence, and there was nowhere any noise, if I except an occasional odd tap-a-tap, which seemed to come from the side of the ship. And so, taking hold of my courage, I stepped out on to the main deck, and proceeded slowly forrard, throwing the beam of light to and fro continuously, as I walked.

"Abruptly, I heard away in the bows of the ship a sudden multitudinous tapping and scraping and slithering; and so loud and near did it sound, that I was brought up all of a round-turn, as the saying is. For, perhaps, a whole minute, I stood there hesitating, and playing the light all about me, not knowing but that some hateful thing might leap upon me from out of the shadows.

"And then, suddenly, I remembered that I had left the door open behind me, that led into the saloon, so that, were there any deadly thing about the decks, it might chance to get in upon my wife and child as they slept. At the thought, I turned and ran swiftly aft again, and in through the door to my cabin. Here, I made sure that all was right with the two sleepers, and after that, I returned to the deck, shutting the door, and locking it behind me.

"And now, feeling very lonesome out there upon the dark decks, and cut off in a way from a retreat, I had need of all my manhood to aid me forrard to learn the wherefore of the pig's crying, and the cause of that manifold tapping. Yet go I did, and have some right to be proud of the act; for the dreeness and lonesomeness and the cold fear of the Weed-World, squeeze the pluck out of one in a very woeful manner.

"As I approached the empty fo'c'sle, I moved with all wariness, swinging the light to and fro, and holding my axe very handily, and the heart within my breast like a shape of water, so in fear was I. Yet, I came at last to the pig-sty, and so discovered a dreadful sight. The pig, a huge boar of twenty-score pounds, had been dragged out on to the deck, and lay before the sty with all his belly ripped up, and stone dead. The iron bars of the sty—great bars they are too—had been torn apart, as though they had been so many straws; and, for the rest, there was a deal of blood both within the sty and upon the decks.

"Yet, I did not stay then to see more; for, all of a sudden, the realisation was borne upon me that this was the work of some monstrous thing, which even at that moment might be stealing upon me; and, with the thought, an overwhelming fear leapt upon me, overbearing my courage; so that I turned and ran for the shelter of the saloon, and never stopped until the stout door was locked between me and that which had wrought such destruction upon the pig. And as I stood there, quivering a little with very fright, I kept questioning dumbly as to what manner of wild-beast thing it was that could burst asunder iron bars, and rip the life out of a great boar, as though it were of no more account than a kitten. And then more vital questions:— How did it get aboard, and where had it hidden? And again:—*What was it?* And so in this fashion for a good while, until I had grown something more calmed.

"But through all the remainder of that night, I slept not so much as a wink.

"Then in the morning when my wife awoke, I told her of the happenings of the night; whereat she turned very white, and fell to reproaching me for going out at all on to the deck, declaring that I had run needlessly into danger, and that, at least, I should not have left her alone, sleeping in ignorance of what was towards. And after that, she fell into a fit of crying, so that I had some to-do comforting her. Yet, when she had come back to calmness, she was all for accompanying me about the decks, to see by daylight what had indeed befallen in the night-time. And from this decision, I could not turn her; though I assured her I should have told her nothing, had it not been that I wished to warn her from going to and fro between the saloon and the galley, until I had made a thorough search about the decks. Yet, as I have remarked, I could not turn her from her purpose of accompanying me, and so was forced to let her come, though against my desire.

"We made our way on deck through the door that opens under the break of the poop, my wife carrying her loaded revolver half-clumsily in both hands, whilst I had mine in my left, and the long-handled axe in my right—holding it very steadily.

"On stepping out on to the deck, we closed the door behind us, locking it and removing the key; for we had in mind our sleeping child. Then we went slowly forrard along the decks, glancing about warily. As we came fore-side of the pig-sty, and my wife saw that which lay beyond it, she let out a little exclamation of horror, shuddering at the sight of the mutilated pig, as, indeed, well she might.

"For my part, I said nothing; but glanced with much appre-hension about us; feeling a fresh access of fright; for it was very plain to me that the boar had been molested since I had seen it —the head having been torn, with awful might, from the body; and there were, besides, other new and ferocious wounds, one of which had come nigh to severing the poor brute's body in half. All of which was so much additional evidence of the for-midable character of the monster, or Monstrosity, that had attacked the animal.

"I did not delay by the pig, nor attempt to touch it; but beckoned my wife to follow me up on to the fo'c'sle head. Here, I removed the canvas cover from the small skylight which lights the fo'c'sle beneath; and, after that, I lifted off the heavy top, letting a flood of light down into the gloomy place. Then I leant down into the opening, and peered about; but could discover no signs of any lurking thing, and so returned to the main deck, and made an entrance into the fo'c'sle through the starboard doorway. And now I made a more minute search; but discovered nothing, beyond the mournful array of sea-chests that had belonged to our dead crew.

"My search concluded, I hastened out from the doleful place, into the daylight, and after that made fast the door again, and saw to it that the one upon the port side was also securely locked. Then I went up again on to the fo'c'sle head, and re-placed the skylight-top and the canvas cover, battening the whole down very thoroughly.

"And in this wise, and with an incredible care, did I make my search through the ship, fastening up each place behind me, so that I should be certain that no Thing was playing some dread game of hide and seek with me.

"Yet I found *nothing*, and had it not been for the grim evidence of the dead and mutilated boar, I had been like to have thought nothing more dreadful than an over vivid imagination had roamed the decks in the darkness of the past night.

"That I had reason to feel puzzled, may be the better understood, when I explain that I had examined the whole of the great, tarred-canvas screen, which I have built about the ship as a protection against the sudden tentacles of any of the roaming giant octopi, without discovering any torn place such as must have been made if any conceivable monster had climbed aboard out of the weed. Also, it must be borne in mind that the ship stands many feet out of the water, presenting only her smooth iron sides to anything that desires to climb aboard.

"And yet there was the dead pig, lying brutally torn before its empty sty! An undeniable proof that, to go out upon the decks after dark, was to run the risk of meeting a horrible and mysterious death!

"Through all that day, I pondered over this new fear that had come upon us, and particularly upon the monstrous and unearthly power that had torn apart the stout iron bars of the sty, and so ferociously wrenched off the head of the boar. The result of my pondering was that I removed our sleeping belongings that evening from the cabin to the iron half deck—a little four-bunked house, standing fore-side of the stump of the main mast, and built entirely of iron, even to the single door, which opens out of the after end.

"Along with our sleeping matters, I carried forrard to our new lodgings a lamp, and oil, also the dark-lantern, a couple of the axes, two rifles, and all of the revolvers, as well as a good supply of ammunition. Then I made my wife forage out sufficient provisions to last us for a week, if need be, and whilst she was so busied, I cleaned out and filled the water beaker which belonged to the half deck.

"At half-past six, I sent my wife forrard to the little iron house, with the baby, and then I locked up the saloon and all of the cabin doors, finally locking after me the heavy, teak door that opened out under the break of the poop.

"Then I went forrard to my wife and child, and shut and bolted the iron door of the half deck for the night. After that I went round and saw to it that all of the iron storm-doors that shut over the eight ports of the house, were in good work ing order, and so we sat down, as it were, to await the night.

"By eight o'clock, the dusk was upon us, and before half-past, the night hid the decks from my sight. Then I shut down all the iron port-flaps, and screwed them up securely, and after that, I lit the lamp.

"And so a space of waiting ensued, during which I whispered reassuringly to my wife, from time to time, as she looked across at me from her seat beside the sleeping child, with frightened eyes, and a very white face; for somehow there had come upon us within the last hour a sense of chilly fright, that went straight to one's heart, robbing one vilely of pluck.

"A little later, a sudden sound broke the impressive silence—a sudden dull thud against the side of the ship; and, after that, there came a succession of heavy blows, seeming to be struck all at once upon every side of the vessel; after which there was quietness for maybe a quarter of an hour.

"Then, suddenly, I heard, away forrard, a tap, tap, tap, and then a loud rattling, slurring noise, and a loud crash. After that, I heard many other sounds, and always that tap, tap, tap, repeated a hundred times, as though an army of wooden-legged men were busied all about the decks at the fore end of the ship.

"Presently, there came to me the sound of something coming down the deck, tap, tap, tap, it came. It drew near to the house, paused for nigh a minute; then continued away aft towards the saloon—tap, tap, tap. I shivered a little, and then, fell half consciously to thanking God that I had been given wisdom to bring my wife and child forrard to the security of the iron deckhouse.

"About a minute later, I heard the sound of a heavy blow struck somewhere away aft; and after that a second, and then a third, and seeming by the sounds to have been against iron—the iron of the bulkhead that runs across the break of the poop. There came the noise of a fourth blow, and it blended into the crash of broken woodwork. And therewith, I had a little tense quivering inside me; for the little one and my wife might have been sleeping aft there at that very moment, had it not been for the providential thought which had sent us forrard to the half deck.

"With the crash of the broken door, away aft, there came, from forrard of us, a great tumult of noises; and, directly, it sounded as though a multitude of wooden-legged men were coming down the decks from forrard. Tap, tap, tap; tap-a-tap, the noises came, and drew abreast of where we sat in the house, crouched and holding our breaths, for fear that we should make some noise to attract THAT which was without. The sounds passed us, and went tapping away aft, and I let out a little breath of sheer easement. Then, as a sudden thought came to me, I rose and turned down the lamp, fearing that some ray from it might be seen from beneath the door. And so, for the space of an hour, we sat wordless, listening to the sounds which came from away aft, the thud of heavy blows, the occasional crash of wood, and, presently the tap, tap, tap, again, coming forrard towards us.

"The sounds came to a stop, opposite the starboard side of the house, and, for a full minute, there was quietness. Then suddenly, 'Boom!' a tremendous blow had been struck against the side of the house. My wife gave out a little gasping cry, and there came a second blow; and, at that, the child awoke and began to wail, and my wife was put to it, with trying to soothe her into immediate silence.

"A third blow was struck, filling the little house with a dull thunder of sound, and then I heard the tap, tap, tap, move round to the after end of the house. There came a pause, and then a great blow right upon the door. I grasped the rifle, which I had leant against my chair, and stood up; for I did not know but that the thing might be upon us in a moment, so prodigious was the force of the blows it struck. Once again it struck the door, and after that went tap, tap, tap, round to the port side of the house, and there struck the house again; but now I had more ease of mind; for it was its direct attack upon the door, that had put such horrid dread into my heart.

"After the blows upon the port side of the house, there came a long spell of silence, as though the thing outside were listening; but, by the mercy of God, my wife had been able to soothe the child, so that no sound from us, told of our presence.

"Then, at last, there came again the sounds—tap, tap, tap, as the voiceless thing moved away forrard. Presently, I heard the noises cease aft; and, after that, there came a multitudinous tap-a-tapping, coming along the decks. It passed the house without so much as a pause, and receded away forrard.

"For a space of over two hours, there was an absolute silence; so that I judged that we were now no longer in danger of being molested. An hour later, I whispered to my wife; but, getting no reply, knew that she had fallen into a doze, and so I sat on, listening tensely; yet making no sort of noise that might attract attention.

"Presently, by the thin line of light from beneath the door, I saw that the day was breaking; and, at that, I rose stiffly, and commenced to unscrew the iron port-covers. I unscrewed the forrard ones first, and looked out into the wan dawn; but could discover nothing unusual about so much of the decks as I could see from there.

"After that, I went round and opened each, as I came to it, in its turn; but it was not until I had uncovered the port which gave me a view of the port side of the after main deck, that I discovered anything extraordinary. Then I saw, at first dimly, but more clearly as the day brightened, that the door, leading from beneath the break of the poop into the saloon, had been broken to flinders, some of which lay scattered upon the deck, and some of which still hung from the bent hinges; whilst more, no doubt, were strewed in the passage beyond my sight.

"Turning from the port, I glanced towards my wife, and saw that she lay half in and half out of the baby's bunk, sleeping with her head beside the child's, both upon one pillow. At the sight, a great wave of holy thankfulness took me, that we had been so wonderfully spared from the terrible and mysterious danger that had stalked the decks in the darkness of the preceding night. Feeling thus, I stole across the floor of the house, and kissed them both very gently, being full of tenderness, yet not minded to waken them. And, after that, I lay down in one of the bunks, and slept until the sun was high in the heaven.

"When I awoke, my wife was about and had tended to the child and prepared our breakfast, so that I had naught to do but tumble out and set to, the which I did with a certain keenness of appetite, induced, I doubt not, by the stress of the night. Whilst we ate, we discussed the peril through which we had just passed; but without coming any nearer to a solution of the weird mystery of the Terror.

"Breakfast over, we took a long and final survey of the decks, from the various ports, and then prepared to sally out. This we did with instinctive caution and quietness, both of us armed as on the previous day. The door of the half deck we closed and locked behind us, thereby ensuring that the child was open to no danger whilst we were in other parts of the ship.

"After a quick look about us, we proceeded aft towards the shattered door beneath the break of the poop. At the doorway, we stopped, not so much with the intent to examine the broken door, as because of an instinctive and natural hesitation to go forward into the saloon, which but a few hours previous had been visited by some incredible monster or monsters. Finally, we decided to go up upon the poop and peer down through the skylight. This we did, lifting the sides of the dome for that purpose; yet though we peered long and earnestly, we could perceive no signs of any lurking thing. But broken woodwork there appeared to be in plenty, to judge by the scattered pieces.

"After that, I unlocked the companion, and pushed back the over-arching slide. Then, silently, we stole down the steps and into the saloon. Here, being now able to see the big cabin through all its length, we discovered a most extraordinary scene; the whole place appeared to be wrecked from end to end; the six cabins that line each side had their bulksheading driven into shards and slivers of broken wood in places. Here, a door would be standing untouched, whilst the bulkshead beside it was in a mass of flinders—There, a door would be driven completely from its hinges, whilst the surrounding wood-work was untouched. And so it was, wherever we looked.

"My wife made to go towards our cabin; but I pulled her back, and went forward myself. Here the desolation was almost as great. My wife's bunk-board had been ripped out, whilst the supporting side-batten of mine had been plucked forth, so that all the bottom-boards of the bunk had descended to the floor in a cascade.

"But it was neither of these things that touched us so sharply, as the fact that the child's little swing cot had been wrenched rom its standards, and flung in a tangled mass of white-painted ironwork across the cabin. At the sight of that, I glanced across at my wife, and she at me, her face grown very white. Then down she slid to her knees, and fell to crying and thanking God together, so that I found myself beside her in a moment, with a very humble and thankful heart.

"Presently, when we were more controlled, we left the cabin, and finished our search. The pantry, we discovered to be entirely untouched, which, somehow, I do not think was then a matter of great surprise to me; for I had ever a feeling that the things which had broken a way into our sleeping-cabin, had been looking for us.

"In a little while, we left the wrecked saloon and cabins, and made our way forrard to the pig-sty; for I was anxious to see whether the carcass of the pig had been touched. As we came round the corner of the sty, I uttered a great cry; for there, lying upon the deck, on its back, was a gigantic crab, so vast in size that I had not conceived so huge a monster existed. Brown it was in colour, save for the belly part, which was of a light yellow.

"One of its pincer-claws, or mandibles, had been torn off in the fight in which it must have been slain (for it was all disembowelled). And this one claw weighed so heavy that I had some to-do to lift it from the deck; and by this you may have some idea of the size and formidableness of the creature itself.

"Around the great crab, lay half a dozen smaller ones, no more than from seven or eight to twenty inches across, and all white in colour, save for an occasional mottling of brown. These had all been killed by a single nip of an enormous mandible, which had in every case smashed them almost into two halves. Of the carcass of the great boar, not a fragment remained.

"And so was the mystery solved; and, with the solution, departed the superstitious terror which had suffocated me through those three nights, since the tapping had commenced. We had been attacked by a wandering shoal of giant crabs, which, it is quite possible, roam across the weed from place to place, devouring aught that comes in their path.

"Whether they had ever boarded a ship before, and so,

perhaps, developed a monstrous lust for human flesh, or whethe
their attack had been prompted by curiosity, I cannot possibl
say. It may be that, at first, they mistook the hull of the vesse
for the body of some dead marine monster, and hence thei
blows upon her sides, by which, possibly, they were endeavour
ing to pierce through our somewhat unusually tough hide!

"Or, again, it may be that they have some power of scent
by means of which they were able to smell our presence aboar
the ship; but this (as they made no general attack upon us in
the deck-house) I feel disinclined to regard as probable. An
yet—I do not know. Why their attack upon the saloon, an
our sleeping-cabin? As I say, I cannot tell, and so must leave
there.

"The way in which they came aboard, I discovered that sam
day; for, having learned what manner of creature it was tha
had attacked us, I made a more intelligent survey of the side
of the ship; but it was not until I came to the extreme bows
that I saw how they had managed. Here, I found that some o
the gear of the broken bowsprit and jib boom trailed dow
on to the weed, and as I had not extended the canvas scree
across the heel of the bowsprit, the monsters had been able t
climb up the gear, and thence aboard, without the least ob
struction being opposed to their progress.

"This state of affairs, I very speedily remedied; for, with
few strokes of my axe, I cut through the gear, allowing it t
drop down among the weed; and, after that, I built a temporar
breastwork of wood across the gap, between the two ends o
the screen; later on making it more permanent.

"Since that time, we have been no more molested by the gian
crabs; though for several nights afterwards, we heard then
knocking strangely against our sides. Maybe, they are attracte
by such refuse as we are forced to dump overboard, and thi
would explain their first tappings being aft, opposite to th
lazarette; for it is from the openings in this part of the canva
screen that we cast our rubbish.

"Yet, it is weeks now since we heard aught of them, so tha
I have reason to believe that they have betaken themselves else
where, maybe to attack some other lonely humans, living ou
their short span of life aboard some lone derelict, lost even t

memory in the depth of this vast sea of weed and deadly creatures.

"I shall send this message forth on its journey, as I have sent the other four, within a well-pitched barrel, attached to a small fire balloon. The shell of the severed claw of the monster crab, I shall enclose,[1] as evidence of the terrors that beset us in this dreadful place. Should this message, and the claw, ever fall into human hands, let them, contemplating this vast mandible, try to imagine the size of the other crab or crabs that could destroy so formidable a creature as the one to which this claw belonged.

"What other terrors does this hideous world hold for us?

"I had thought of inclosing, along with the claw, the shell of one of the white smaller crabs. It must have been some of these moving in the weed that night, that set my disordered fancy to imagining of ghouls and the un-dead. But, on thinking it over, I shall not; for to do so would be to illustrate nothing that needs illustration, and it would but increase needlessly the weight which the balloon will have to lift.

"And so I grow wearied of writing. The night is drawing near, and I have little more to tell. I am writing this in the saloon, and, though I have mended and carpentered so well as I am able, nothing I can do will hide the traces of that night when the vast crabs raided through these cabins, searching for —WHAT?

"There is nothing more to say. In health, I am well, and so is my wife and the little one, but . . .

"I must have myself under control, and be patient. We are beyond all help, and must bear that which is before us, with such bravery as we are able. And with this, I end; for my last word shall not be one of complaint.

"ARTHUR SAMUEL PHILIPS."

"Christmas Eve, 1879."

---

[1] Captain Bolton makes no mention of the claw, in the covering letter which he has enclosed with the MS.—W. H. H.

THE DEVIL AND THE OLD MAN
by John Masefield

In common with several other writers represented in this collection, John Masefield (1878–1967) followed an early inclination to go to sea. At the age of thirteen he was a ship's apprentice. Later, he sailed to New York to join a ship as third officer—but changed his mind and worked at a variety of fanciful jobs before returning to England in 1897 to pursue a literary career. His first published volume, *Saltwater Ballads* (1902), a book of poems, was followed by a collection of short stories, *A Mainsail Haul* (1905), from which "The Devil and the Old Man" is taken. Subsequent works include *Captain Margaret* (1908), *Multitude and Solitude* (1909) and *The Midnight Folk* (1927). In addition to receiving recognition as an outstanding poet, Masefield attracted a popular readership with a series of rumbustious novels of adventure such as *Sard Harker* (1924), *Odtaa* (1926), *Dead Ned: The Autobiography of a Corpse* (1938) and *Live and Kicking Ned* (1939). John Masefield was appointed Poet Laureate in 1930 and became a member of the Order of Merit in 1933. He is generally regarded as being amongst the most versatile and "accessible" Poet Laureates that England has known. Towards the end of his life he wrote of himself: "I have done ... much other work of different kinds, yet always with the love (and the hope) of story-telling deep within me, as the work beyond all other work, to which my nature called."

Up away north, in the old days, in Chester, there was a man who never throve. Nothing he put his hand to ever prospered, and as his state worsened, his friends fell away and he grew desperate. So one night when he was alone in his room, thinking of the rent due in two or three days and the money he couldn't scrape together, he cried out, "I wish I could sell my soul to the Devil like that man the old books tell about."

Now just as he spoke the clock struck twelve, and, while it chimed, a sparkle began to burn about the room, and the air, all at once, began to smell of brimstone, and a voice said:

"Will these terms suit you?"

He then saw that someone had just placed a parchment there. He picked it up and read it through; and being in despair, and not knowing what he was doing, he answered, "Yes," and looked round for a pen.

"Take and sign," said the voice again, "but first consider what it is you do; do nothing rashly. Consider."

So he thought awhile; then, "Yes," he said, "I'll sign," and with that he groped for the pen.

"Blood from your left thumb and sign," said the voice.

So he pricked his left thumb and signed.

"Here is your earnest money," said the voice, "nine and twenty silver pennies. This day twenty years hence I shall see you again."

Now early next morning our friend came to himself and felt like one of the drowned. "What a dream I've had," he said. Then he woke up and saw the nine and twenty silver pennies and smelled a faint smell of brimstone.

So he sat in his chair there and remembered that he had sold his soul to the Devil for twenty years of heart's desire; and whatever fears he may have had as to what might come at the end of those twenty years, he found comfort in the thought that, after all, twenty years is a good stretch of time, and that throughout them he could eat, drink, merrymake, roll in gold, dress in silk, and be carefree, heart at ease, and jib sheet to windward.

So for nineteen years and nine months he lived in great state, having his heart's desire in all things; but, when his twenty years were nearly run through, there was no wretcheder man in all the world than that poor fellow. So he threw up his house, his position, riches, everything, and away he went to the port of Liverpool, where he signed on as A.B., aboard a Black Ball packet, a tea clipper, bound to the China Seas.

They made a fine passage out, and when our friend had only three days more, they were in the Indian Ocean, lying lazy, becalmed.

Now it was his wheel that forenoon, and it being dead calm, all he had to do was just to think of things, the ship of course having no way on her.

So he stood there, hanging on to the spokes, groaning and weeping till, just twenty minutes or so before eight bells were made, up came the captain for a turn on deck.

He went aft of course, took a squint aloft, and saw our friend crying at the wheel. "Hello, my man," he says, "why, what's all this? Ain't you well? You'd best lay aft for a dose o' salts at four bells tonight."

"No, Cap'n" said the man, "there's no salts'll ever cure my sickness."

"Why, what's all this?" says the old man. "You must be sick if it's as bad as all that. But come now; your cheek is all sunk, and you look as if you ain't slept well. What is it ails you, anyway? Have you anything on your mind?"

"Captain," he answers very solemn, "I have sold my soul to the Devil."

"Oh," said the old man, "why, that's bad. That's powerful bad. I never thought them sort of things ever happened outside a book."

"But," said our friend, "that's not the worst of it, Captain. At this time three days hence the Devil will fetch me home."

"Good Lord!" groaned the old man. "Here's a nice hurrah's nest to happen aboard my ship. But come now," he went on, "did the Devil give you no chance—no saving clause like? Just think quietly for a moment."

"Yes, Captain," said our friend, "just when I made the deal, there came a whisper in my ear. And," he said, speaking quietly, so as not to let the mate hear, "if I can give the Devil three jobs to do which he cannot do, why, then, Captain," he says, "I'm saved, and that deed of mine is cancelled."

Well, at this the old man grinned and said, "You just leave things to me, my son. *I'll* fix the Devil for you. Aft there, one o' you, and relieve the wheel. Now you run forrard, and have a good watch below, and be quite easy in your mind, for I'll deal with the Devil for you. You rest and be easy."

And so that day goes by, and the next, and the one after that, and the one after that was the day the Devil was due.

Soon as eight bells was made in the morning watch, the old man called all hands aft.

"Men," he said, "I've got an all-hands job for you this fore-noon. Mr Mate," he cried, "get all hands on to the main tops'l halyards and bouse the sail stiff up and down."

So they passed along the halyards and took the turns off, and old John Chantyman piped up:

"There's a Black Ball clipper
Comin' down the river."

And away the yard went to the masthead till the bunt robands jammed in the sheave.

"Very well that," said the old man. "Now get my dinghy off o' the half deck and let her drag alongside."

So they did that too.

"Very well that," said the old man. "Now forrard with you, to the chain locker, and rouse out every inch of chain you find there."

So forrard they went, and the chain was lighted up and flaked along the deck all clear for running.

"Now, Chips," says the old man to the carpenter, "just bend the spare anchor to the end of that chain and clear away the fo'c'sle rails ready for when we let go."

So they did this too.

"Now," said the old man, "get them tubs of slush from the galley. Pass that slush along there, doctor. Very well that. Now turn to, all hands, and slush away every link in that chain a good inch thick in grease."

So they did that, too, and wondered what the old man meant.

"Very well that," cries the old man. "Now get below, all hands! Chips, on to the fo'c'sle head with you and stand by! I'll keep the deck, Mr Mate! Very well that."

So all hands tumbled down below; Chips took a fill o' 'baccy

to leeward of the capstan, and the old man walked the weather
poop, looking for a sign of hell-fire.

It was still dead calm—but presently, towards six bells, he
raised a black cloud away to leeward and saw the glimmer of
the lightning in it; only the flashes were too red and came too
quick.

"Now," says he to himself, "stand by."

Very soon that black cloud worked up to windward, right
alongside, and there came a red flash, and a strong sulphurous
smell, and then a loud peal of thunder as the Devil steps
aboard.

"Mornin', Cap'n," says he.

"Mornin', Mr Devil," says the old man, "and what in blazes
do you want aboard *my* ship?"

"Why, Captain," said the Devil, "I've come for the soul of
one of your hands as per signed agreement; and, as my time's
pretty full up in these wicked days, I hope you won't keep me
waiting for him longer than need be."

"Well, Mr Devil," says the old man, "the man you come for
is down below, sleeping, just at this moment. It's a fair pity to
call him till it's right time. So supposin' I set you them three
tasks. How would that be? Have you any objections?"

"Why, no," said the Devil, "fire away as soon as you like."

"Mr Devil," said the old man, "you see that main tops'l yard?
Suppose you lay out on that main tops'l yard and take in three
reefs singlehanded."

"Ay, ay, sir," the Devil said, and he ran up the ratlines, into
the top, up the topmast rigging, and along the yard.

Well, when he found the sail stiff up and down, he hailed the
deck:

"Below there! On deck there! Lower away ya halyards!"

"I will not," said the old man, "nary a lower."

"Come up your sheets, then," said the Devil. "This main
topsail's stiff up and down. How'm I to take in three reefs when
the sail's stiff up and down?"

"Why," said the old man, "*you can't do it*. Come out o' that!
Down from aloft, you hoof-footed son. That's one to me."

"Yes," says the Devil, when he got on deck again, "I don't
deny it, Cap'n. That's one to you."

"Now, Mr Devil," said the old man, going towards the rail, "suppose you was to step into that little boat alongside there. Will you please?"

"Ay, ay, sir," he said, and he slid down the forrard fall, got into the stern sheets, and sat down.

"Now, Mr Devil," said the skipper, taking a little salt spoon from his vest pocket, "supposin' you bail all the water on that side the boat on to this side the boat, using this spoon as your dipper."

Well!—the Devil just looked at him.

"Say!" he said at length. "Which of the New England States d'ye hail from anyway?"

"Not Jersey, anyway," said the old man. "That's two up, all right; ain't it, sonny?"

"Yes," growls the Devil as he climbs aboard. "That's two up. Two to you and one to play. Now, what's your next contraption?"

"Mr Devil," said the old man, looking very innocent, "you see, I've ranged my chain ready for letting go anchor. Now Chips is forrard there, and when I sing out, he'll let the anchor go. Supposin' you stopper the chain with them big hands o' yourn and keep it from running out clear. Will you, please?"

So the Devil takes off his coat and rubs his hands together and gets away forrard by the bitts and stands by.

"All ready, Cap'n," he says.

"All ready, Chips?" asked the old man.

"All ready, sir," replies Chips.

"Then, stand by. Let *go* the anchor," and clink, clink, old Chips knocks out the pin, and away goes the spare anchor and greased chain into a five-mile deep of God's sea. As I said, they were in the Indian Ocean.

Well—there was the Devil, making a grab here and a grab there, and the slushy chain just slipping through his claws, and at whiles a bight of chain would spring clear and rap him in the eye.

So at last the cable was nearly clean gone, and the Devil ran to the last big link (which was seized to the heel of the foremast), and he put both his arms through it and hung on to it like grim death.

But the chain gave such a *yank* when it came to that the big link carried away, and oh, roll and go, out it went through the haweshole, in a shower of bright sparks, carrying the Devil with it. There is no Devil now. The Devil's dead.

As for the old man, he looked over the bows, watching the bubbles burst, but the Devil never rose. Then he went to the fo'c'sle scuttle and banged thereon with a hand spike.

"Rouse out, there, the port watch," he called, "an' get my dinghy inboard."